GOTH OPERA

GOTH OPERA

Paul Cornell

First published in Great Britain in 1994 by
Doctor Who Books
an imprint of Virgin Publishing Ltd
332 Ladbroke Grove
London W10 5AH

ISBN 0 426 20418 2

Cover illustration by Alister Pearson

Typeset by Galleon Typesetting
Printed and bound in Great Britain by
Cox & Wyman Ltd, Reading, Berks

Preface

Welcome to the first of a new series of Doctor Who novels.

I'm sorry. You've probably heard all this before, several times. But for the benefit of those of you who have been in suspended animation for the past five years, here it is again. The last new Doctor Who television story was broadcast in Britain at the end of 1989. A little less than two years later, having published novelizations of just about every one of the stories shown on television since the series started in 1963, we launched the New Adventures: original, full-length Doctor Who novels that related the Doctor's continuing exploits, picking up the trail where television had abandoned it.

Indulge me for a moment: let me tell you about a publishing success story. Yes, the series has become established, extending across ever-wider stretches of book-shops' shelves. But that's not the point. As a Doctor Who fan, I find the most satisfying aspect of the New Adventures is that they have helped to keep Doctor Who alive (and kicking, sometimes) – and not in a nostalgic, introspective way, but by setting the Doctor in stories that are, I hope, interesting and challenging for the mature and sophisticated audience that Doctor Who fandom has developed into.

And as a publisher, I find the New Adventures exciting because they have provided a showcase for a gang of talented young authors who deserve to be in print. Our policy has always been to encourage book proposals from anyone – absolutely anyone – who's prepared to follow our guidelines. In these straitened times the New Adventures constitute one of the few places where new SF writers can work, experiment, show off – and get published.

And now: here we go again.

Except that the Missing Adventures are not the New Adventures all over again. Yes, they will be full-length original novels, written for a readership that is older than you and I were when we started to watch Doctor Who on television. And – of course – we will continue to encourage new talent.

But these are new stories with old Doctors. Each Missing Adventures will slot seamlessly into a gap between television stories, and we will attempt to ensure that the Missing Adventures have the flavour of the television stories in which they are embedded.

This book, *Goth Opera*, the first of the Missing Adventures, demonstrates the principles of the series. It is written by Paul Cornell, one of the brightest stars of the New Adventures galaxy (his first published novel was the fourth New Adventure). But he hasn't written just another New Adventure. In *Goth Opera* you will find a complex story beautifully told – but you won't find experimental techniques, ultra-fast cutting between scenes, enigmatic dialogue, and the other modern styles featured in some of the New Adventures. The Doctor Who television stories weren't like that, and neither will the Missing Adventures be.

As an added bonus, this first Missing Adventure and the simultaneously published New Adventure share a storyline. *Goth Opera* is, in a way, the sequel to *Blood Harvest* by Terrance Dicks, although they can be read and understood separately. Except that *Goth Opera* features the fifth Doctor, while *Blood Harvest* has the seventh Doctor, so in a sense *Blood Harvest* is the sequel to *Goth Opera*. It certainly confuses me.

There'll be a month without a Missing Adventures after this one, and after that there will be one Missing Adventure a month, all being well. Look out for the distinctive blue diamond logo and more stunning Alister Pearson artwork.

Finally – yes, really, we're getting near the end – I must stress that when I say 'we' I sometimes mean Virgin Publishing as a whole, and even its predecessor companies. But usually I mean myself, Rebecca Levene who edits, and Andy Bodle who assists. And these days, of that triumvirate, I play the smallest part.

Peter Darvill-Evans
Fiction Publisher, Virgin Publishing Ltd.

With thanks to:
Kini Brooks, Sarah Groenewegen, Claire Longhurst,
Trog, Mark Wyman

FOR TERRANCE

GOTH OPERA

Prologue

The beacon on top of the Siemens Tower blinked red every twenty seconds. At a certain eye-level, it formed part of a chain of blinking lights, igniting one by one as the sun set over the city. Russet light sparkled off Piccadilly station, ran in a great amber river down Oxford Road, made the crescent estates of Moss Side into tangles of lengthening shadows. In the city, people were going home, pulling on coats and gloves, and locking shops. The pubs were filling up and the bus station was busy with commuters.

In the chilly clear autumn air two figures danced, swooping past the tower like sparrows, calling and laughing. Against the darkening blue of the sky they were like two charcoal sketches, the drifting debris of some distant bonfire. They didn't care if they were seen.

Madelaine lowered her arms to her sides, holding down her long black dress, and sped towards the beacon tower. She grabbed it as she shot past, spinning around the pole at a speed which made the bones in her arm pop out of their sockets. She let go again, her hand a floppy glove, and whizzed off into the sky under her own momentum, shaking her joints back together. Her black lipsticked grin was wide with laughter.

Jake stopped, standing a few feet above the roof of the skyscraper. 'Manchester!' he called, spreading his arms wide. 'So much to answer for!'

'I like it!' Madelaine flew to him, embracing him so

1

that they both fell onto the roof. 'Thank you for bringing me here.' They'd slept on the journey up, in a freight wagon on a train out of Bristol.

'No need to thank me, like.' Jake cradled her head with his arm, and they lay back against the concrete, looking up at the sky. 'This is where I come from. Mum and Dad still live here, down in Rusholme.'

'Want to visit them?'

'No. Best not to.' He frowned quickly, because he'd thought of bad things to do with his past. He tried not to show her all that.

Madelaine had met Jake one night at the King's Bridge Inn, a pub in Totnes. She'd lived in the town with her Mum and Dad, spending more time with her friends than at home. The town was what kept her going, a round of gossip and people she'd always known. You hung around Vire Island, out in the middle of the river, or down at the Rumour bar. You could be really buoyed up by it some nights, or sometimes you could be very lonely in it, held back when everybody else said they'd be leaving soon. The inn had a ghost, it was said, a serving maid who'd died on the premises. That, and the books you could grab off the shelves above the tables, and the little corners and stairwells for gossip was enough to attract her crowd, the goths and the metal-heads. They had bands upstairs too, one of the few places left in town that did. They used to have a laugh, but Madelaine always thought that there was something missing in her life, and as soon as she saw him she knew that that thing had been Jake.

He'd been with a group of mates, and they'd said they were down for the surfing, with a VW van parked somewhere. But they didn't look like surfers. The other lads had treated her like she was invisible, talking over her and ignoring her. He was different. He had a face that held a permanent grin somewhere, even when he was sad. His hair was all over the place, a mess of black and shiny stuff that set off his grey eyes. He had a lovely northern accent and shoulders that looked like he'd stuffed a pair of great wings under his leather jacket.

'Come on over to the beach with us,' he'd said. 'You'll be all right.' His friends had bellowed with laughter at that and Madelaine said no, asking if he was going to be around the next day. He'd shrugged, grinning again, and grunted something non-committal. As she got back into conversation with her friends he left, not looking back. His mates stayed at the bar, drinking pints down in one gulp and then getting another round in. They didn't seem to be getting pissed, either.

She stopped in at Rumours on her way back home, but nobody she wanted to see was about. Then she'd wandered down through the dark walkway behind the supermarket, heading sadly back to her house. The walkway had a square gap in it beside the railing where people chained their bikes. Maddy always stopped in the gap to look up into the sky. She'd been into astronomy when she was little, always wanting to go into space. Wouldn't mind now, really.

The lads stepped forward. They were standing on the roof, around the edge of her gap, looking down at her with intent.

'What're you doing up there?' she'd asked.

They swooped on her. They grabbed her by the hem of her skirt and pulled her up into the sky. High up, until she could see the whole of the peninsula in the moonlight, the sea and everything. They went through a cloud, and it was like a cold mist, soaking her. She was screaming through all this, strange as it sounded now.

One of the men had started to suck at her fingers. The most horrible part of it all was that they weren't

3

threatening her or telling her to be quiet or anything. They were just ignoring her.

He arrived as they were pulling the scarf away from her neck. His entrance, rising up through the cloud until it looked like he was standing on it, was spectacular enough, but he didn't attack them or even shout at them.

'Come on lads,' he said. 'Not this one, eh?'

'Frigging hell, Jake . . .' one of the creatures moaned. 'It's only a woman. Have an arm, if you want.'

'I was talking to her, lad. I don't like to talk to my food.'

'Oh, and she was really interesting, I suppose. Really of great interest, all her stories about travel.' The last word raised a laugh from the others.

'She's never gone anywhere,' Jake mumbled, looking down at the cloud. 'But she's all right, okay? She's just a nice girl.'

'I'm sure she is, my son, but, in case you haven't realized, that's the whole point of being vampy. She's a nice girl, and we – don't – care.' The man holding her had an accent like Michael Caine, an affected Cockney. The little details of it all were continually scaring Madelaine out of the idea that this was a dream.

'Look, how about if I – '

'Make her one of us and live happily ever after? You can only do that to three people in your whole existence, mate. I've met kids like you before. You've got the teeth, but you're still back in the daylight in your head. You dream about cashpoints and Sega and foreign travel.'

Jake nodded. 'You're right there. I had this dream yesterday about going on an 18–30 holiday. Woke up sweating.' He spread his arms out towards the others. 'Give her here, I'm claiming her as one of my three.'

'It all gets written down, you know. You won't thank

4

me when she goes on telly and shows off her teeth.' The man who'd been holding her pushed Madelaine away, and she fell.

Falling from high up, fluttering on the edge of unconsciousness, she'd been more scared than ever before in her life. She'd spun, over and over, her skirts and hair fluttering like a falling flag.

He caught her as quickly as he could. She shouted again, beating at him with her hands.

'Are you happy at home? Get on with your Mum and Dad, like?'

'Yes!' she screamed. 'Yes!'

'Then I'm really sorry. Can't do anything else. Calm down, now, calm down.'

Their eyes met, and like a big hand had grabbed her head, she was suddenly calm. A strange taste rushed into her mouth, all that biological fear with nowhere else to go. 'You're a vampire,' she said.

'Yeah.'

'What's all that stuff about travel?'

'Something humans do. Go on package tours, watch TV, buy crisps. Whatever the running joke is this week.'

'Let me go. Let me go home.'

'Sorry. I can't.'

He pushed her hair back, and leaned forward to her neck. There were two sharp injections, a sudden small pain, and a powerful sucking sensation. Madelaine was paralysed. She tried to move her fingers as the sucking went on, but she couldn't. She could feel his teeth, his normal teeth, against her skin.

It went on too long and she opened her mouth, wanting to laugh or cry, or at least give some sign that she didn't believe in this. 'Don't kill me, don't kill me,' was all she could whisper.

When it was over, he turned his face aside and wiped

5

his mouth on the back of his hand. 'You're one of us now,' he'd said.

They landed in Dartington and walked through the gardens, Jake explaining all the rules and the dangers. She'd hated him for five days.

On the roof now, Madelaine laughed and put Jake's fingers to the old wounds on her neck. They'd been together four years now. 'I was just thinking about how it all happened,' she told him. 'It doesn't turn you on, being bitten, like in the films.'

'It can.' Jake grinned. 'If you make it like that. But I wanted it to be honest. You'd got into a mess, I sorted it the only way I knew how. You're still glad, aren't you?'

'Yeah. It's the flying that I like. That's still great.'

'Aye, you never lose that. Right, then – ' Jake clapped his hands and stood up, taking a deep breath of night air. 'Dinner?'

'Dinner.' She took his hand and he pulled her upright. 'Chinese?'

'Indian.'

'All right, Indian then. But can we find one with leukemia?'

'Leukemia? That's a long shot, an Indian leukemia victim. They're not going to be out and about, are they? Where'd you get a taste like that?'

'Party of Alec's. He passed a cup round. That's what he said it was.'

'We'll try, all right? But only if we find one walking down the street. I don't want to work too hard. I was thinking of a kid, myself.'

'A pretty young Indian girl? You be careful.' She punched him playfully in the chest, breaking one of his ribs.

He flexed his back and the bone melted back together with a theatrical popping sound. 'Aye, well, I was thinking I might convert a couple more of you soon, build myself a harem.'

Madelaine pretended to sulk. 'I'd leave you.'

'Never. We're together forever, you and me.' He whistled a couple of bars of an old pop tune. 'Long as you keep on leaving me the drumsticks.'

'Perhaps we could find somebody famous? I wouldn't mind a bit of Morrissey. What do you think his blood would taste like?'

'Milky tea, love. You know we can't off anybody famous, it'd draw attention to ourselves, get us on the news and all that. Do you remember the article in that magazine?'

Maddy laughed. ' "Vampire hunters in Stoke-on-Trent report that British vampires now number 1225, up 65 on last year's figure!" D'you think they watch us with binoculars and put tags on our ankles when we're not looking?'

'I wonder if Russ down in Burslem's seen it? He might go and give them a fright. Make it 67 up on last year. 1225 indeed, it must be more like 300. 400, maximum.'

Maddy laid her head on Jake's shoulder. 'I've started to think about kidneys . . .' she murmured. 'Stop me, won't you, you know they're bad for me.'

Jake patted her head. 'I'll take both of them, and you can have some nice healthy liver instead.'

They would have flown off to find meat then, but a new sound split the air atop the tower: the sound of time and space being ripped apart.

It was a sound the lovers had never heard before. They watched in amazement as a new pylon appeared on the roof top, a red light flashing on top of it. The light stopped flashing when it was fully materialized.

The side of the pylon opened, and out stepped a woman.

She was tall and straight-backed, wearing a neat black trouser-suit and a silver belt. From it hung a number of utility packs. Her hair was bound severely back to her head, and her features were sharp and inquisitive. Strangely, she sported a bruise across her cheek. She'd done nothing to hide it. The only ostentation about her was a necklace of golden spheres. 'Ah,' she said to Jake, smiling politely. 'There you are.'

'You were expecting us, like?' Jake advanced with a cheeky grin, the courage that indestructability gave you.

'Somebody like you, yes. My name is Ruathadvoro-phrenaltid. Call me Ruath. And you are?'

'Jake Hedges, this is Madelaine Worth.' Jake waved a hand at Maddy, who curtsied, adopting that look of dangerous hunger which always produced such a good effect in their prey.

Ruath didn't blink at it. 'You are vampires, am I right?'

Jake laughed. 'Well, we don't like to boast.'

'Good. I thought this would be the right time to find some of you. Always at the high points, overlooking the feeding grounds. This is a good omen.' She noticed the curiosity on their faces, and indicated the pylon behind her. 'I'm a Time Lady of Gallifrey. That's a TARDIS. Do you know what one of those is?' Jake and Madelaine shook their heads. 'How soon they forget.'

'Why did you want to find us?' asked Maddy.

'I've made a study of you. You're so important, as a species that is. Great things are about to happen. Can you summon some more of your kind?'

'If you want. It's possible that they'll rip you apart, like.'

'No it isn't. I'm here because of destiny. They'll listen to what I have to say.'

'You asked for it. Madelaine, do you want to do it?'

'Okay.' Glancing suspiciously at the stranger, Maddy

stepped to the edge of the roof. She took a deep breath and clenched her teeth. There came a little popping sound from her throat. She let go the breath, and blew out a bright stream of red, a bloody mist that dissipated on the wind. She ran round the roof, spitting it as she went, until a circle of the stuff had disappeared into the night air. 'Eck.' She stopped, and put a hand to her throat. 'Now I really need my dinner.'

'Here,' Jake opened up his wrist and offered it to her. 'Have some of mine for a bit, I want to see how this turns out.' Maddy dashed over and sucked quickly on the open vein, gargling with it.

Ruath watched them, shaking her head, a sad smile on her face. 'Beautiful,' she whispered. 'Beautiful.'

They only had to wait a few minutes. Ruath spent the time examining Jake and Madelaine with an enthusiast's glee, feeling their teeth, peering into their eyes and generally fussing over them in a way which Maddy found disturbing. Jake seemed entertained by it, though.

The first one to arrive was a fat, bald man. He materialized out of a mist that had been hanging around the edge of the roof. 'What's this then, party?' he chuckled, rubbing his hands together at the sight of Ruath.

'No,' Ruath told him, 'I bring – '

'Where are you two kids from, then?'

'Down south. We're here for the beer.'

'Listen to me – ' Ruath began, her voice rising a notch.

The man shot out a finger, embedding it in Ruath's throat. 'Shall I be mother?' he asked.

Ruath calmly pulled something from her belt, and thrust it into the man's face. It was a book with an elegantly designed round symbol embossed on its ancient cover.

The newcomer threw up his hands and stepped back, bellowing in shock. Jake and Madelaine took a step back as well. They could feel the force of the symbol.

'The Great Seal of Rassilon!' shouted Ruath. She advanced on the man until he stood on the edge of the roof, on the verge of flying away. 'I do not have time for these games. I know the secrets of your past, and have important news concerning your future. If you listen to me, you can rule this world and others. If you prey on me, you will remain ignorant and vulnerable. I am of the Time Lords. I come from another world, do you understand?'

'I understand.' The voice came from behind Ruath. Standing there was an elegantly dressed young man in leather gloves and sports jacket. He doffed his cap to Ruath. 'Pleased to meet you. The children of the Great Vampire are bound to the ring and the tradition.'

Ruath quickly reached into her pouch again, and slipped a ring onto her finger. She held it out in the direction of the gentleman. 'Thank goodness somebody knows the form. Kiss the ring.'

'Of course.' He went down on one knee and gently touched the silver band with his lips. Then he looked up at the others. 'I advise you to do the same. Haven't you read the books? This lady is the herald of our jolly old saviour.'

Ruath held the ring high over the other vampires. They all knelt. 'Bring me the blood of a virgin,' she told them. 'And I will show you the truth of what I say.'

Jake glanced at Madelaine. 'It's the night for tall orders, isn't it?'

They spread the pool of blood in a circle on the roof, directed by the man in the cap, who introduced himself as Jeremy Sanders. He'd shaken hands with the bald man, pleased to meet his 'competition in the Withington area'. Ruath expected more vampirekind to arrive, but Jake explained to her that only a couple per major city was the norm.

'More than that, and it gets out of control. You get everybody biting each other, passing it on without killing. Soon your food supply's gone and you all starve. You're taught that by whoever initiates you, only make three of the kind as you go. Space them out as well, so you're not all fighting over the same meat.'

'Ah, but do you know who the father of you all is?' Ruath looked around the group. 'The only vampire on Earth at one point. Anyone?'

'Count Dracula?' suggested Maddy sarcastically.

'No. No, that legendary figure's progeny all died out.'

'The Great Vampire.' Jeremy smiled. 'You wear the ring of his cult.'

'Not the Great Vampire. But I'm impressed by your knowledge.'

'Ah, when I was initiated into the Undead back in the forties, everybody knew the form. We were expecting you almost immediately. Got a little miffed by the passing of the years, it must be said.'

'Let me show you.' She took a bottle from her pouch and let three drops of a clear liquid fall into the pool of blood. The red liquid shifted and stirred, as if it suddenly had a life of its own. Colours and textures swirled across its surface. 'Activation code. Bioplasmic data-processors, go go go.' She looked up as the blood started to glitter and swirl faster. 'It has to be virgin blood, no hint of anybody else's genes. My little datapod virus structures hook into the memories of individual cells and go back into racial memory, interrogating it and following the trail back until they find what I've told them to find. Somewhere back in this person's ancestry, somebody will

11

have touched somebody who's seen what we want to see.'

The vampires looked blankly at her.

'It's magic,' she told them.

'That's all right then,' the bald man muttered. 'For a minute, I thought it were going to be something complicated.'

The pool shimmered and suddenly flattened into a vibrating flat surface. 'There he is!' gasped Ruath.

In the pool, a picture had formed. A bearded man, running and snarling. The background was some sort of store-room. There was a flash of a crate. The man sped across what looked like a casino, past card tables and the like, and threw himself through the glass of a window, shattering it. The scene changed. Now they were in a darkened alleyway, beside a street sign of American design. Something about the look of the place suggested the nineteen thirties. The man lashed out at the viewer, and the picture whizzed aside in a burst of red.

'Like his style,' whispered Jake. 'Who is that?'

'Yarven,' Ruath breathed, rippling the pool. 'Lord Yarven. The assassin of Veran and the last Undead survivor of E-Space.'

'Thought that was a car.'

'Hush. Watch.' The picture switched to the hold of a ship. The point of view was peering down into an earth-filled box. A hand shot up and pulled it into darkness.

'That's an initiation,' Jeremy murmured. 'Too much style for a killing.'

A series of attacks followed, all from the victim's point of view. The setting changed from aboard ship to a familiar background of Big Ben and the Thames. But the details were strange, old-fashioned cars and men in trilbies shuffling by in the night.

'This is the early nineteen forties, by your calendar.

12

Yarven came to this country during that decade, and initiated many of your kind into being. He was not exercising your restraint. He sought to create an army of the night. But what happened to him?'

The picture shifted suddenly to the hold of an aircraft. Somebody was grabbed, struggled in the darkness. A hatch was pulled open. Yarven stood suddenly framed in the doorway of the aircraft, an elegant figure in a dressing-gown and cravat. The viewpoint dropped away, down into the night. Yarven fell with it, spinning past in an elegant dive.

'Where's he going?' murmured Ruath.

The next viewpoint was crouched in a forest, a Sten gun propped in front of it. Yarven was running towards the bushes. The observer stood up and apparently shouted a warning, for Yarven turned and looked. He said something with a curl of his lip.

The observer opened fire. Yarven's body flew backwards, bloody debris blasted out of his torso. The observer stepped forward.

Yarven stood up again, roaring, and snapped the gun with his fingers. He thrust a claw straight at the observer, and the picture became black and red. Suddenly, another point of view on the same scene, a partisan in a heavy coat and scarf kneeling before Yarven, his face a mess of blood. The vampire was caught unawares, looking around him in surprise. Into the picture was thrust a crucifix. From the forest all around came serious-faced countrymen, holding up the silver crosses they carried around their throats.

'Oh no, I can't look . . .' whispered Madelaine. 'This is like a horror movie.'

The burly men grabbed Yarven and dragged him through the forest. He was roaring and struggling, but their grip seemed to increase with his resistance.

'They've got faith, the sods,' said Jake.

'I'm beginning to recognize this,' grinned Jeremy, smoothing his moustache. 'Just as the prophecies predict, what?'

The observer was watching as two of his countrymen dug out a pit. Yarven was offered a blindfold, which he declined angrily. He seemed more irritated than frightened. A couple of the partisans were tying logs together.

Yarven stood before the pit, and bullets burst once more across his body. He fell back into it, and the partisans rushed forward, throwing silver crucifixes after him. A giant cross made of two great logs was thrown down on top of him, and the pit swiftly filled in. The last scene was of one of the men blessing the ground. He crossed himself before he turned away.

The picture clouded and became blood once more. Jake laughed in amazement. 'The idiots. They haven't cut off his head, there's no stake. Bloody hell, he must still be conscious down there.'

'That's so cruel.' Madelaine shook her head in anger.

'I see what you mean,' Jeremy straightened up. 'That's the story of – '

Ruath raised a finger. 'Let me read it.' She opened the book with the Great Seal on its cover, and found the place she'd marked. 'Here it is. "And those who will the destruction of the vampiric races must be ever vigilant. The records of the Dark Time state that there shall come among their number one who was never completely killed. He will be entombed in a pit, not alive and not dead, on the world that will be called Ravolox." ' Ruath looked up. 'That's another name for Earth.' She found her place again. ' "He will be joined with a Prydonian Lady, and the two of them shall cause much suffering, for he is the one the Great Vampire predicted at his meeting with

Rassilon, the one who will succeed him and be consumed in the maw of time that his people may prosper. They will call him the Vampire Messiah." '

She closed the book triumphantly. 'The Dark Time was when my people used their abilities to discover what should not be discovered. This isn't mystical nonsense, but an actual report of the future. I am that Prydonian Lady, and it is my destiny to set your people free.'

'The Vampire Messiah . . .' The bald man smiled broadly. 'Even I've heard of him. Chap who initiated me said he'd come and save us all.'

'Indeed.' Ruath put a finger to the pool of blood, and it curled into a ball in her hand. 'This will show us where to find him.' She pointed to her TARDIS. 'Shall we?'

Ruath's TARDIS materialized in the shelter of a low stone wall, its shape now that of an old well. She pushed aside the wooden well cover and hopped out. 'Come on out,' she called back. 'It's dark.'

A dense mist rose out of the well and resolved itself into the four vampires, who looked around themselves in amazement. They were at the edge of a forest. Nearby was a town with a battered clock tower. Across the night, tracer fire was rattling down out of the hills onto the buildings. Every now and then a small explosion bloomed in the square. The noise was terrifying.

'Bosnia,' Madelaine sighed. 'Cheers.'

'It's not Bosnia,' Ruath glanced at her map. 'It's technically Croatia, but that's the whole nature of the current dispute. Now, we need to go . . .' she felt the ball of blood move in her palm, 'that way.' She set off. The others followed.

'That thing,' the bald man whispered, pointing back to the well. 'It's bigger on the inside than the outside.'

* * *

15

They made their way through the trees cautiously, Jake stopping to sniff the air at intervals. 'There's a lot of people about, all different sorts, all over the place.'

'And judging by what happened to Yarven,' Jeremy purred, 'they've got a lot of faith. Fighting men generally do.'

'Those we saw were Catholic partisans, one of the many factions assembled under the banner of one General Tito in the nineteen forties.' Ruath pursed her lips. 'Which shows what a strong leader can do, considering that the country eventually chose Communism. The local culture has been heavily influenced by vampires, there must have been a great number of them in the area at one point. That's why the partisans knew some of the lore. Fortunately not enough.'

'Well, they won't believe in us any more, will they?' Maddy muttered. 'Nobody does.' She was getting irritated by the clear sky. Sometimes she liked the little pricking sensations that stars, distant suns, produced on her skin. But not tonight. There were people in these woods who might be able to actually do them harm. After years of invulnerability, that was a very worrying thought.

Ruath smiled. 'Really? In this current conflict, Serbian spokesmen have alleged that an army of the Undead will arise to help them in their final battle.'

The vampires laughed. 'The cheek of them!' chuckled Jake. 'We'll mop up afterwards, ta very much.'

As the others moved forward, fanning out to better sniff the air, Madelaine tugged at the arm of Jake's jacket. 'Why are we doing this?' she whispered.

Jake shrugged. 'Something to do. Where would you rather be?'

'Back in Manchester or somewhere. That woman's out of her tree, you can see it in her eyes.'

'Listen.' He put a gentle hand on her shoulders. 'If things get rough, we'll just take off and go somewhere else, okay?'

Madelaine smiled, not particularly convinced. 'I just don't want to lose you. I don't want us to get hurt for nothing.'

'No chance. I'm not signing up for anything, I just want to see what this is all about.'

Ruath had looked back to them, a sharp little glance that Madelaine felt was directed at her. 'Hurry up,' she said. 'We haven't got all night.'

After ten minutes or so, the party came to a familiar clearing. The ball of blood in Ruath's hand pulsed and fell into liquid. She wiped it from her hand, conscious of the sudden attention of the Undead around her. 'We're here. Look for the pit.'

The bald man fell to his knees and sniffed the ground, scuttling about like a hunting dog. At one point, he raised his head. 'Eric,' he said.

'Sorry?' Ruath frowned.

'Eric Batley, pleased to meet you. Forgot to mention it in all the excitement.'

'Yes, yes . . .' Ruath waved her hand impatiently. 'Do get on with it.'

Jeremy raised a hand. 'Think I've found it.' He was staring down at a depression in the soil by a young sapling. 'Look at this tree.'

The vampires gathered around. The little sapling was covered with fleshy black flowers. Ruath clenched her fist round its stem and pulled it out of the ground. The roots thrashed and stretched, trying to reach the flesh of her face. 'One of yours, I think.' She threw the plant onto the ground, drew a small staser pistol and reduced it to ashes with a pulse of light.

17

She pointed to the soil where the plant had been growing. 'Vampire DNA on the move. Dig.'

Ten minutes later the vampires had reached the rough wooden cross. It had rotted greatly, but they still couldn't touch it. They'd burned their hands on quite a few silver crucifixes on the way down.

'Got a scientific explanation for that, then?' Eric asked.

'Yes. It's all to do with faith and how it affects the transition between the quantum and classical states of physics in the humanoid mind. An Ice Warrior wouldn't be able to perceive any of you, you know. It'd think that I was talking to myself.'

'Many a true word . . .' whispered Maddy.

'I'll go into the details of it with you at some point,' Ruath snapped, stepping forward to haul the rotting wooden cross out of the ground. She dropped it a few metres away.

Beneath it, the top of a skull-like head was visible, a few tufts of ragged hair poking out. 'There he is!' She helped the vampires with the final scrabble at the earth, carefully heaping the soil away from the parched skull. They revealed a furrowed brow and the top of a face, deathly pale. The eyes were closed.

'He's still conscious, he must be.' Ruath bent closer, reaching out to touch –

The corpse's eyes opened.

A hand shot out of the ground and grabbed her sleeve, pulling her down. Her face hit the earth by Yarven's head.

He was inching up out of the soil, his neck craning like a man thirsting for water. His teeth moved in a mechanical biting motion, his arm pulling Ruath inexorably towards his soil-filled mouth.

'No, master, no!' Jeremy pulled the gnarled old hand off Ruath.

18

She leapt to her feet. 'Get him out of there,' she whispered, a look of excitement on her face. 'Yarven must feed. But not on me. Not yet.'

Jeremy and Jake pulled the shuddering and naked figure up out of the soil. Yarven was as thin as a skeleton, skin hanging off him in flaps. Ragged bullet holes formed a series of white craters across his wizened chest. His eyes were caked shut, and soil fell from his mouth and nose in a steady stream. After the effort of grabbing for Ruath, he seemed weak as a baby.

'The Messiah.' Ruath knelt. 'Open your veins for him.'

Ruath's TARDIS console room was all oak panelling and elegant black leather padding. The console itself was silver and black, burnished metal and slate-like work surfaces. The Time Lady closed the doors behind the vampires as they carried Yarven in, and activated another control. A panel in the ceiling swept open and a silver hammock descended, a twisted umbilical of pipes leading down to it.

Jake was feeling quite weak, having made his contribution to the blood that the vampires had squirted down Yarven's throat. With a final effort, he managed to heft the inert body into the hammock. A plastic screen inflated around it and nutrients poured down the tubes, making them pulse with liquid.

'Second-hand blood doesn't do you much good,' Jake told Ruath. 'He needs the real thing.'

'He does indeed.' Ruath tapped some co-ordinates into the console and the TARDIS took off, the central silver column rising and falling. 'But for what I've got planned, human blood won't do.'

'You what?' Eric frowned. 'You expect the Messiah to drink the blood of animals? Why, the lowest Undead wouldn't stoop to that.'

19

'Animals? By Rassilon, no. Yarven needs a very rich brew if he's going to be good for my purposes.' The Time Lady flicked another control and the scanner screen spun out of the wall, a globe of the Earth flashing up on it. A cursor was blinking away below Australia. 'Another TARDIS, on the island that you call Tasmania. As I thought. Now, if I've got my timing right . . .' Her hand became a blur of motion as she asked her TARDIS's systems log to identify the user code of that particular vehicle. 'Yes.' She smiled up at the screen triumphantly. 'I missed him on Gallifrey, but I've certainly got him now.'

On the screen had appeared a picture of a fresh-faced blond young man, frowning a pained frown at the troubles of the world.

'The Doctor, in his fifth incarnation.' Ruath grinned triumphantly.

'So he's . . .' Madelaine raised a finger.

'A Time Lord. Oh yes . . .' Ruath stared at the screen in anticipation. 'That's why we need his blood.'

One

Tegan Jovanka leaned back in her deckchair and yawned. She had her legs stretched out in front of her, hoping for a bit of a tan, but Tassy's cloudy skies didn't look too hopeful. 'Bloody place,' she muttered, adjusting the brim of her redundant sun hat. 'Might as well be in Kent.' The countryside around Launceston was green and lush in a restrained, home counties sort of way. It was the first time Tegan had been to Tasmania. Apart from the plants and the shape of the houses, she couldn't see a lot of difference between it and England.

Tegan had, after all, become an air stewardess to see the world, the world being points to the north east and south west, having had enough of Brisbane and London. When her Aunt Vanessa had been murdered by the Master, the young Australian had teamed up with the tall, curly-haired adventurer in time and space known as the Doctor. However, before she'd got to know him that well, he'd fallen off a radio telescope and changed into a really dull Romper Room reject who'd rather play bloody cricket than do anything entertaining.

She didn't always think of him like that, but at this particular moment Tegan was sitting with her back to a cricket scoreboard. It indicated that the Doctor was currently enjoying a mind-numbing 88 not out. She had been marched into this guest enclosure, with access to the pavilion, thank God, and presented with a deckchair. A woman called Frances had chatted to her for a while, but

21

Tegan wasn't in the mood.

'You'll enjoy it, Tegan,' the Doctor had said. 'You're Australian.' She'd told him there and then that a charity cricket tournament in Tasmania was about as exciting to her as a Basic TARDIS Maintenance course would be to him, and about a quarter as useful. But he was already running around the console in excitement, tapping out co-ordinates like a vicar with the runs.

If she'd never met him, she'd have had a career by now. She'd had the chance to go back and have a real go at it, but then he'd showed up again. The least he could do would be to take her to some alien planets, let her meet some interesting people. Some monsters.

Tegan glanced at the Doctor as he carefully stepped forward to block a ball. His face was a study in concentration. For somebody so open, it was sometimes hard to tell what he was thinking.

She turned back to her book, Primo Levi's *If This Is A Man*. She'd lost her place. It'd been hard to read, these last few days. Like she ought to be doing something more important. But the book demanded that she finish it. It was the story of the author's confinement in a concentration camp. How he'd managed to survive such staggering inhumanity. What people could do to other people.

And how invasive it all was.

She put the book down again and put on her sunglasses. Why did the Mara have to have been a bloody snake? She could picture it, she kept on picturing it, wrapped around her brain.

Always there, he'd said. Maybe he'd been making some metaphorical point about the nature of evil, but that wasn't the way she saw it. She saw it like she was somebody with a terminal disease. Always waiting for the relapse. Just a question of bloody time.

Somebody was standing at her shoulder.

She looked up. It was Nyssa, in her blue and white dress. 'Hi,' Tegan muttered. 'What's up, you got bored with checking out the scoreboard?'

'I think I've got it . . .' Nyssa glanced up at the black slab behind them. 'You see, the number up there – '

'What I don't understand about cricket,' Tegan interrupted her, 'is that it's a sport where most of the team stay back in the pavilion and stuff their faces. They ought to be made to sit out here and suffer with the rest of us. I'll bet they've got a few tinnies back there.'

'Tinnies?' Nyssa sat down beside her, cross-legged.

Tegan sighed. 'Cans of lager. Alcohol, you know.'

'Yes. We had ale on Traken.' Nyssa came from a distant planet that, Tegan had come to believe, was the interstellar equivalent of Public Service Broadcasting. 'We had several sayings about it.'

'I'll bet.' Tegan opened her book again and pretended to read.

Nyssa began to play with her bracelet, a ring of Trakenite gold that she'd quietly taken to wearing after the death of Adric. 'Tegan . . .' Her voice had taken on that head prefect tone.

'What?'

'How are you feeling?'

'Fine.'

'About the Mara, I mean.'

'Yeah, I understood that that was what you meant. I'm fine.'

'Only you seem to have become very – '

Tegan threw down the book. 'I'm okay. Do you know what it's like to have all your doors thrown open? No you don't. And it's still in here, right? So you be careful, or I'll bite your head off.'

Nyssa was silent for a moment. 'I think you just did,' she said carefully. She stood up and walked away.

'Rabbits.' Tegan stamped her foot, angry at herself. Nyssa seemed to expect her to whinge about what she'd gone through, and that was annoying. Tegan just wanted to get on with something, anything. It was sitting here that was the problem.

Nyssa had gone into the pavilion. Tegan stood up and stretched, getting between several of the other spectators and a fine cover drive from the Doctor's batting partner, a man called Boon who had a stupid moustache. 'Sorry,' she muttered to them.

As she made her way towards the exit, there came a sudden shout and a gasp from the crowd. The spectators in the guest enclosure got to their feet and applauded.

The Doctor was walking back to the pavilion, his bat held high. Out for ninety.

'Serves you right,' said Tegan.

By the time she'd checked out the shops of Launceston's little centre, bought a bag of apples and tried on some bright flowery shorts, the light had started to fade. So had her anger. She'd say sorry to Nyssa and try to explain. It wasn't like the kid hadn't suffered herself. The Master was currently going around wearing her Dad's body like an off-the-peg suit. It was just that she was so level-headed and logical. On a camping holiday, Nyssa would have been the one with the emergency matches and the insect repellant. Tegan would have been the one without a tent.

1993 wasn't that different from the eighties, thank God. A glance in a bookshop cheered her with the news that the cold war was over, and it was great that that creep Hawke was out of office. Maybe things towards the end of the century were looking up. Book prices were still too bloody high, though.

The TARDIS had landed out by the nets that morning. The Doctor had explained to the organizers of the competition that the police box was a small part of his collection of thirties memorabilia. They'd been delighted, such behaviour being just what they'd expected from the writer of *By Lord Cranleigh's Invitation, Seventy Years Of Charity Elevens*, a piece that the Doctor had, apparently, had published in *Wisden*. Tegan had flicked through a pile of the Doctor's cricketing magazines at one point, and had been delighted to discover a ferocious letters-page dispute concerning the details of one of the Time Lord's historical reminiscences.

As she approached the nets in the dusk, she could see that he was practising alone, facing a steady stream of balls from a bowling machine. His cream coat hung from it, leaving him in his shirtsleeves, ignoring the chill of the evening air like he ignored the poor light. He was adjusting his stance, his blond hair catching the last light of the descending sun. His face was creased in a frown, but it wasn't the frown of somebody who was worried about duties or careers or anything serious. It was the frown of somebody free, somebody whose whole concentration was on enjoying the game. That could change, of course. Sometimes Tegan had glimpsed a giant old pain on that face, a sort of despair at how all the universe's hopes could end in violence. He'd always try to do something about that. But he preferred to just be free to play. He'd once said to her, and she thought he was quoting somebody: 'What do they know of cricket, who only cricket know?'

She could never be angry at him for long.

The latest ball spun in, hitting the ground at a low angle. The Doctor stroked it aside with sudden force and broke into a grin. 'Got it!' he exclaimed. He turned to Tegan, as if he'd been aware of her presence all the time. 'My eye wasn't quite in today.'

'Did your side win?'

'Oh yes.' The Doctor switched off the machine. 'We're in the quarter-final tomorrow, against Mike Gatting's side. How was your day?'

'Oh, I walked around a bit, did some shopping.'

The Doctor had pulled on his coat. He unrolled his panama hat from his pocket and knocked it into shape before perching it one-handed on his head. 'Nyssa said that you'd – '

'Yeah, well, I'm going to say sorry.'

'Been feeling bored.' He'd stuffed his hands in his pockets and met her gaze with that frown again. 'Would you prefer to go somewhere else?'

'No.' Tegan kicked a twig back into the band of forest that bordered the nets. 'It's just that she keeps going on about the Mara.'

'Ah.'

'I'd like to be able to forget it, but she wants to care and share. I snapped at her a bit.'

'Well, you've been through a very trying experience, it's only natural that you should – '

'Don't you start.'

'Sorry. Did you want to get something from the TARDIS?'

'No. Came to find you.'

'Tea, then, I think.' He picked up his cricket bag and headed back towards the pavilion, Tegan following. His face was lit with a brisk jollity that she knew was for her benefit but appreciated anyway. 'I'm told that our boarding house provides a bottomless pot.' He frowned again. 'Before eight o'clock.'

As they doubled their pace across the finely cut grass, the Doctor plucked the hat from his head and dropped it onto Tegan's. She put a hand on it to keep it there.

Nyssa was reading a thick volume of chemical abstracts

that she'd propped open on the small bedside table the boarding house had provided. Nyssa had never left Traken before the Doctor's future self, the Watcher, had appeared to spirit her away. She liked Earth, and could see why it was the Time Lord's favourite planet. It had the potential to be like her homeworld, but didn't have the enforced peace that had made Traken . . . dull. That was a hard word to apply to such a paradise, especially one that was now just a memory, but . . . things were always better when they were difficult to achieve. If two people on Earth were good to each other, it was because they'd made that decision.

There was a knock on the door. 'Come in,' Nyssa called.

Tegan popped her head round the door, looking abashed. She was carrying the Doctor's hat. 'Hi.'

'Hello, Tegan.' Nyssa smiled. 'I shan't ask you how you are.'

'Yeah, right . . .' Tegan glanced at the volume of abstracts. 'Hey, I think I saw the movie. Great twist ending.'

'I think the ending's quite obvious. The dissolution and cooling of the universe.'

'I wanted to say sorry.' Tegan sat down on the bed and dropped the hat on the bedpost. 'I shouldn't have snapped at you.'

'That's all right. You've been through a – '

'Don't say it. I was just as bloody-minded before the Mara.'

'Yes,' Nyssa agreed. 'But we worry about you. It is hard to tell whether you're really suffering or whether you're just, as you put it, moaning.'

'Thanks.' Tegan grinned. 'I'm just not used to people coming right out with all this concern. I thought that the poms were soft, but you two – '

27

Nyssa was staring at her. 'You thought that the apples were soft?'

'No, poms, Brits, English people.'

'Ah. I think that the TARDIS's power of translation sometimes has trouble between Australian and Trakenite. Perhaps that's where the difficulty lies.'

'Perhaps.' Tegan gave her friend a quick hug. 'Cheers, anyway. Good night.'

'Good night, Tegan.' Nyssa shook her head as the older woman left, and returned to her book. Perhaps the Doctor's impulse to take Tegan to Australia had been the right one after all. She glanced at the panama hat at the foot of the bed and smiled.

Nyssa read for another five minutes, and found her concentration faltering. She put down the book, locked the door, and got ready for bed. She'd closed the curtains, and thought about leaving the window open ... on Traken, you could have done the same with the door, but freedom had its price. She closed it. Finally, she settled down to sleep.

It began during a dream. Tremas, her father, was telling her that she must get out of their house, that there was no longer any place for her at his hearth. He'd found a new wife, and she was going to have a baby.

Nyssa protested. She'd always been a loving daughter to him, it was wonderful that he was alive and himself, could she not stay?

No, Tremas waved a finger. She must go and sleep in the hut on the hills, with only a rough blanket to cover her. When the baby was born, they would have to treat it as an only child too, so it would be exactly like her. So she could not be in the house with it.

At night, and it was night now, Nyssa would creep up to the window of her father's house and stare in at him and his new bride, slowly dancing by the fire. She had a face, but Nyssa couldn't recognize her.

Something was moving across the wooden floor. A naked baby.

It looked up at the window. It could see her!

The baby rushed across the room, its tiny limbs working like an insect's. With one leap, it was atop the chair, and had its palms and giant face against the window. Its eyes were full of watery desire. They were blue, but they could change colour any day. Its stubby little palms were white against the glass. Its full lips were sucking at the window, making a little cloud of white on red.

'Let me in,' he said.

Nyssa wanted to know what the baby's name was, so she carefully undid the window catch, and let it inside.

The cold air woke her up.

She was standing by the window in her night-dress.

And the baby was holding her hand.

Nyssa stifled her urge to jump back. The baby would have fallen from the window-sill where it stood. It was a little, naked, blue-eyed boy, about a year old. No, more than that. It was standing on the window frame, swaying. Only its grip on her finger was keeping it upright. It was smiling at her and pointing, in that curious way of babies, with one finger and all the others spread out, at the Doctor's hat. She looked quickly round the room, expecting for an insane moment to see a mother who'd handed her the child. Nyssa knew enough about Earth children to realize that the baby couldn't possibly have got here on its own.

'Somebody must have broken in here,' she said to the child, uncertainly. 'And sat you on the window-sill. Thank goodness I woke up, I might have knocked you over the edge.' The story sounded ridiculous as she said it, but it was the only way she could make the facts fit.

She picked the baby up. 'Come on then, let's go and see the Doctor. He'll know what to do with you.' The little boy breathed hot baby breath against her cheek. She reached for the dressing-gown that hung from the wardrobe door, and in doing so exposed the mirror on the front of the cabinet.

In the mirror, she wasn't carrying anything.

Nyssa looked down at the weight in her arms. The baby opened his mouth. Out of his pink, smooth, upper gums, two elongated fangs emerged.

With a convulsive jerk of her arms, she threw the thing onto the bed.

It bounced immediately back at her, flying through the air and grabbing the arm of her night-dress. It spun onto her throat, its little hands pulling at the material around her collarbone.

Terrified, Nyssa found that she couldn't scream. She couldn't will herself to make the sound. She ran at the wall, all instinct not to hurt the baby gone. Its head hit the plaster and rebounded, uninjured.

They fell into a corner and the baby succeeded in ripping open the material at her shoulder. Nyssa grabbed the infant with both hands, trying to pull it off her, but it had enormous strength. Tiny fingers grasped her ear and pulled so hard that Nyssa opened her mouth wide, unable to yell out the pain of it.

The baby's other hand grabbed her bottom lip, pulling it until it was white. Nyssa hit the baby with her fists, punched its body frantically, rolled around the floor, trying to dislodge it as the pain in her face grew greater. She could taste the child's fingers and they were like earth, like old mud in a playground. She tried to bite them but couldn't bring her teeth to bear on the little vice that held her lip. The baby's warm mouth descended to the flesh of her neck, and she thrashed again, kicking against the door in the hope that somebody would hear her.

It would hurt so much, it would hurt too much for her to stand. She wanted to scream, she wanted to beg the baby to at least let her scream.

Two injections into the jugular vein.

She thought of the smell of bottled anaesthetic when she felt the sharp, quick sting, of inoculations at her father's hands.

A huge relief washed over her at the lack of pain.

Then the baby began to suckle.

It was sucking and licking the blood out of her neck, its little tongue working at the wounds. She could lie here until it had taken all of it, until she'd had her life eaten away. An awful calm descended on her, and she realized that the baby wasn't just taking her blood out, it was putting something in, a calming agent, a premed. The animal had to be calm.

There was a gentle knock on the door behind her. 'Nyssa? You okay?' Tegan's voice.

There was another little pain as the baby disengaged itself from her vein, and looked up at the door. It smiled, its lips coated in red, and then bent to resume its task. The teeth injected themselves once more, and the sucking resumed.

Nyssa made a great effort of will, and slammed her feet against the door again.

'Nyssa?' Tegan asked, more concerned now. 'Can you open the door?'

She couldn't reply. Her legs wouldn't move again.

'I'm coming in.' The door vibrated twice with the impact as Tegan kicked at the wood. It was a narrow corridor, she wouldn't have been able to get much leverage. The door stood firm. 'Hold on!' she shouted. 'I'll go and get the Doctor!'

Nyssa shivered as the baby detached itself from her throat once more. It looked at her, calmly, a look of well-fed peace. It smiled a red smile. Then it rose from her, floated up to the ceiling and, like a summer wasp, out of the window.

Nyssa put her hand to her throat, gingerly, as one inspects a tooth after dentistry. There were two tender puncture wounds, but they weren't bleeding. Her neck was bruised around them. Her lip hurt far worse, and her ear was throbbing red. Coughing, she stood up, and tottered to her bed.

She pulled the covers up over her and grabbed her pillow, pressing her neck down into it.

There was a clunking sound from the door and it sprang open. The Doctor strode in with Tegan behind him, replacing a skeleton key in the pocket of his dressing-gown. 'Nyssa?' he asked, urgently. 'Are you all right?'

'Yes . . .' she was surprised to hear herself say it, and to hear the measured tones she said it in. 'I'm fine.'

'Oh . . .' he seemed almost embarrassed. 'Sorry. Tegan said she heard a commotion. Must have been a nightmare.'

'Yes, it must have been. I was asleep.' No, she wanted to shout, I was awake, I was assaulted.

'Just as well I didn't kick down the door,' Tegan muttered. 'Did you bash on it, though?'

'I have been known to sleep-walk.'

'Yes . . .' The Doctor frowned, glancing around the room. He went to the end of the bed and recovered his hat, staring at it curiously. 'Well,' he decided, folding his hands behind his back, 'we'll leave you in peace. Tegan – '

'Before you go,' Nyssa's voice rose in pitch. She felt like she was speaking properly for the first time. 'Could you do something for me, please?'

'Yes, of course.'
'Close the window.'

Ruath stood on a tree-covered hillside above Launceston, her arm outstretched. Her squad of vampires stood behind her, looking about them with bemusement. They'd made another stop after their trip to the Balkans, in Sunderland, where they'd picked up their unusual passenger. Ruath's TARDIS, disguised as a bush, was standing behind them, its open door throwing a triangle of golden light across the scrub.

'I'm tired,' sighed Madelaine.

'You would be,' nodded Ruath. 'You've spent more than one night-time awake. Get used to it.'

'Who's this lad gone after?' asked Eric. 'One of your lot, is it?'

'Correct. A fellow Time Lord. His name is the Doctor.' Ruath pushed a wayward hair back off her forehead. 'He likes to think of himself as human, and so he hangs around this world, pursuing all sorts of trivia.'

Madelaine smiled nastily at the tone in the Time Lady's voice. 'You two go back a long way, then?'

Ruath didn't react. 'We have history, yes. Ah, here comes the Child.'

In the sky, a tiny speck was floating towards them. It resolved itself into the figure of a baby, giggling and kicking its legs happily. The Child was one of Jeremy's acquaintances. He'd recommended him to Ruath as something that might get past the guard of whoever she was hunting, and the Time Lady had agreed.

The baby settled on Ruath's arm like a hunting falcon.

'Well?' she asked it. 'Have you a belly full of his blood?'

The baby burped and smiled.

'He, ah, doesn't talk . . .' Jeremy murmured. 'Sorry and all that, but he was taken at a very early age. He mainly

33

acts on instinct, but if you point him in the right direction and give him a sniff of your victim . . .'

'I did provide him with a sample of the Doctor's DNA, stolen from the bio-data files.' Ruath frowned. 'I want to know. Could one of you . . ?'

Jake sighed and put a finger to the baby's lips. He then applied it to his own. 'You're all right,' he nodded. 'That's not human blood. I never tasted anything like that before.'

'Good!' Ruath patted the baby on the head. 'Let's make use of it.'

They took the baby back to Ruath's TARDIS, Madelaine holding it by the foot like a balloon. Inside, Ruath checked on Yarven's condition and declared herself satisfied.

'How much blood will the Child have metabolized?' she asked Jeremy.

'Not much. He generally only feeds once a week or so.'

'He can't have the stomach to carry a full nine pints!' laughed Eric.

Ruath looked at him sharply. 'Like my TARDIS, vampires are bigger on the inside. Didn't you know?'

Madelaine put a hand on her stomach. 'I feel all hollow now.'

Ruath took a thin tube from the silver hammock in which Yarven hung, and unreeled it, attaching a needle to the end. She slipped this into the baby's wrist, at which it only giggled, not allowing itself to feel pain. She repeated the process with the other wrist, so the Child floated, two lines attaching it to the hammock. Then she pressed a button on the console. The lines ran red as the blood was drained from the baby to the sleeping vampire, and back again.

'It's a filtration system,' Ruath explained. 'Yarven gets the alien blood, and the Child gets his own passed back to him.'

'What will this stuff do?' asked Jake.

'It will enable Yarven to take up his rightful place as Lord of Vampires. He is, after all, the last representative of a vampire nobility created by the Great Vampire himself.' Ruath sighed, apparently deciding that this would be a good point for a history lesson. 'Recently, certain rather misguided elements on my planet, that's Gallifrey, aided an attempt to resurrect that grand creature. They weren't interested in the cause of the Undead. They were foolish enough to think that Gallifrey as it stands now could rule space and time, with a man called Borusa at its head. I watched, amused, as they attempted to gain the services of the being called Agonal – '

'Agonal!' Jeremy gasped. 'The fools!'

The other vampires looked at each other. 'Is he hard, then, this Agonal?' asked Madelaine.

'The hardest. Not hard enough, however, to pose a serious threat to the omnitemporal power of Rassilon. The cosmos is now one Eternal poorer. No, in order to restore Gallifrey to its former glory, to secure its future, we must follow my path. The books I have consulted say that the final end of the Great Vampire, its death by sunlight, will be the prelude to the arising of the Vampire Messiah. That event has just occurred. The books also say that the means of his triumph will be his enemies. He escaped to Earth in the Doctor's TARDIS. I realized that was what had occurred just after the said TARDIS had left Gallifrey. If I had worked it out a few moments earlier, I would have stowed away with him, and all this would have happened in the nineteen thirties. But even that, even that was foreseen by the ancient sages who saw how the future was to progress.'

Maddy glanced sidelong at Jake. They were both concealing smiles at the Thatcheresque tones that were driving Ruath's voice higher and higher.

'I ran into the Time Lady called Romana,' she was continuing. 'And she volunteered to tell me of her experiences with the Undead. She fell, let us say, before the force of destiny.'

'But not without smacking her one ...' whispered Jake, indicating Ruath's cheek.

'I made her help me with the controls of the Time Scoop before I disposed of her, used it to view the paths of the Doctor's many incarnations, and when I saw that he was on Earth now, in his most vulnerable form, with many vampires ready and waiting ... I knew that the time of the prophecies was at hand. Hence all I have done, hence Yarven.' She raised her hands triumphantly, as if expecting applause.

'Well, that's very impressive, like,' nodded Jake.

There came a sudden shout from the hammock, which began to buck and twist as if the occupant was in agony.

'Yarven!' shouted Ruath, running to him. She hit a control to cut off the blood supply, and the convulsions subsided. She turned on Jake, furious. 'That was not Time Lord blood!'

'Well how was I supposed to know? I don't know one lot of alien blood from another.'

'The Child does, ah, mainly work on instinct,' murmured Jeremy apologetically. 'He might have got a bit mixed up.'

Ruath made a spire with her fingers, visibly calming herself. 'Well. This is a set-back. It means that I shall have to do something that I didn't want to do. Rather a last resort, in fact.' She unhooked the Child from the blood circulation system, a look of quiet determination on her face. 'I knew that it might come to this. I shall have to give Yarven my own blood.' She opened a hatch on the console and pressed a series of controls.

The console room darkened as power drained away from the walls. A door opened overhead and a crystalline probe descended, a glowing series of interlocking cylinders.

From the wall a metal chair emerged, with a heavy rubber tube connected to each arm rest. The chair had metal cuffs at the hands and feet. Ruath quickly sat in it, and began locking the ankle cuffs. 'During this process, I must ask you to ignore any pleas for help I might make,' she told the vampires. 'It's not going to be pleasant, but one has to make sacrifices for the cause. It's about time somebody did.' She looked up at Madelaine suddenly, while securing the first wrist cuff, and shrugged. 'I mean, it may be fine. All I'm saying is, if I scream and plead, please ignore it. It's all for the best.'

Madelaine nodded. 'We understand.'

Jeremy helped to connect up the other cuff. 'Be careful,' he advised.

'Sorry, no,' Ruath took a deep breath. 'Activate speed plasma drill, then full rejuvenation. Thank you, all. Goodbye.'

There was a sudden thump of machinery and Ruath sucked in a breath, slamming her back up against the chair. A sharp sound came from the cuffs, and she bit her lip.

A powerful liquid throbbing resonated through the fabric of the console room, and Ruath closed her eyes. She was getting whiter as the vampires watched, blue veins starting to stand out on her neck. Her skin became flaccid and dull, and her lips were the grey of death.

She was silent throughout, her chin held up and still.

The roaring stopped. Ruath's head fell forward, the muscles no longer strong enough to hold it.

'She's given everything,' whispered Jeremy. 'All her blood.'

Suddenly the crystal lattice in the ceiling began to pulse, and the grating sound of take-off filled the room. The walls reflected the beat of the light, the whole craft booming with noise and glare.

Ruath's face took on the colour of the light, an orange glow that enveloped it and held to it like a second skin. The glare spread to cover her body. The vampires staggered, their senses suddenly full of a rich, organic scent.

The glow flared to white light around Ruath, and she was gone. Then, everything stopped. The light faded, all was silent. The cuffs opened, and somebody fell forward from Ruath's seat.

Somebody dressed in a red velvet gown and long gloves. Her hair was different too, black and flowing to her waist.

Jeremy ran to the new arrival and helped her stand. 'Who are you?' he asked, amazed.

'Why, Jeremy,' the voice was rich and full of laughter, 'it's me. Ruath. Ruath number three. A new body, a whole new me.' Even the bruise had vanished. She raised her elegant hands to her face and grinned at them. 'Isn't it wonderful!'

'I agree!' The new voice caused the vampires to spin around. It was powerful and dark, with a cultured edge to it. It came from a patch of shadow and mist that had risen around the remains of the silver hammock, now a pile of tatters on the floor. The darkness resolved itself into a cloaked figure, a thin, sharp-faced man with shining eyes and a neatly pointed beard. He was dressed in the garb of an aristocrat, waistcoat and boots set with silver buckles and purple silks. He held his hand out in demand. 'Give me the ring,' he commanded.

Ruath quickly reached into one of the pouches her

new gown had around its waist, and threw the silver band to the man. It sped through the air and spun onto his upraised finger.

'I am Yarven,' he said. 'Lord of the House of Yar. Last survivor of the Great Vampire's progeny, father to all the Earth's Undead. I am the Vampire Messiah. Kneel before me.'

They all did so. Even the Child.

'Good . . .' Yarven looked around slowly, delighting in his new strength. 'You have done well, my children, to free me from my long imprisonment. Especially you, Ruath, who are of the same blood as that insolent wench Romana. You honour the Time Lords with your actions.'

Ruath looked up at Yarven, her green eyes glittering. 'You have been treated with Numismaton gas, my Lord. Your body is awash with symbiotic nuclei. Do you not feel the joined power of both Time Lord and Vampire?'

Yarven threw his head back and laughed in joy. 'Yes! I do feel it. It is a magnificent sensation, the ability to travel through time and space. Name your boon, Ruath, for I would grant anything to the one who has given me such freedom.'

Ruath licked her lips. 'I desire nothing more than for our bloodlines to be joined. I have done this for you, Lord. Do the same for me.'

'Very well.' Yarven opened his arms. 'Come to me.'

Ruath stood and walked to him, still unsteady.

He put a hand on both of her shoulders. 'You will be my consort,' he told her. 'We shall be King and Queen of the Night, and we will unite all of human and Time Lord society in the great communion of the Undead. We shall feed through all time and space. There will be no limit to the letting of blood in our name, and no power in the universe to challenge us. You, with the wisdom of your people, have brought us this far. Together, nothing is beyond our reach.'

He bent forward and bit her, drawing his cloak around her as she cried out at the sensation. History being born, a grand marriage of peoples and destinies. Her own wish made flesh. Ruath could feel the new principles taking root in her, the new abilities rushing to remake her genes.

Holding her against him, Yarven raised his head once more and bared his bloody fangs. Her blood was dripping off them, Ruath realized with a little shudder of delight.

'Thus it begins!' bellowed Yarven, his voice full of the lust of blood. 'The time of humanity on this world has come to an end. The long night is starting!' He spread his arms wide and shouted a berserker shout. 'The age of the Undead is upon us!'

Two

Meat meat meat meat meat.

The trouble was that they had stopped bands performing at the Civic Centre. Dr Claypole were very upset about it.

I will rule the world.

Nyssa woke, gently, to find that she had gathered the sheets into a knot in her hands.

Surely last night had been a dream. She felt fine now. She put a hand to her neck, smiling to herself.

It was bruised. Why should that be? Her mouth didn't hurt, her ear didn't hurt, why should her neck actually feel like the experiences of last night had been real? It had been some sort of repression dream, a lurid message from her unconscious concerning the death of her planet. Her father, after all, was now in some senses a vampire, therefore she had invented a vampire child to punish herself with. It was all perfectly simple. Nothing that a better diet and a few brisk walks couldn't cure.

Probably a crick in her neck. Something with salt was required for breakfast. Poached eggs would be appealing. Mrs Capricelli would certainly provide some if asked.

She couldn't stay in bed all day. Now that she had understood cricket, Launceston had a library that she wanted to explore. Perhaps there would be something interesting about marsupials.

So. Get up.

She did so, throwing aside the sheets and wandering into the bathroom.

Well, that showed that she was being silly. There she was in the mirror. A little pale, but reassuringly solid. And her neck had –

Two small holes in it.

Nyssa shook her head, irritated. 'It can't be true,' she said. 'I would feel different if it were true.'

The Doctor was peering at a teapot over the breakfast table, holding it gently in both hands. His spectacles were on the bridge of his nose. 'Mrs Capricelli has a Georgian teapot,' he told Tegan, who was reading the paper.

'How nice for her . . .' murmured the Australian absently, taking another bite of toast. 'What's your star sign?'

The Doctor lowered the teapot and frowned at her. 'My what?'

'What star sign were you born under? There's one here that sounds so like you I'll bet you're a Cancerian.'

The Doctor hopped up and glanced over Tegan's shoulder, taking a corner of the paper in his hand. 'The constellations one sees from Gallifrey are different from those seen on Earth, Tegan. Add to that the fact that Time Lords make no note of what ancient stellar pattern happens to be on the horizon when they're born, and the fact that astrology is an unscientific and unprovable system based on blind chance, and – ' His face fell as he saw the entry for Cancer. 'Stuffy?' He let go of the paper and glared at her.

'Never mind.' Tegan carefully kept a straight face. 'There's an opportunity for romance on Wednesday.'

The Doctor sat down again, still regarding her suspiciously. 'Does your paper have anything to say about tall, dark strangers?'

'You're worried about the Master?'

'No, I should think the Xeraphins took care of him. It's the Black Guardian that concerns me. Of late, I've been piloting the TARDIS to deliberate destinations such as this one quite often. The more I do that, the greater the chance that he'll launch some attempt at revenge.'

'Let him try,' Tegan smiled. 'Hey, Nyssa!'

Nyssa had entered, wearing a high-necked Traken jacket over her dress. 'I'm sorry if I disturbed you last night,' she said.

'Not at all, Nyssa!' The Doctor pulled out a chair for her and she primly sat. 'How are you feeling this morning?'

'Better. I was dreaming about the past, about Traken. That can sometimes be very traumatic.'

'You were bucking like a horse,' Tegan told her. 'Do you often sleep-walk?'

'Lately, yes.' Nyssa raised a hand to her face as the landlady pulled back the curtains. She felt suddenly sun-burnt, as if she'd gone to sleep with her hand outside the shade on a beach. 'Goodness, that's bright.'

'Is it? Yes, I suppose it is rather.' The Doctor gently moved Nyssa's head from side to side with his hands, looking into her eyes. 'Have you been having headaches?'

'No. As I said – ' Nyssa had raised her voice. She paused, and when she spoke again it was more level. 'I'm fine. I'm a little embarrassed about all this. It isn't the first time that I've been overcome by my memories, and I'm sure it isn't the last. Please don't dwell on it.'

'No . . .' The Doctor glanced back to the teapot, rather abashed. 'Mrs Capricelli,' he called, 'is there any chance that we might have another pot of tea?'

Night in another place. Total silence. Yarven spread his

43

arms wide. The landscape around him was a flat and windy heath, surrounded in all directions by muddy wastelands. The only thing breaking the flatness of it all was Ruath's TARDIS, a tall white rock atop which they stood. The Time Lady was behind Yarven, hooded, enjoying his delight.

'Magnificent!' he was laughing. 'It rather reminds me of home. You mean to say that this is the future of Earth? Why, my dear, this takes all the sport out of it!'

'This is one possible future,' Ruath told him, 'that the Earth may come to at some distant point in its calendar. I brought you here to encourage you, darling, not to reassure you. Step off the rock at your peril, for touches like that make futures fixed and destinies finite. My ring allows me to change timestreams, I wouldn't be here if it didn't, but we really shouldn't push it. The Time Lords may be watching us even now. They have a special interest in this place.'

'Let them see . . .' Yarven chuckled. 'They should learn to fear me. Tell me, are there creatures here?'

'Yes. They live totally under the chemical swamps. They should have smelled us, or the blood that I splashed about. Ah, look, here they are, the lovely things!'

From the flat sludge ahead, a gnarled blue head rose. Puckered lips flexed inquisitively under bright eyes. The creature wore the tattered remains of some ancient uniform.

'A Haemovore,' Ruath smiled. 'The natural evolutionary inheritor of a pollution-ravaged Earth. They live in the saline solution of the oceans, plankton feeding, and occasionally they gang together to ambush a great whale. This is my point, Yarven. Even without us, the humans become vampires. History is on our side. The only pity is that the transformation comes too late, when the planet's in decline, rolling around a bloated star. Our job, my dear, is to bring the future on more swiftly.'

The Haemovore stared at them, blinking. Yarven stroked his beard, studying the creature. 'Yes . . . Do you have any thoughts on how we're going to go about it?'

'I was hoping you'd ask. I do have a plan, it's really quite simple. It involves the Doctor, as a matter of fact.'

'What!' Yarven spun and stared at her. 'The Doctor . . . the one who became a hero to those vile peasants. The one who staked the Great Vampire. He is on Earth?'

'Yes. Do you hate him?'

'Hate him? Not as a man, no, I have never met him. But as a symbol for resistance, a figurehead . . . when I was a child, his name was the one the servants used as an example for their wretched hopes. Ruath, you have told me of all these prophecies concerning me, and I have . . . my own reasons for believing them to be true, reasons which are only becoming clear to me now. Am I destined to kill this Doctor, this destroyer of the Undead?'

Ruath paused, biting her lip in concentration. 'Not exactly, my Lord. The books are clear about your role. You are to capture the Doctor, and then leave him to my mercy. I'll torture him over a period of days, and share out his blood amongst your lieutenants. You have a greater destiny to fulfil, by sacrificing yourself to – '

'Yes, yes, you keep mentioning that. Since you did me the service of murdering the one called Romana, I am sorry that I cannot return the favour. As for the Doctor, it may not be my destiny to kill him, but I will enjoy seeing him suffer for the harm he has done my people.' He turned to Ruath and regarded her with a piercing gaze. 'But never presume to manipulate me with this prophecy of yours. I am not this Agonal who was so easily tricked by the wiles of Gallifrey.'

'No, sir.' Ruath dropped to one knee. 'You are the Messiah. I follow only your cause now.'

'Good. Rise now.' Yarven lifted her to her feet and they stepped back down into the TARDIS.

After the rock had faded away, the Haemovore gave a long sigh and sank back into the warm mud.

A day went by, back when the Doctor was. He played badly. Twenty six. Out to an ordinary-looking ball, caught the edge of the bat and the wicket keeper got it. The others scraped to a hundred and seventy, but Boon glanced at the troubled look in the Time Lord's eye and refused to let him bowl. They still won.

Tegan took a bus to the countryside and wandered about. She'd asked Nyssa to come with her, but the Trakenite had just shaken her head and retreated back to her room to read. Tegan was kind of hoping that she'd have come along. For once, she could have done a bit of the explaining.

There was a particular slope that Tegan would have liked to have helped her with. An earthy hill with a cluster of trees on top. Tegan threw her bag up and launched herself up towards it, climbing with her hands, getting her shorts dirty. If Nyssa had been there, she could have pulled her behind her. They'd done all right with the Doctor's zero cabinet back on Castrovalva.

She grabbed a tree trunk at the top, and hauled herself upright, taking a deep breath of the Tasmanian air. Like a lot of urban Australians, Tegan had never seen any of the poisonous spiders or insects of her country. There were probably hundreds of them out here.

Not to mention snakes.

The view from the top of the hill was wonderful.

Nyssa looked out from her bedroom window and calculated the distance across to the cricket ground and then the TARDIS. All that ground to cover in the sunlight before she could gain access to her laboratory. She could put herself through a full diagnostic program. If only there wasn't so much sunlight.

She could run from shadow to shadow, perhaps. Wear a big hat and stay out of the worst of it.

Wait until nightfall.

Nyssa slumped onto the edge of the bed, her hands bunched in her lap. If only she could tell somebody about all this. It seemed silly to be so feverish in bright summer. She lay back, tired through worry. Before she knew anything else, she was asleep.

Night fell, and all was well across the island, insects chirruping, the town alive with the sound of people in bars and on streets. Tegan had returned for tea, armed with a strong grin, ready to shake some fun into Nyssa. But the Trakenite had already retired, she was told, so she accepted the Doctor's invitation to dinner. Best frock job because it was a long table for several of the tournament's guests, with Mike Gatting and his wife at the head. Thankfully they talked about things other than cricket, and Gatting kept on doing tricks with the wine glasses, making them sing with his finger. Tegan and the woman called Frances exchanged looks and made impressed noises. Gatting grinned at them.

'The Doctor,' Frances said, proposing a toast at one point. Those around the table echoed her. 'I wouldn't dream of calling it affectation not to have a real name, but I do worry about your past. You haven't done anything criminal, have you?'

The team laughed. 'We can, ah, offer asylum if you have, Doc,' David Boon said, straight-faced.

Tegan glanced at the Doctor. He'd stopped in the middle of taking a spoonful of soup, looking around as if genuinely accused of something. His mind had been on other things. Slowly, a grin broke across his face. 'I don't think I've done anything that would disgrace the TCCB. Not lately, at any rate. And, as in the small matter of being out, W. G. Grace didn't always admit to a name either.'

There was general laughter. After the meal had ended Tegan and the Doctor walked home. The Doctor had his hands stuck in his pockets, deep in thought under the brim of his panama.

'Penny for your thoughts?' asked Tegan.

'Not a bargain at that price I'm afraid. I'm worried about Nyssa.'

'Yeah, so am I. She's going all weird. Maybe it's the sun.'

'Perhaps. Ah well, only three days left to go, unless it rains. Then we can go somewhere more exciting.'

Tegan smiled. 'I thought you were having fun?'

'I am. But neither of you seem to be – '

'I like it here. It's Nyssa you ought to be worrying about.'

'Yes . . .' The Doctor returned to his musings and increased the speed of his stride to the point where Tegan was tottering along on her heels to keep up with him.

Nyssa had woken up a few hours ago to watch the sunset. Inside her, it felt like dawn. She opened the window of her room and sat on the sill, feet dangling over the edge. She watched the Southern Cross appear overhead, and held up her palms to the great tingling spread of the Magellanic Clouds.

If she had a powerful optical telescope, she would be able to see Traken's sun from here. The light from it was still travelling. She'd be seeing some prehistoric solar flares, the state of the star as it lighted the day while . . . she did a quick calculation: the first Union agreement was signed.

48

She had stopped herself feeling bitter about it very early on. The Master had destroyed Traken as a side effect of what he was doing, a farcical sub-plot. Sometimes she dreamed of him as a Melkur, calcified, sweating away his childish evil. But if they ever met again, she knew that she'd try to communicate with the good man inside him, rather than take any sort of revenge. She had time enough to meet him again, after all. She was going to live forever.

The knock on the door made her leap back from the window and close it. Tegan was at the door again, Nyssa realized without knowing how. She crossed the room and opened it. 'Hello. How was dinner?'

'Great. You missed out. I just wanted to make sure you were okay. No more nightmares?'

'No.'

'Okay.' Tegan paused, as if expecting something more. 'I'm really enjoying the book you lent me.'

'Good. I'm glad.'

'Do you want to talk about something?'

'About what?'

'Oh . . . nothing. Listen to me, I'm doing to you exactly what I didn't like you doing to me. Sorry.'

Nyssa managed a smile. 'That's all right.'

'Okay, sleep well tonight, yeah?'

'I'll try. Good night, Tegan.' Nyssa closed the door and leant on it, her hand reaching up to her neck.

Tegan watched a bit of Tassy TV, repeats of old British comedy shows and stuff, and then settled down to read before going to sleep. She got through a few pages of Primo Levi before the hand holding the book began to tire and her eyes lost their concentration. She dropped the book on top of the Gideon Bible on the bedside table and switched off the light, turning over to sleep.

Hours passed. The room creaked as the wood and

plaster contracted with the declining heat. Tegan moved in sleep, turning from one side to the other and pulling the blankets after her.

Around three o'clock a mist hissed in under the window. It collected itself into the form of Jeremy Sanders, who stood at the end of Tegan's bed, looking down at her hungrily. He moved silently around the bed and sat on the corner by Tegan's head. He reached out a hand and stroked her cheek. 'Tegan Jovanka? That's what Ruath says you're called. Rather an Australian name, eh? Wake up. Gently now.'

Tegan opened her eyes. Her muscles had all tensed. A voice had got in her ear, her sleeping mind told her, and was trying to tell her things. Be quiet, it was saying.

Be what?

She sat upright, slapping the hand away from her face. 'Who the hell are you?' she shouted.

'My name's Jeremy. Delighted. I was just going to bite you on the neck, if that's all right. That is all right, isn't it?'

His eyes closed on hers, and a dozen hard suggestions thudded into her brain. Tegan suddenly imagined a snake inside, roused ever so slightly, raising its head out of sleep with a wicked gleam in its eye. The image distracted her. He was talking into her again, trying to make her submit to what he said. They were inches apart now, his eyes bearing down on hers.

'Are you a vampire?' she asked. Back in Brisbane, before he died, Tegan's old Serbian grandfather had told her endless stories about vampires. She hadn't believed a word of it, even when she was little.

'Oh yes,' Jeremy replied. 'Wouldn't ask otherwise.'

'Yeah, okay then, go ahead.' Tegan suddenly turned aside and unbuttoned the collar of her nightgown. 'Careful about it, I don't want to have to go around with a jacket on all summer.'

50

Jeremy frowned, a trifle unsatisfied. 'Very well. Pardon me.' He bent to his task.

Tegan's hand had reached behind him, and stealthily grabbed one of the books on her table. As Jeremy closed on her neck, she slammed the spine of the Gideon Bible into the back of his head.

The vampire screeched and swished off the side of the bed like a cartoon character. Tegan leapt out of bed, brandishing the Bible before her. It seemed that a lot of the stuff Grandad had said was spot on.

Sanders was clutching his skull in pain. Amongst his immaculate hair, a tiny white cross had burnt through to the flesh, a reflection of the one on the book's spine. 'Very clever of you,' he told her. 'But that only worked because you thought it would. You have no real religious faith, certainly not in that collection of pious lies you're holding. You can't hold me back with it.' He took a step forward.

'Yeah, but you couldn't hypnotize me, could you?'

'Indeed. You have great strength of will. All that means is that this is going to be more unpleasant for you.'

'I've got faith in lots of things. Qantas, the republic, James Reyne.'

'None of which you can bring strongly enough to mind at present. You'll have a go, fail, and then I'll eat you. Wouldn't it be better to go out with some dignity, old girl?'

Tegan glanced about the room, looking for some familiar icon. If she'd been at home, it'd be easier, but hotel rooms weren't full of objects of faith. Exactly the bloody opposite. Then she glanced down at the book she'd knocked onto the floor. She squatted quickly and grabbed it. 'Try this!' she called, making herself step towards the advancing vampire. 'I've got faith in the words of Primo Levi!'

51

Sanders faultered. 'You really shouldn't – '

Tegan flicked open a page and began to read at random and with force, drowning out the vampire's words. She kept on walking until she was nose to nose with the creature. 'You can't lay a finger on me, can you?' she told him. 'I've got a good book in my hands, and a dirty great snake in my brain, so get back!' She emphasized the point with a finger stuck very nearly up Jeremy's nose. 'Or I'll bite your head off.'

Jeremy looked around, distraught. 'We'll return,' he told her. 'You can't keep this up forever.'

'Yeah? Well, my mate's a Time Lord, and if I had any Aussie wine handy it'd be like holy water, so you just flap off and terrorize someone else, you big wuss.'

Sanders stared at her for a moment, and then gave a little snarl of defeat. He dispersed into a mist again, and swiftly hissed out under the window.

Tegan sagged and sat down on a chair, near to tears. Vampires were real. That was all she needed. Just as well he hadn't seen through all that rubbish. If he knew how scared she'd been –

There came a cry from another room, a male shout.

'Doctor?' cried Tegan, jumping to her feet. 'Hang on, I'm coming!' Primo Levi held before her, she ran out of the room.

The door of the Doctor's room was, surprisingly, open. Tegan burst in to find the Time Lord, in his dressing-gown, holding a conversation with a bald man who was standing in the corner. The man was surrounded by several small pieces of bread.

'Ah, Tegan!' The Doctor didn't look at her, but concentrated his concerned gaze on the visitor. 'This is Eric. Eric's a vampire. This is my friend Tegan. She's not. I hope.' He glanced at her and nodded. 'Good.'

'I'm not telling you owt.' Eric folded his arms. 'Let me out of this circle and we'll see who's boss.'

'Sorry, but I think that would be a very unwise thing to do. Mrs Capricelli's garlic bread is particularly strong. Garlic affects our perception of vampires, Tegan, rather like faith. The herb chemically interferes with the process by which the quantum world, the world in which anything including vampires is possible, is translated into the world of classical physics in our brains. It increases one's ability to see the straight and narrow, rather like an anti-psychedelic, and has thus become renowned as a defence against the supernatural.'

'Faith works like that too?' Tegan took a look at the rather ordinary-looking vampire and tried to stop herself shaking.

'Oh yes.' The Doctor looked down his nose at the man called Eric. 'In big enough doses, either can make a vampire vanish from this world entirely. But what worries me, Eric, is what you're doing here in the first place. I dealt with the last vampires in the cosmos only recently, or so I thought. Tell me, are you from E-Space?'

'I'm not telling you anything.'

'You already have. You're from the south of England – '

'The south?' The vampire laughed. 'I'm from Manchester, lad!'

The Doctor nodded. 'I thought so. And your clothes suggest a modern origin. Early nineteen nineties.'

'I was attacked by one too,' Tegan muttered. 'They're working together.'

'So, teamwork amongst a predatory species. That's interesting, isn't it? Tegan,' the Doctor's voice hardened, 'go and find Nyssa.'

* * *

Nyssa was talking to Madelaine. She'd been expecting somebody for hours. It was a relief when the young woman had appeared at the window and tapped to be let in.

'What is happening to me?' Nyssa had asked her.

'You're becoming a vampire.' Madelaine reached out and smoothed back Nyssa's hair protectively. 'The Child was interrupted in his feeding, but by then he'd taken enough to pass it on to you. Don't worry. It's really good. You can do what you want and live how you like.'

'But you prey on other people!' Nyssa clasped her hands distractedly.

'Yes, that worried me at first. But, listen, you get the idea really quickly. Jake says that we're the next step up from mea . . . from humans, okay? So we treat them like they treat cows and sheep and things. They're going to die anyway, and we're not, so we get to feed on them. And we're in the position to offer them a gentle and painless death. Fear makes blood taste revolting, anyway. We're not sadists, Nyssa.'

'I can't do this. I can't.'

'You can hear me in your head already, can't you? Feel where I am in the room? You're never going to be lonely again. You meet great people. You can fly! I know you feel awful now, I mean, I did as well, but you soon realize that you've got no choice, not after the next full moon at least, and then – ' Madelaine glanced up. 'Company's on the way. Do you want to come with me, let me introduce you to everybody?'

'No. Just go.'

'Okay. I understand. We won't let you tell, though, all right? Bye for now.' Madelaine leapt for the window and vanished like a rocket into the black.

A second later there was a knock at the door. Holding

her emotions in with every ounce of Trakenite reserve, Nyssa opened it.

'Have you been – ?' Tegan glanced around the room. 'No, you're okay. Come quick, the Doctor's got a vampire with him.'

'Has he?' Nyssa heard herself say, reaching for her dressing-gown. 'How interesting.'

When the two women entered, the Doctor was pacing up and down his room, his hands thrust deep into the pockets of his dressing-gown. His gaze was fixed on the stoic vampire.

Eric looked at Nyssa as she came in, and smiled slightly. Nyssa looked away.

'So,' the Doctor was saying. 'You're not local and you're part of a team, which tends to indicate that you came after myself and my companions deliberately. Am I right?' Eric ignored him. 'I don't know you, so you must be working for somebody who does. Who?'

'He knows you all right,' Eric muttered. 'But you don't know him.' He furrowed his brow, suddenly. Inside his head, a voice had started asking him where he'd got to and what was happening to him.

'Interesting! Somebody from my past, then.' The Doctor stopped, hit by a sudden thought. His hand emerged from his dressing-gown in a pointing gesture, and his voice took on sudden conviction. 'Or somebody from my future, hm?'

The muscles of Eric's face twitched, and the vampire grimaced. 'Oh no . . .' he murmured. 'He's got nowt, he won't find out anything like this! No, you can't!' He seemed to be shouting at some unseen force that was making the flesh of his face twist and distort.

Eric's hands sprang up in front of him, suddenly independent and possessed by life.

The Doctor realized what was about to happen. 'No!' he shouted to the ceiling. 'Whoever you are, your argument is with me, not him!'

Eric's hands grabbed his own head, fingers stretched against the temples. The Doctor sprang forward, knocking aside the breads, and wrestled with the man, pulling at his arms. One solid palm shot out and sent him sprawling backwards.

'He's free!' the Doctor shouted from where he lay. 'He can escape, I won't stop him!'

But it was too late. Eric's hands were pulling at his own skull, his face going white. Tegan grabbed Nyssa and made her look away. She had been staring at what was happening with a kind of distant shock that the Australian didn't like the look of at all. Not that she was enjoying this all that much herself.

'Let me go!' Eric shouted, and the shout became a scream. His fingers were holding his skull like a ball, pushing it upwards, thumbs hooked under his jaw. His features creased in a mask of fear.

There was a sudden cracking sound.

Eric pulled his head from his shoulders and flung it upwards. It hit the ceiling. The body fell, lifeless. The head landed on top of it.

There was no blood. For a moment, Eric looked like an ordinary dead man, his features relaxed in very human surprise.

'Don't look.' Tegan held Nyssa close. 'Look away.'

As she and the Doctor watched, the corpse crumbled, the chest collapsing and the skull crumpling in on itself. The body dissolved into ashes, disintegrating into smaller and smaller fragments until only a fine dust remained.

'There was no need . . .' The Doctor stepped forward, shaking his head in horror. 'Absolutely no need . . .'

* * *

56

Yarven unclenched his fist. 'There was every need, Doctor,' he whispered. 'He betrayed my intentions. And served as a messenger of the fear I wish you to experience.'

He turned from the corner of the console room where he'd been standing, concentrating. His face was full of sadness before Ruath, Madelaine, Jake and Jeremy. The Child floated over the console, interested only in the flashing lights. 'Eric is . . . dead,' Yarven told his people. 'The Doctor killed him.'

'What!' Sanders cried. 'Why then, let's go over there and punish him for it! You can't let one of us die without vengeance! It's against the whole blasted code!'

'I agree. Of course there must be vengeance.' Yarven took Jeremy by the shoulders and smiled kindly. 'I feel the insult as much as you do, believe me. But Madelaine says that one of the Doctor's party is becoming one of us. Let this Time Lord see her transformation before we take him. Let him feel the loss of that.'

Jeremy took a deep breath and nodded his assent. 'Yes, Lord. Sorry, it's just that these particular humans . . . well, they're rather good at this sort of thing.' He felt the cross marked on his skull. 'It's not good form at all.'

Jake and Madelaine were standing a little apart from the others. 'What's the kid like?' Jake asked.

'She's sweet,' Maddy whispered. 'I sort of wish that she wasn't involved in all this. We could give her some more help. She's quite innocent, the sort who might try and stake herself or something. It's going to be hard for her.'

'Harder than it was for you?'

'It was just you and me, then,' Maddy murmured, carefully smiling at the others.

Ruath was lounging on a couch by the wall, examining her new fingers closely. She had painted the nails blood red. 'We will all have the revenge we desire,

57

Jeremy.' She looked at Yarven. 'Won't we, my dear?'

'Of course!' laughed Yarven, turning away from Sanders. 'You were born to be Undead, my dear. Now . . .' he waved a hand airily, 'the details of your plan, please.'

'My Lord!' Ruath hopped up and activated the monitor. 'Let me tell you, my friends, how we are to humble this arrogant adventurer called the Doctor, and incidentally how we are going to gain control of this planet. The first things we need . . .' She punched a button and a map appeared on the screen. 'The first things we need are a place to settle and a large food supply. Does anybody have any suggestions?'

Jake raised a hand lazily, despite Maddy's quick glare. 'I think I know a place,' he said.

The Doctor stared down at the ashes as they scattered across the floor in the breeze from the window. 'I have to find out who did this,' he told Nyssa and Tegan.

Tegan had let Nyssa go. The young Trakenite bent to examine the ashes. 'I've never seen such swift cellular decay,' she murmured. 'Why does it happen?'

'A vampire's bioplasmic field, like that of a Time Lord, is diffused through its whole body,' the Doctor explained, squatting down beside her, 'though it isn't controlled by symbiotic nuclei. It's centred on the human brain stem, at the top of the spine. Sever that stem from the controlling brain, and the whole system collapses. Certain sources recommend keeping the head and body separate, and stuffing the neck with garlic.'

'Who says that?' Tegan muttered. 'Delia Smith?'

'Tegan . . .'

'Sorry. Who are this lot, anyway? You said something about, what was it, E-Space? Isn't that where Adric came from?'

'Yes. Sometime before we met, Tegan, I encountered a planet in E-Space that was ruled by vampires. They were created by the Great Vampire itself, a being of legendary power. At that point, I thought that they were an isolated community, that Rassilon himself had wiped out all the original Undead.' He picked up a handful of ashes. 'It seems that I was wrong.'

'So what do we do?' Tegan asked. 'If they're after us . . .'

'This has the feel of an opening gambit, a demonstration of power. Just what you'd expect of somebody with an old grudge. Pack your bags. We should move on.'

'You mean we're running away?' Tegan had thoughts of getting their landlady to start baking garlic bread around the clock.

'Hardly, Tegan.' The Doctor stood up, clapping the dust from his hands. 'I want to find out where these two creatures came from, and follow them back to whoever's in charge. If we stay here, nobody on the island's going to be safe.' He frowned. 'I'd better tell David that he's going to have to find another opening bat.'

Tegan left to pack. The Doctor opened his wardrobe and started to throw clothes into a bag.

Nyssa stood in the middle of the room, looking down at the ashes that had coated her bare feet.

Three

———

Victor Lang sat behind a large oak desk, its surface clear and shiny. He was handsome and silver-haired, with a richly cragged face and large hands. These were clasped in prayer before him, his eyes closed.

On the other side of the desk sat a woman in a business suit. She was praying too.

'Oh Lord,' began Lang, 'make this day a happy and useful one. Let's do good works in your name, and do them well.' His voice was gentle Texan, a great power evident in the slow roll of consonants. 'Amen.'

'Amen,' echoed his P.A. She opened her eyes and smiled brightly.

'Would you like a decaf, Olivia?' Lang got up and headed for the coffee machine in the corner of the office.

'No thank you, sir. I gave it up.'

'Did you? Well, maybe I should.' Lang poured himself a cup. 'Tell me how the publicity's going.'

Olivia called up some figures on her laptop computer. 'We're now fully postered. Stephen went to the top local firm and they sorted it.'

'I love the way you say that,' Lang smiled. 'Sorted. Is that a Manchester thing?'

'Yes, sir, I suppose so. We've got North West Tonight on Friday, a recorded interview.'

'Did we get it straight about final edit? I don't like what some of the media here do with this stuff.'

'They refuse to budge on editing, sir, but they're

60

making noises about the interview being "dignified". I think that was the word they used. If they mess it up, we'll talk to Granada instead. They're both interested. It's not every day that a man of God sells out Old Trafford.'

Lang waved a hand, looking down at his feet uncomfortably. 'It's not getting them there that matters, Olivia, it's what they come away with. Have we heard from that poor young girl again?'

'She called the office last night, pretty late. Stephen didn't think it was a good idea to wake you. They asked her to keep in touch, to come in if she needs to. I've got a transcript here. Terrible stuff. She keeps going on about how she can't remember anything awful happening to her when she was little, but she's sure something did.'

'False memory syndrome,' Lang nodded, taking the sheaves of printout and studying them. 'We see this with a lot of victims of Satanic Abuse. They feel there's a hole in their lives, but can't figure out what's missing. It can take months of hypnotherapy for them to remember.' He tapped the paper with his finger. 'This is the heart of evil, Olivia, the biggest problem in this country of yours. And only a few people, people like you and I, are trying to do anything about it.'

'There's the New Light group, sir.'

'Yes, yes . . .' Lang raised a hand and forced a smile. 'I'm not going to let the tricks of Satan get me down. The weekend's going to see a lot of people turning away from that nonsense. If we could get that young woman up on-stage . . . Tell Steve to try and get a contact number. We can come and get her if she wants. I don't want her going through another day without help.' Lang took another sip of his coffee and looked at the cup worriedly. 'I'm beginning to see what you mean about this stuff. Maybe they should do de-decaf.'

* * *

The Doctor stood outside the TARDIS, holding his hat against his lapel. He replaced it on his head as it started to drizzle. He sniffed the air. Not good. A lot of pollution, though not as much as in the seventies. Ground-level ozone up and atmospheric levels down, of course. The whole decade was upside down.

The TARDIS had appeared in a side-street, nearby to a multi-storey car-park and the backs of several shops. The Doctor had identified the place as Manchester, a city he had some experience of. His companions had never been there, but at least Tegan wouldn't stand out from the crowd. She wandered out behind him, having changed into jeans and pullover for a British November.

'Tegan . . .' The Doctor grinned. 'You're ordinary.'

'Thanks.'

'This is a major city, a smorgasbord for the Undead. Wander around a bit and check up on things. Listen to rumours, buy a few newspapers.'

'Okay. They're not going to be about in daytime, are they?'

'No. Vampires can't stand sunlight.' He saw Tegan's nonplussed glance skywards. 'And they have an overwhelming urge to sleep during the daytime. Take Nyssa with you.'

Tegan shook her head. 'She's locked herself in the lab and won't come out. Doctor, you don't think that she – '

'I'll go and call her.' The Doctor spun on his heel and headed back into the TARDIS. 'Stay there.'

Tegan sighed, and popped her umbrella open.

Nyssa would normally have compiled a record of her experiments, but that would have been too much of a risk this time. She had been pleased to find out that in the other-dimensional interior of the TARDIS, she didn't feel an urge to sleep or wake at any particular time, so she'd gone to bed at the same time as the others when they'd left Tasmania. The Doctor had stayed up for a while working with the TARDIS navigation equipment, telling her that he was trying to find a way to track vampires. Nyssa wondered if she should listen to such conversations. Soon she might be telling the enemy everything. Or perhaps she already had, if they were as telepathic as they claimed.

She didn't hear the door behind her opening.

The Doctor had deactivated the lock from the console room, feeling rather awful about it even as he'd done so. Now he walked carefully into the laboratory and took a couple of soft paces forward. Nyssa had left her jacket on a hook on the back of the door and was working in the sleeveless vest she favoured for the hot atmosphere of the lab. The Doctor examined the curve of her neck carefully. Nothing on either side. No sign of a mark. Thank goodness.

He coughed loudly and walked quickly to her. Nyssa turned round, surprised but not shocked. 'I was wondering if you could give Tegan a hand?' the Doctor asked. 'Keep her company.'

'Of course.' Nyssa put down the flask she'd been holding over a Bunsen burner. 'Doctor, this reaction gets dangerously volatile. I thought that I'd locked the door.'

'Oh? Local power coupling failure, I expect. The old girl's getting old. I've been thinking of redesigning the console, actually, stabilizing a few of the linkages. Well, Tegan's waiting outside, so – '

'I'll get my jacket.' Nyssa followed the Doctor to the door. Before she left the room, she glanced back.

The ball of plastic skin she'd kicked under the table had rolled into a shadowy corner.

* * *

63

Nyssa stepped carefully out of the TARDIS and shivered despite the bulky coat she'd put on. She felt suddenly exhausted, like she'd been up all night and was working at dawn. The backstreet was cold and murky, like some parched dream. Cautiously, she looked up at the sky. The terrible sun was obscured, thank the Keeper.

'Good to see you,' Tegan smiled, looking relieved. 'Come on then, we'll go and do some shopping.'

The Doctor watched them walk off down the street, and turned back to the TARDIS. He was going to take the air himself, but first there were some preparations he had to make.

'What do all the flowers mean?' Nyssa asked as they passed by the Arndale Centre. By the steps that led up to the restaurant, a pile of bouquets had gathered. There was another pile in the entrance to the centre itself.

'I guess that's where somebody's died,' Tegan told her. 'But two in the same place? That's bizarre.'

They wandered down to the Exchange Theatre complex, moving with a crowd of shoppers across the traffic signals.

Nyssa was shivering more every moment, but at least her coat kept that from Tegan. She felt sensitive to every footstep and atom of exhaust gas. And at any moment the sun might come out. She didn't know what that would do, but it would be horrible.

She wanted desperately to tell Tegan. But every time she even thought of it, a great wall of shame and embarrassment rose up in front of the words. Their way of stopping her, she supposed. If they could plant such a powerful suggestion in her mind, why didn't they use her limbs, make her into a weapon, or at least a purveyor of false information? Obviously they couldn't yet, so she was still free in that regard.

64

On the steps of the Royal Exchange, there were more flowers. Tegan bought a copy of the *Evening News*. The headline read: 'How Can We Stop This Madness?' Beneath it were pictures of parents grieving.

'They're here,' Tegan muttered.

Nyssa bit her lip, and shuddered.

She'd drawn blood.

They walked to the Town Hall and sat on a bench in front of its great gothic shape, Tegan reading extracts from the paper. There were, of course, piles of flowers in dark corners. 'The city's in the middle of a wave of violence,' Tegan muttered. 'Not riots or anything, just individual assaults. Lots of missing kids. I wouldn't like to be around here when it gets dark.'

'Can we go back to the TARDIS now?' Nyssa asked. 'I'm hungry.'

'Yeah, I could do with some munchies as well. We could go to a pizza place or something.'

'No, I'd like to make something myself.' Nyssa seemed to be concealing some great urgency. 'There are some dishes that I used to have on Traken, that I'd like to prepare. And the ingredients are in my room. So if we could go back – '

'What, are you scared? It won't be dark for hours yet.' Tegan stared at her.

'I'm going on my own.' Nyssa stood up.

'Hey, wait up, what's wrong?'

'I don't like this place at all. You can't feel there's evil here, all around us, Tegan! You're not sensitive like I am, you weren't brought up to know how people are feeling because they'll always be feeling kind!' She turned and ran off towards the shopping centre.

Tegan followed as quickly as she could, but by the time she'd turned the corner that the Trakenite had disappeared around, there was no sign of her. 'Damn . . .' she muttered. 'What's got into her?'

The Doctor had returned to the TARDIS carrying shopping bags. He frowned at the graffiti that had appeared on the side of the blue box, a big multicoloured signature with artistic sparkles and highlights. Then he inclined his head and grinned. It was actually rather good. Besides, one trip in the vortex would erase it.

He opened the door and went inside, placing the bags at the foot of the hatstand. A flashing light on the console indicated that the task he'd set the TARDIS computers was complete. The intelligent listening program had been checking all broadcast news bulletins in the last two hours and preparing a digest of what was happening. There wouldn't be any direct references to vampires, of course, but hopefully he'd be able to make some inferences of his own. He'd sent Nyssa and Tegan out to get more human reactions . . . and, he admitted to himself, to make sure that Nyssa could go out in daylight. That, at least, wasn't a problem.

He pressed a control. The first few reports concerned various assaults and murders in the Greater Manchester area. As they came in, the Doctor used a light pen to pin-point them on a map on the viewscreen. No pattern emerged. On any night of the week, in any particular area of town, it was possible to be attacked. That in itself was worrying. If the Undead no longer felt constrained by the need for secrecy, not to mention the desire to limit their numbers, they must be feeling very confident. A spokeswoman from a neighbourhood watch group came on an afternoon phone-in and told the story of how a gang of youths had leapt over fences from garden to garden down her street, jumping higher and faster than she thought possible. A policeman urged the public not to go out alone at night. A father whose son had gone missing made a desperate plea for him to be returned. The Doctor closed his eyes, then flicked the control impatiently. Other news. American TV evangelist Victor Lang's appearance at the Old Trafford stadium had jammed the switchboard of the ticket office. His organization were now advising that the event was sold out.

There was Lang himself: 'As far as I can see, the city's under siege by the forces of evil. Now you may smile, but what else do you call it when ordinary people can't go anywhere for fear of what might happen? I haven't got a profit motive here, we're as full as we can be. I just want to tell everybody out there: it only takes a minute. Put your hands together, close your eyes or, if you're driving, just think of Jesus. The power of prayer can turn this around.'

Well, that would help with the matter of belief, at least. Hopefully the Sikh, Hindu and Muslim communities in the city would have similar gatherings. Between them, they were going to need all the faith they could get.

Nyssa had run down the street far faster than she expected to. It was as if her body was a paper aircraft that her legs were blowing along. If she'd lifted them, she would have flown like a dart, she knew she would.

But she didn't want to fly.

All her protests to Tegan had been lies, though she could feel a sleeping presence of evil about the city. She was hungry, but she knew just what the hunger was.

She'd seen a healthy young man in an Umbro shirt go by. She'd imagined sinking her teeth into the muscles of his arm, and sucking the hot and nourishing soup inside.

She had to eat something ordinary, but the thought of normal food . . . it would be like eating hay. Nyssa wasn't sure she could do it any more. The urge to kill something –

Why had she come so far from the TARDIS?

She sped into a darker side street, grateful that the clouds had come down and heavy rain was gushing into the gutters. Her hair was heavy with water, and streams of it were running down her nose, but at least she could feel it. A human thing to feel.

'Spare some change?' He was sitting in a sleeping bag, curled up in the doorway of a boarded-up shop. He wore an anorak hood, and beneath it his face was pale and unshaven. 'Nice day for it, eh?' His hand was held out towards her.

Nyssa stared at him. A shudder racked her body again. With a great effort of will, she said, 'Do you know anything about the people who have disappeared?'

The boy raised his eyebrows, surprised. 'Yeah, everybody has. Pitches going everywhere these days. For a while, people were saying that there was a new shelter, but nobody knew where it was. Hey, stop looking at me like that. What's that look mean, then?'

Nyssa closed her eyes and made herself concentrate on a rural idyll on Traken. It wasn't as if this man was one of her own kind. He was just a beggar. He'd probably die of the cold soon anyway. She didn't even have to kill him, because now there was no law – it sang inside her, a distant edict that might have been something she'd dreamt – you could convert as many as you wished now, for soon the feeding would be enough for everyone.

He'd like it. He wouldn't be cold any more. He would taste really good.

She opened her eyes again, and saw that the man was shouting at her. She couldn't hear what he was saying, because that didn't interest her. What was interesting was the different emotional smells rising from him, anger and sadness. She could almost see the wave of them around his body.

68

'Has anybody come back?' It felt like a flirtation, talking about something else when they both knew what they were actually thinking. His scent was that of something that knew it was prey.

'Why should I tell you anything? What are you on, anyway? You enjoying this, are you, standing there on whatever you're on!' He was yelling, shaking a gloved hand at her.

'Stop.' Nyssa froze him with a glance, hit his brain motionless with her eyes. 'Tell me the exact details of who you've heard of that has returned after going missing.'

He began to do so, in a halting voice, the voice of a rabbit. Nyssa listened to him impassively. She was interested in what would happen when he stopped.

Tegan got back to the TARDIS soaked and angry.

'Where is she?' she asked, flapping the umbrella outside the doors before hanging it on the hatstand.

'If you mean Nyssa, I've no idea.' The Doctor looked up from a cricket bag that he was packing with provisions. 'You mean that you've left her alone out there?'

'I've left her – ! Listen, she gave me the slip. I don't know what she's playing at but shugglubburghhh . . .'

The Doctor had slipped a capsule of some sort into her mouth. He breathed into his hand and waved it in front of her nose. His palm reeked of garlic. 'I've been chewing the real thing,' he explained. 'You've just swallowed a concentrated dose of the stuff.'

'Thanks a lot.' Tegan wrinkled her nose. 'Did I say romance on Wednesday? You'll be lucky.'

They both turned around as a dripping figure staggered in through the doors. Nyssa stared at them pitifully, and hid her hands by folding her arms around herself. 'I have . . . some information,' she muttered.

'Where on Earth did you get to?' Tegan asked as the Doctor closed the doors. 'I was worried sick.'

'I told you I was hungry . . .' Nyssa leant heavily on the console, and turned to look Tegan in the eye. 'I found something to eat.'

The Doctor had popped out of the console room. He returned carrying a large towel, which he handed to Nyssa. 'So what did you discover?'

'A large number of people that live on the street have gone missing.' Nyssa began to dry her hair. 'And they are starting to return. Once they do, they're not like their old selves. They can be violent and unpredictable. They don't seem to keep their old lifestyle for long. The man I talked to said that there were fewer homeless people on the streets every day. He added that nobody would take any notice until students started to go missing. Does that make sense?'

'Yeah.' Tegan flapped her newspaper to dry it off a bit. 'That's just what's starting to happen. The children are being taken, and unwary students, people who live alone. The city's in a real panic.'

'Interesting . . .' The Doctor took the paper from Tegan. 'Normally vampires don't exhaust their food supply by overfeeding. They're aware of their vulnerabilities and don't like to make their existence known. It seems that these individuals don't worry about such considerations any more. Oh, Nyssa – ' He took another garlic capsule from his pocket and absently popped it in her mouth. 'Here you are.'

Nyssa swallowed in a reflex action. It felt like a stone going down, and she fought to stop herself from retching. 'What is it?'

'Garlic. Slow-release capsule. Should keep you going for several days.'

Nyssa took a deep, slow breath. 'Good,' she said. 'Well,

if you'll excuse me, I have some things to do. Call me if you come to any conclusions.'

Tegan shook her head. 'I'd say something about bad breath, only it'd be true.'

Nyssa ran straight to the laboratory. Thankfully the experiment she'd left was still intact. An attempt to construct synthetic haemoglobin, an artificial blood substitute. They still didn't suspect, and swallowing the garlic had probably cleared up any lingering suspicions. It was just as well she was still able to do that. Perhaps the properties of the herb would slow down her transformation.

If she could complete this experiment successfully, then no harm would come. She could manufacture as much as she liked, and use her new abilities to help the Doctor defeat the other vampires. It would, she thought with a survivor's chilly optimism, be interesting to be a vampire. For one thing, the Master would not be able to evade or control her next time they met. She would be able to reach into him, to hypnotically bring Tremas to the surface. She and her father could work together then on the problem of vampirism, perhaps come up with a cure that might be used on other people.

She worked for six hours, using the chemistry skills she'd learnt at her father's side. Traken had made great advances in biochemistry, far beyond Earth's level of achievement, and their scientists had designed an artificial plasma years ago. The trouble was that it generally needed large vats and high pressures to produce. Nyssa was hoping to simplify the process.

Finally she held in her hand a beaker containing a thick red emulsion. She placed an electric stirrer in it at intervals as it cooled, making herself wait until it was a reasonable temperature to drink. Her throat already felt full and heavy, as if she had a glandular infection.

71

She sniffed the beaker. It certainly smelt like blood, but it didn't excite her as she'd expected. Still, perhaps that was a result of being back in the TARDIS. She hadn't felt such a disabling urge to feed since she'd returned, just a nagging hunger.

Nyssa carefully drank the contents of the beaker, licking her lips afterwards to make sure there was no sign of it on them. A pleasingly warm drink. She washed out the beaker and put it back on the bench.

The Doctor was circling the console, selecting controls like a choosy aunt might pick chocolates. 'Nyssa!' he smiled, glancing up. 'How are you?'

'I'm fine.' Nyssa wandered into the console room, feeling slightly stronger than she had. 'I'm sorry if my behaviour has seemed strange. As I told Tegan, it's because I can feel the evil in the city. I almost want to run and hide.' She glanced towards the doors. 'There must be hundreds of them out there.'

'Yes, which is why I'm fine-tuning the TARDIS defence systems. We shall conduct our campaign in daylight, while making sure . . .' he flicked a final switch, 'that nothing can reach us here at night.' He stood back, satisfied. 'I worry about you. So does Tegan.'

'I understand that. I'll try to be more sociable.' She felt the blood substitute warming her. 'I was meaning to tell you, there are tales of vampires in Traken legend.'

'Are there?'

'Before the Union was formed, all manner of evil things happened. The story goes that there was a village where the dead would return to their relatives at night, and tell them awful stories that sent them mad.'

'What happened?'

'A party of Proctors was formed, and they put a silver stake through the heart of every grave in the village.

Nobody was ever troubled again.'

'Well, it's possible that those were real vampires, but legends of the Undead persist in several cultures without any foundation. The dead are always with us, and in conditions of poverty or hunger, it's often tempting to think that there's another existence after this one.'

Nyssa paused. 'Do you think vampires . . . are necessarily evil?'

'Well, that's a very difficult question. You might as well ask if a shark or a tiger is evil. They're predators, I don't think they have much choice in the matter. It's best to think of it as an unfortunate medical condition. Who knows, perhaps some day there'll be a cure.'

Nyssa stood there for a second, and smiled. 'Perhaps. Good night.' Then she left.

'Good night.' Feeling slightly more at ease, the Doctor glanced at the console one last time, and adjusted a dial slightly. 'Let's hope we won't be disturbed.'

Nyssa's eyes opened.

She had been lying in the darkness, drifting through something like sleep. She had been thinking of falling up into the sky, of being lost in that emptiness.

Something had happened in her throat. There was no pain, but something had suddenly moved or torn or . . .

She sat up, and went to the mirror on her dressing table. She pulled aside the shawl she'd thrown over it when she went to bed. Her reflection had been a ghostly blur then, and she didn't want to see it deteriorate. She was still just as faded. 'Lights up, please,' she called. The TARDIS responded, flooding the room with light.

Nyssa winced. There was blood all down her nightdress. It was coming from her mouth.

She stretched her jaw open and tried to see her gums. Suddenly she doubled up. No pain, just an all-powerful muscular spasm. From her mouth poured another gout of blood.

She fell off the chair onto the floor. A shudder started in her stomach and rammed up to her mouth. She spat something out in another rush of fluid.

The garlic capsule. Surrounded by a hard knot of fatty deposits. It lay on the rug in a fan of red. She didn't want to touch it.

She pushed herself up to a sitting position. The blood on the floor had that different smell to it. Her chemical substitute. Her body hadn't absorbed it at all.

She was hungry. Desperately hungry.

She must have food now.

She must have blood.

She'd sit here and die. She'd make herself sit here and die.

She started to sweat, a fast boiling like every drop of liquid in her was dissolving away. There was still no pain. Pain would be welcome, rather that than this terrible craving.

She stood up, like a puppet jerked to its feet. Her hands were curling into animal shapes. Sobbing, she stumbled towards the door.

The corridors of the TARDIS had dimmed with night. Nyssa marched along, her bare feet making no noise. She wasn't cold in her bloodied night-dress. Her head was fastened straight forward, her eyes brimming with salty swift-evaporating tears.

The first door was Tegan's.

She knocked on it. Three quick knocks.

'Who is it?' came the call.

'It's me. Nyssa.' The voice was her own used as a trick. Calm and normal. This is beyond my control. I can't help it. It's not my fault.

'Wait a second.' The door opened. 'Hi, what – ' Tegan

was still dressed, she'd been reading. She looked down in horror at the blood. 'My God, what happened?'

'Help me, Tegan!' Nyssa stepped forward, falling into her friend's arms. They staggered back into the room and the door swung closed behind them.

'I'll get the Doctor,' Tegan muttered, trying to guide her to a chair.

'No, don't.' Nyssa grabbed Tegan's arm.

Tegan stared at her, suddenly scared by the young Trakenite's strength. 'I was right,' she gasped. 'You're – '

'Help me, Tegan, don't let me die. Let me have some of your blood. You won't feel any pain, I won't harm you. Please, I need it!' Nyssa gently pulled Tegan towards the corner of the room, her voice imploring her.

Tegan shook her head, dazed. 'No, I can't . . .' she muttered, watching the depths of Nyssa's eyes. They were trying to make her dream. 'No!' She gave the Trakenite a sudden shove, sending her sprawling onto the floor, and ran for the door.

Nyssa was there first, ricocheting up from the floor. Her palm slammed the door closed.

'How could you ask me that?' Tegan shouted, backing away. 'After all that stuff with the Mara!' She made a visible effort to concentrate. 'I have faith in Primo Levi, in your book! I have faith in you, Nyssa. You can't touch me.'

Nyssa reached forwards, her arms open in a pleading gesture. 'You haven't got faith in what I've become, Tegan. As you say, you've gone through it yourself. You understand it too much. Your faith isn't enough to hold me back. I have to eat. I need blood. I can't help myself. Please – ' She stepped forward.

'Get away from me!' Tegan lashed out, catching her across the cheek with her fist.

Nyssa turned, her eyes full of sudden rage, and pinned

75

Tegan to the wall. She lunged at her neck, snarling.

'Nyssa! Nyssa, don't!' Tegan screamed, kicking and punching uselessly. 'Doctor!'

Nyssa's mouth paused, a millimetre from where her sharp teeth would touch the soft flesh of Tegan's throat. A muscular spasm shook her.

With a great roar, she threw Tegan onto her bed and dived out of the door. A great breeze followed her, causing books to leap from shelves and papers to flutter around the room.

Tegan curled up where she'd been thrown, and started to cough out big sobbing breaths.

Nyssa burst out of the TARDIS and ran down the street, weeping. Around her, whirlwinds erupted, scattering cans and rubbish across the pavement. She sprinted around the corner, heedless of where she was going, and bounced off the bonnet of a taxi as it sped down the street.

Nyssa flew into the air. The vehicle skidded to a halt.

She kept on flying, spinning over and over as she fell up into the chilly night.

By the time the driver had got out, Nyssa was a white and red speck in the sky, lost in the neon glare.

'Is that Mr Lang?'

'Speaking. How are you? Are you okay?'

Pause. 'No. I've been thinking about things, and I think I can remember . . . bits of it. Names, places and stuff. They take children, you know, they take children . . .' The voice rose a fraction in pitch.

'Let us come and get you. Just tell me where you are, and we'll be there within half an hour.'

'I can't tell you, I have to get back – '

'No, wait.' Lang's voice was calm and reassuring.

'Don't go. I don't mean to come over there all guns blazing. I just want you to know that you're not alone, that there are people who can help you.'

'Can you get me soon?'

'Of course we can. Tell me where and when.'

'I'm not sure. I'll call and tell you. I can tell you all about them, what they do and where they do it. It's a whole . . . coven, is that what it's called? They're taking all the kids right now. I'll tell you all about them. I have to go now.'

'Okay. Be sure to call me tomorrow night.'

'I will.'

'Goodnight, Madelaine.'

'Good night.' Madelaine dropped the phone back onto its hook and opened the door of the phonebox. On a deserted suburban pavement, a circle of dark individuals stood round her in the streetlight.

'Well?' asked Jeremy Sanders.

Madelaine sighed, brushing her hair back with a hand. 'We've got a bite.'

In the shelter of a shop doorway, a homeless boy reached into the pocket of his coat. The streets that night were deserted. No club-goers to ask for cash. It was just him and the cold.

He wished that he hadn't been so narky with her, but you got like that sometimes. You didn't want to answer stuff like that. She'd been coming off something, having a really hard time, but at least she'd talked to him. They'd had a long conversation in fact, not that he could remember much about it. At the end of it, she'd leaned close to him, and for a minute he'd thought that she was going to kiss him. He wouldn't have minded that.

She'd whispered her thanks in his ear, her breath hot on his cheek, and had slipped a golden bracelet off her wrist. He spun it in his hands now, wondering how much it was worth. A few meals, no problem. Maybe more.

She'd given it to him and said that she was going to go on a long journey. And he wasn't. He'd taken it as cruelty at the time. But, thinking about it, maybe she was just being kind. From the look in her eyes, the boy didn't think that he wanted to end up wherever she was going.

Four

'Vun, vun gothic battlement! Two, two gothic battlements! Ah, ha ha hah ha!' Jake hopped around the stonework happily, looking down on the forest below. The castle was elegantly dark, with slim towers and moody battlements. Gargoyles leaned out from the walls and an imposing drawbridge was drawn up to isolate the place inside its moat. In the hummocks and low hills of the forest, with a light evening mist rising, it was an eerie sight.

Madelaine lay along the slated roof of the kitchens with her sunglasses on, bathing in the moonlight: the only way for a vampire to get a tan. She sighed at Jake. 'You're really into all this, aren't you?'

'Yeah, 'spose so.' Jake looked crestfallen for a moment. 'Something different, isn't it?'

'But we can still go if we want, can't we?'

'Of course we can. We don't want to end up like Eric.'

'Couldn't we go back to Australia? I liked that. We could have fun there.'

'Yeah, fine, any time you want to go, but what about the stuff you're doing for Yarven, the phone calls?'

'He can find somebody else, the melodramatic sod. Every call I make it feels more dangerous.'

'Probably is. So why're you doing it?'

'It's something about the man. Lang. I'm curious. I want to know what his angle is.'

Jake frowned at her. 'Christianity. That's his angle.'

79

'Yeah. Only in his case, I think it's . . . I can just sniff something about him, that's all. If I met him, I'd know.'

Jake took a long, contemptuous snort of the night air. Trees and small woodland creatures. Clear and fine. He grinned. 'Hope it's on your terms, love. Good castle though, eh?'

'Mm.' Maddy sniffed one of the chimneys on the kitchen roof. 'They're dishing out in a minute. You want to go down and join them?'

'Why, you want to do something else?'

Maddy raised her eyebrows pleadingly. 'We could pop out and get a take-away.'

Yarven stood on the balcony, looking down into a magnificent banqueting hall. Tapestries hung from the walls, depicting humans running and cowering before an army of the Undead. Below was a long table, at which sat nearly fifty vampires. Some of them were locals, answering the call that Ruath had put into the night air over the last few evenings. Some were new converts, amazed at the society they had become part of. A few had even journeyed from the continent, hearing the news that something important was going on.

They were enjoying Yarven's hospitality, his larder a result of the continual raids that his followers were conducting. Each course was brought to the table bound but not gagged. The noise was part of the festivities, screams mingling with laughter and music. There was blood everywhere, and the heady scent of human fear. This was how it should be, Yarven reflected, the path that his homeworld should have taken. Here was a demonstration of the pure fact of power. Tonight's new Undead were enjoying it. They were always slow at first. Yarven had learnt to watch the decision in their faces, as their hunger overcame their old ethics. Once they'd bitten, ripped or gouged, it was over, there was never a decision to make again. The taste of blood held them, told them what they were: the future.

The humans who had been his ancestors had thought that going into space was somehow a conquest, that when they made landfall on some distant planet, they were advancing the species. A species that had ceased evolving at the level of an ape. Yarven had grown up in E-Space, knowing that somewhere there were more stars than the handful he saw in the sky. His parents had been of the nobility, friends of Lord Veran, that poor, fearful old man. Yarven was just old enough to remember the end of what the peasants called the Dark Time, when everything he was part of was overturned. His father had hidden the children in a secret room while he negotiated with his servants that night. Yarven had heard his father's voice, distantly, pleading and cajoling. It was not the voice of a noble man. It was at that point, looking back on it, that he had become convinced of his bastardry. Veran's troops had arrived, an unlikely and swift mixture of Black Guards and peasant militia, and Yarven's family had been spared an ignominious death.

He had never seen the Three Who Rule except as an image in stories. But Veran's son, Vetar, said he had. The two of them had met at a distance from Yarven's father's grave, during the funeral. 'Death is not the end,' Vetar had said. Yarven had asked him what he meant. Vetar had looked into his eyes with that otherworldly stare of his, and Yarven knew. They'd walked that night in the forest, under the clouds of swirling bats, and they had talked of the past that the nobles were trying so hard to forget. Vetar said that he was also unsure of his parentage, for Veran gave concessions to the rabble every day. Veran was going to ask Yarven to take the place of his late father as his most trusted aide. How did Yarven feel about that?

Yarven said that he was horrified, that he could never join such a cause, believing what he did. He would have to decline.

Vetar told him to accept the offer. There was a way that, in such a position, he could serve the last feeble remnants of the Great Race. If he could find a way to turn the peace process around, to throw the planet back into chaos then the Children of the Night, the handful that remained, might begin to prosper once more.

Yarven had offered Vetar his neck, there and then.

Nights later, he had woken with a sudden start, his hand clutching his chest. He felt the stake, and knew that Vetar was dead. It was the same place, oddly enough, where he now carried the mark of that peasant's arrow. The arrow that had wounded him before he'd had his second, his most disturbing encounter with Agonal.

Ruath entered the balcony behind him. She'd changed into a black ball gown. She was chewing on a bone. 'Enjoying yourself?' she asked.

'Yes, my dear. It is good to see so many new converts.'

'One from Pakistan, just arrived.'

'Really? Good, good, I'll welcome him later.'

'It was a brilliant decision of yours to repeal the edict against uncontrolled feeding. We're getting random bite victims as well as deliberate converts. They come here out of instinct. The little dears feel that this is their spiritual home.' She kissed him, transferring a little meat to his teeth.

'And how is your research progressing?'

'It's very boring.' Ruath hopped up onto the rail of the balcony, taking a sip from the goblet of blood that Yarven was holding. 'Oh, thank you. My Lord, you know we must really see about getting some human slaves. The youngsters down there are content to serve in shifts, but it really isn't fitting.'

'No.' Yarven stroked her chin. 'I'll do something about that. Boring, you were saying?'

'Yes. I wasn't prepared for that, the idea that regeneration would sap me of all interest in science. Still, dull or not, it has to be done. It's just a question of calibration, of getting the details right. What I'm attempting is something that normally takes the full executive powers of Gallifrey. And a bit of a variation, at that. Not easy, my love.'

'Indeed. I appreciate that. So we have your work in the cellar, we have Lang . . . ah, yes, we do have Lang, I can feel the power of his desire even at this distance. What else do we need?'

Ruath handed him the cup again, grinning red. 'We need a little service from you, and we need the Doctor.'

'Ah yes.' Yarven stepped forward, and raised his voice over the noise of his guests and their food below. 'The Doctor!' he called, raising the goblet in a toast.

The call came bellowed back: 'The Doctor!'

'What?' The Doctor was staring straight ahead, sitting on the edge of his bed.

'She's a vampire, Doctor.' Tegan was pacing about the room, her arms wrapped around her. 'She tried to have a go at me, and ran away when she smelled the garlic. Her room's full of blood.'

'Are you certain she's – '

'She's got fangs. What are those, Traken wisdom teeth?'

'Well . . .' The Doctor took a long breath, and frowned down at his slippers. 'I seem to have erred. I should have taken more notice of the signs – '

'Oh, don't just sit there blaming yourself. What can we do about it?'

'As I was about to say,' the Doctor hopped up, grabbing

his pullover from a nearby stool, 'a vampire only properly becomes a vampire on the next full moon after they've been converted. That gives us a week or so.'

'A week to do what?'

'To find whoever's in charge, stop them and rescue Nyssa.' His tone was deceptively light, but Tegan could tell how seriously he took the words. 'I've lost one companion already this regeneration. I'm not about to lose two. Now,' he folded the pullover in his arms, 'if you'll give me a moment to put my trousers on . . .'

'What?' Tegan glanced down at his dressing-gown. 'Oh. Sure. Sorry.'

They met a few minutes later in the console room, Tegan having dressed also. The Doctor stood by the console for a few minutes, listening to the details of Tegan's story, tapping his lips with a finger as if waiting for inspiration. 'I see,' he concluded. 'Now, help me think, Tegan. Where would Nyssa have gone?'

'To find food?'

'Exactly! But she doesn't want to grab innocent bystanders. No, judging by the way you describe it, she's still almost herself. She can just about keep her urges under control unless provoked. What are the central facets of Nyssa's character?'

'Erm, caring? She cares about people?'

'True, which means she's not going to go hunting if she can help it. Apart from that?'

'Learning. She always wants to learn things.'

'Correct. So she'll go to where she can find out most about vampires. The headquarters of whoever we're up against. Find that and we find her.'

'So how do we find that?'

'We follow Mrs Beeton, Tegan.'

'What?'

'First catch our vampire.' The Doctor hit the door control, and chilly night winds blew in. He pointed to the cricket bag. 'Let's see if my shopping expedition's been successful, shall we?'

Nyssa folded the ferns about her. The gully was just a crack in the rock, and she was aware of some slight cold. That was one good thing, that the chill night air was no longer so harsh on her skin as she sat here. She wiped the blood from her lips. A cow, anaesthetized and gently asked for as much as she could safely give. Nyssa wasn't sure if that would pass on the condition, but the idea of a vampire cow seemed ridiculous enough for safety. Animal blood wasn't very satisfying. She thought that she would need much of it and often, and she was aware that she'd grow thin and weak on such unsuitable food. But at least it kept the terrible hunger at bay.

Her first flight had been a sickening thing. She'd spun up into the sky, uncontrolled as a leaf on the wind, arms spiralling randomly. She'd kept on going up until she was above the clouds, the moonlight reflecting on them like islands in the darkness. The city was an expanse of tiny lights far below. If she continued to rise, she realized, she'd go straight out of the atmosphere and into space. Surely this was impossible?

The thought stopped her. She hovered, gazing down at the cloud layer quite placidly. It wasn't cold. She wasn't afraid of falling. It was like a dream, because it was all so imposs –

She fell straight through the cloud and found herself hurtling down towards the city.

Good! This was impossible! Impossible! Nobody could fly, she couldn't fly, she'd hit the ground and –

A picture of her father flashed into her head and she stopped and stood on air. She couldn't die while there

85

was still a chance of seeing him again. Besides, there was no guarantee that hitting the ground would harm her any more. And she might hit some innocent bystander.

Reluctantly hovering, as she was, Nyssa smelled it for the first time. A faint scent on the breeze, something that touched her emotions like the smells of family life or, more accurately, the urgent smell of fire or gas. She had to find out what it was, she couldn't be content without that knowledge.

She glanced down at Manchester. She should go back to the Doctor and explain, say sorry to Tegan. But what could they do? Just suffer every time she got an urge for blood. She couldn't put Tegan through that again.

The scent came to her once more. There was something interesting on the end of it, something informative. She flew after it, learning how to modulate and control how she moved through the air.

She hadn't expected it to tire her, but it did. That's why she'd landed in the forest, a long way south of the city. She half wanted to sleep, but that might mean waking in the sunlight, and she was terrified of doing that.

There was a cough from behind her. 'Well, hello . . .' Jeremy Sanders smiled down at her from the rock where he stood. 'What you're looking for isn't far from here. Come with me.' He held out his hand.

After a moment's pause, Nyssa took it.

On the bench by the Cathedral, opposite the Mitre Inn, Russell sat. He was a student, went for Salford 'cos of the night-life, and he'd found some. Like tonight, when this girl down at the Banshee said that she'd see him here in Cathedral Close after hours. Three, she'd said, and of course she was having him on. Maybe it was just to spite her boyfriend, a moody sort who'd stood at the bar all night looking cool. Maybe she wanted somebody a bit

86

more intellectual. Still, where was the loss? He'd drunk six pints of cider and was having a good time looking at the architecture. In a minute, he'd wander down to the road and catch a cab back to Withington. Or he could walk. No problem.

'Oh, there you are, you waited!' She sat down on the bench beside him, like she'd just dropped out of the sky. Her hair was a mass of black, and her face was powdered white over a spiked choker. On her neck she'd painted circles around two fake fang marks.

'Nothing else to do,' Russell grinned. 'I was just looking at the church, I'm an archaeology student.'

'Really. That must be so exciting.'

'I like the way you look. It's dead good.'

'Thanks. Well, have you heard the news, what they're saying about vampires?'

'No. Well, the two girls in our house have stopped going out and all, but it's drugs, gangs and stuff, isn't it? Nobody's taking all those rumours seriously.'

'Oh, Russell. Perhaps they should.' The girl looked down at her lap, somewhat embarrassed. 'If somebody said to you: "join us or die?" which would you choose?'

'Oh, I'm a man of principle. I'd choose death.'

'What about: "live forever or die?" '

'Who wants to live forever?'

The girl paused, flummoxed. 'All right, how would you react to: "Join us and live forever?" '

Russell frowned. 'You a Jehovah's Witness or something?'

The girl raised her hands, defeated. 'You'll thank me later,' she decided. 'Now, do you want to snog or what?'

'What.' Russell reached for her, but she diverted her mouth towards his neck. Goth through and through, Russell thought. What the hell.

'Now Tegan!' A cricketer with a mad stare leapt out

of an alleyway, and flung what looked like a loop of hosepipe in their direction. The girl jumped off Russell, startled, and the loop landed around her like she was a goldfish at a fair.

Russell stared at it. It was a hosepipe, a length made of two pipes bound together, opening out into a ring which encircled his would-be goth snog. Behind the cricketer, a young woman with short hair was standing beside a water main. She had turned on the valve. She must have opened it with one of those tools that firemen use. Russell's cider-addled brain tried to stack all these facts into an order of priority and failed completely.

'Get this off me!' The girl shouted at him.

'I wouldn't do that if I were you.' The cricketer stepped quickly forward, a searching expression on his face. He stuffed his hands in his pockets. 'If she wants to be free, ask her why she can't lift it off.'

Russell looked between them.

'Ask her!' repeated the man.

'I can't move it, Russell, because I'm a vampire,' Madelaine smiled at the student sweetly. 'And we have an inability to cross running water. Why don't you go home now? I think this is going to get rather messy.'

The young man jumped up, staring at her, and sprinted off down the cobbled street, towards lights and taxis.

'I'll pop round later, okay?' Maddy shouted after him.

'You will do nothing of the sort.' The Doctor pointed at her angrily. 'Do you know what damage your feeding does, what innocent lives it — '

Maddy interrupted him. She'd been sniffing the air, intrigued. 'You're not human,' she whispered. 'Oh no, you're this Doctor bloke, aren't you?'

'I'm the Doctor, yes, and you're right, I'm not human. Now, I'm not going to hurt you, I just want to know what's happened to my companion Nyssa.'

'She's one of us, that's what's happened,' Maddy smiled. 'It'll suit her. She's got a lot of pain inside, she deserves the chance to enjoy herself.' She put her hands on the hose gingerly.

'How do you know – ' The Doctor visibly controlled himself. 'Where is she?'

'I don't know. I haven't seen her since Australia.'

The Doctor frowned at her. He seemed to realize that she was telling the truth. 'Who's your leader? Who's behind all this?'

'Good question . . . now Jake!' Maddy had looked up suddenly.

Tegan slammed into the railings behind the bench, propelled by some sudden force. The other end of the hosepipe spilled water over the cobbles at her feet.

Maddy shrugged off the loop.

The Doctor found himself pulled off his feet and held aloft by his collar. Jake stared at him accusingly. 'Don't do that,' he murmured. 'She doesn't like getting closed in.'

'No . . . I'm sure she doesn't. You know, if you put me down, we might be able to talk about the safety of my companion.' He glanced quickly at Madelaine. 'I think we all have her well-being at heart, don't we?'

'Yeah, we might. But you're full of traps. You killed one of us. Can't let you live.' Jake threw the Doctor over the railings, and he landed in the churchyard. 'You all right?' he asked Madelaine.

'Fine, yeah. You finish him off, I'll make it two out of two with the girl.' Maddy dropped to her knees and approached the unconscious Tegan, who was lying against the railings. 'This'll be the Aussie who upset that Sanders. The Doctor isn't exactly Ian Wright, is he?'

'Eh?' Jake hopped over the railings. The Time Lord was picking himself up, gasping. The fall had winded him.

'No trouble scoring at international level.' Maddy

pulled aside Tegan's pullover and undid the top button of her shirt beneath.

Jake laughed, casually knocking the Doctor over again with the back of his hand. 'So what did you do to Eric, then?' he asked.

'I did nothing!' the Doctor shouted. 'He killed himself! If you'd only listen to me – ' He struggled to his feet again.

Jake reached for him, intending to snap his neck.

'Barbara Wright!' the Doctor gasped manically. 'She became a housewife, you know, and makes a rather good upside-down cake! She and her husband Ian have a son called John!'

Jake snatched back his hand as the Doctor moved forward, staggered by the force of his words. The Time Lord was staring intently into his eyes as he pushed Jake back to the railings.

'My granddaughter, Susan! My friend Adric, who gave his life trying to save others! I have great faith in these people, whatever your name is, and if there's one thing that you can count on in this turbulent and uncertain universe it's that I'll never allow any of them to come to harm if I can possibly . . . help it!' He snatched a cricket ball from his pocket and tossed it expertly through the railings.

It smacked against Madelaine's forehead as she bent over Tegan. The female vampire's head flew back, her skull hitting the cobbles with a force totally out of proportion to the impact of the ball.

'I tampered with the seam,' the Doctor advised Jake, backed onto the railings by now. 'It's interlaced with thread from a rather ancient prayer mat, a distillation of faith. Besides, I think you'll find that my companion and I have a touch too much garlic in our bloodstreams for your taste. Tell me who your leader is.'

'Yarven. Lord Yarven. This is all my fault, right? Don't go hurting Madelaine because of what I've done.'

'I didn't kill your friend. I don't intend to kill you. That's my handicap, you see, I try not to kill anybody. Now, tell me – '

From the street behind Jake, there came a great commotion. Torches flared around the corner, and a great noise of shouts suddenly erupted with the sound of running footsteps. 'Great,' muttered the vampire. 'Lot of faith in that lot. You've got some friends there. Got their stakes ready, have they?'

The Doctor looked down at his shoes. 'Take her and go.'

The vampire needed no second bidding. He swept over the railings, grabbed Madelaine and sped off straight up as the first torch beams caught him.

'If you see Nyssa, take care of her!' The Doctor bellowed skyward, watching as the lovers became a tiny silhouette against the stars. Then he was blinded by the torch beams too. He raised his hands. 'So . . . are you friend or foe?'

Jeremy led Nyssa through the forest, keeping up a jolly stream of conversation as he did so. 'You know, I felt rotten when I was converted. I thought that the whole thing was rather, oh, I don't know, seedy. My first instinct was towards self-destruction, but you soon learn to rationalize things. It's not as if you're alone. The Undead have one of the best social circles in the world. It's going to get a lot better shortly as well.'

Nyssa, suspicious at first, had grudgingly come to appreciate his company. She'd felt so alone in the sky and the forest. It was only her familiarity with that feeling that had kept despair at bay. To have a normal conversation with somebody was unexpected. 'Is there any cure for this condition?' she asked.

91

'Cure? Do you know, I've never really asked. In my day, all we had to go on was X-films. The Messiah and his lady will be able to tell you, I'm sure.'

'The Messiah?'

'Lord Yarven. As the title suggests, he's the saviour of all our people, as well as their father. Now he's here, exciting things are going to happen. Ah . . .' They'd come to a clearing, with a clear view of the low hills and hummocks ahead of them. In the middle distance stood the castle, torches on its walls casting shimmering reflections in the moat. The distant sounds of music echoed across the valley.

Jeremy indicated the building with a flourish. 'The Castle Yarven. Let's fly, shall we?'

Madelaine woke up high over the forest, and relaxed in Jake's arms. 'Sod it. What was that thing?'

'Holy relic.'

'Did you kill him, then?'

'No. He got away. Bunch of villagers with torches arrived to rescue him.'

'Really?' Madelaine sniffed at Jake's arms, surprised. 'Oh, hey, that was him. The Christian. We missed him!'

'Yeah, and thank God for that and all. You and your flirting. We could have been killed there, you know? "Let's make a student into a vampire"! Why do I listen to you?'

'You love me. Don't you?'

' 'Spose so. That Doctor said he didn't kill Eric.'

'He would do, wouldn't he?'

'No, he didn't smell of a lie. He was all right too, for a mortal.'

'Not him too. The last thing our lot need is an alien.'

Jake banked and headed down towards the castle. 'That's what we've already got, remember?'

Maddy hugged him. 'I remember,' she said. 'Damn right I do.'

Tegan knocked aside the damp cloth that was being applied to her brow. 'Get off! Doctor, they're – ' She looked around. A concerned young woman was reaching into a first-aid kit. She was sitting in the back seat of a car, parked just beside the pub. The Doctor was leaning in the doorway.

'Ah, Tegan,' he grinned. 'Every now and then I wish you had a thicker skull. How are you feeling?'

'Insulted. What happened?'

'I, ah, don't think we should talk about that now.'

'But did you find out the name of – ?'

'I did. Unfortunately, it meant absolutely nothing to me. Hush now, here comes our rescuer . . .'

'Is she okay?' A tall man in a blue tracksuit peered over the car door, and reached a big hand round into the back seat. 'Victor Lang, Ms Jovanka. How are you doing?'

'Fine, thanks.' She would have started to ask questions, but Lang turned immediately to the Doctor. That, and the back of her head was developing a healthy bruise. She took the moist cloth from the young woman and started to apply her own first-aid training.

'My people are searching in teams,' Lang pointed along the street. 'Do you know who they were?'

'No. Muggers, I suppose.'

'No, my friend, no, that was a rhetorical question. On your way to your costume party, you were ambushed by the forces of evil. We've found them everywhere tonight, as we make our way from church to church. They run from us wherever we cast our light.'

'The forces of evil?' The Doctor asked carefully. 'What exactly do you mean?'

Lang put a hand gently on his shoulder. 'Satanic cultists. I know, I know, to you British it sounds like something out of an old movie. But in the USA we've seen cases like this before. They can infest a city like rats. It's no accident that we find them here around churches – and such wonderful churches you have here – they love abusing places like that.'

A blue-tracksuited group leader jogged up to Lang. 'They're long gone, sir. Does the gentleman want to call the police?'

'No, no . . .' The Doctor waved a hand. 'Victor Lang. Yes, of course, you're the evangelist who's due to appear locally soon, aren't you?'

'Yes. But I haven't just come to this city to preach. I've been helping out local groups like New Light wherever I go. These guys seem to have quite a problem on their hands.'

'We're up to it, sir,' the young man cut in.

'I'm sure you are, Mike.' Lang grinned, gently punching him on the arm. 'Are you sure you don't want to go to a police station? We could drop you off in the refreshment wagon here. I'd love to see one of these guys identified, get him in an identity parade or whatever.'

'I didn't see enough of them to be any use. What do they do, exactly, these cultists?'

'Oh, terrible things.' Lang sat on the car bonnet, his hands clasped together. 'I guess that's part of the reason why this stuff never gets reported. People can't imagine anything so incredible happening in their city. These cults follow their own religious doctrines, usually nonsense that they've invented themselves, but it invariably attracts the attention of Lucifer. They need new blood for their sacrifices, so they harvest babies, either abducting young girls or encouraging their female members to become pregnant, time and time again. It's quicker for them if . . .

well, for the young lady's sake I won't go into details, but they don't generally sacrifice children who've gone full term. On top of that, let me tell you, Doctor, three-quarters of child abuse in Britain is down to these people.'

'Really?' The Doctor looked at Lang seriously, then glanced at his shoes, rocking on his heels. 'You know, I thought that most child abuse happened in very ordinary homes, mainly by a relative of the victim.' His gaze shot up and fastened on Lang's. 'Isn't that true?'

'That's what the media want you to think, Doctor. I mean, I'm not saying it's a conspiracy or anything, but these media people seem to be obsessed by the idea that ordinary fathers are always abusing kids. In actual fact, that's a tiny part of the problem. Most families are still the safest place for a child to be.'

'Well, it's been a pleasure to meet you, Mr Lang, but my companion and I really should – '

'Wait.' Lang reached into the glove compartment of the car and handed the Doctor a calling card. 'That's my office in Manchester. If you want proof about these cultists – I can tell you're sceptical – within a few days we're going to raid a major centre of cult activity. My contact says we should be able to photograph and hope-fully identify at least two dozen of them. You'll see the story of that one in the press. Bet on it.'

The Doctor had turned away, but now he slowly turned back to Lang. 'Do you know,' he breathed, 'I think I'd like to do more than read about it. Tell me, would you have room for two more in your raiding party?'

In the great hall of Castle Yarven, a muscular vampire banged a gong. The revellers fell silent. Jeremy Sanders strode forward from the stairwell that led to the roof, a doorway that had acquired the trappings of a main entrance. 'My Lord Yarven,' he called. 'May I introduce a rather special new arrival?'

Yarven had assumed his place at the head of the table, sitting on a wooden throne with Ruath perched on the arm. 'You may.'

'May I introduce our first novice from another world, Nyssa of Traken!'

Applause echoed around the chamber. Nyssa stepped down the stairs, trying to maintain a regal bearing despite the revulsion that welled up in her at the sight of what lay on the white cloth of the dining table. If she could appear confident, even with the terrible weakness that she felt gaining on her every moment, then she would be in a better position to deal with this Yarven. 'My Lord,' she curtsied. 'I am Traken's last daughter. Thank you for offering me your hospitality.'

'By my blood!' Yarven laughed. 'You show right proper respect! Kiss the ring.'

Nyssa approached him, curtsied again, and kissed the silver band on his finger. It tingled against her lips.

'My Lord, she needs food!' Ruath reached out and examined the pallor of Nyssa's skin. 'My child, let me get you something – '

'No! I mean . . . I can't . . .'

The vampires at the table laughed and made affectionate noises. They thought this was charming innocence, Nyssa realized, something they recognized. Great Keeper, did this mean that she was destined to end up like them?

'We understand, my dear.' Ruath stroked her hair. 'There are more subtle meats for your young palate. You must take something other than animal blood, or you'll fall into a fugue.'

Jake and Madelaine had entered the hall themselves. Madelaine saw Nyssa by the throne and ran forward,

96

quickly bobbing her knee to Yarven. 'My Lord, this is the Doctor's companion, the one whose blood was taken by the Child. Surely he won't have used all that up yet?'

'You're right!' Ruath smiled brightly at Madelaine. She searched the hall for the baby vampire and found him bobbing near the fireplace, then whispered in Yarven's ear. The Lord of the Vampires nodded. 'Madelaine, perhaps you'd arrange for a transfer between them. The Child's metabolism is very slow. He's only little, and I've got no idea what his system will have made of Trakenite blood.'

'Come with me,' Maddy put a hand on Nyssa's shoulder and led her away. Jake grabbed the Child by a foot and pulled the floating baby towards the door.

'Fair Nyssa,' called Yarven as they left, 'after you have fed, I would have words with you concerning your master, the Doctor. Come and see me later, when this gathering has retired for the morning, and we can talk in private.'

The vampires at the table roared with laughter. Ruath playfully flicked Yarven's nose with her finger.

Nyssa turned slowly at the door, pallid and supported by Madelaine's arm. 'Thank you, my Lord,' she managed to say. 'I should like that very much.'

She took three more steps before she fell to the floor, unconscious.

Five

Nyssa opened her eyes.

She was curled against Madelaine, under a giant satin quilt that also encompassed Jake and the baby they called the Child. Everybody else was asleep. In the corners of the elaborate gothic bedroom various other vampires were curled up, with clothes rolled under their heads as pillows. The first light of dawn was redly streaking the leaded glass of the windows. Nyssa didn't feel cold.

Last night, after they'd woken her from her swoon, Madelaine had fussed over her, telling her to look away while she connected her to the Child. She said that she wasn't very familiar with the equipment but they'd have to do a lot of this in the future. Parched and impoverished Undead had started to arrive, and they had to share blood out. Far from looking away in nausea, Nyssa had explained the workings of the circulation pump to her. Madelaine had told her about the shock she'd felt when she found out that Ruath had taken them a few weeks back in time going from Tasmania to here. She kept thinking of flying across the world to see herself. Nyssa had realized how dangerous Ruath's short time-jump had been, but kept quiet.

When the Child was connected, burbling away to itself, to the other end of the equipment, Jake had made a show of throwing the switch. 'Big red switches. Great.' The machine sorted through the various blood groups the Child contained, Nyssa theorized, and –

She nearly fainted when the first Trakenite blood came through to her. Food, her own dear food, after so long starving. She was filled with warmth and strength again, and in being so realized how weak she'd been. Maddy had insisted that she sleep with them, and Nyssa had been too tired to offer any comment. Madelaine had an arm draped protectively around her even now.

Why was she awake at dawn? Was this the last of her humanity making itself felt?

She hadn't wanted to think about the future, about what would become of her. The Traken blood would last a day, a night, and then she'd have to feed or die. The vampires could offer her their second-hand blood, but that had still been originally taken from some innocent. Besides, how long could she prevail upon such hospitality? Nyssa closed her eyes at the thought of her manners forcing her to bite somebody's neck. That would almost be humorous if –

Come to me, child.

That had been clear, a voice right into her ear. Nyssa gently moved Madelaine's arm from her shoulder and eased the cover back, finding her clothes on the floor.

The great stairs of the castle were littered with the sleeping forms of the Undead, dried blood formed in pools round their heads on occasion. Nyssa picked her way down the heavily carpeted steps, glancing at the growing light from the windows. The panes were growing darker as she watched, rejecting the dawn.

She followed the call through the portrait-lined halls, stepping over vampires and, she shuddered, the occasional remains of their food.

Yarven sat on his throne at one end of the great hall, one hand cradling his chin as if deep in thought. Ruath was curled asleep at his feet. A great sheet of ruddy light lay over them, the eclipsing screen of the large window that illuminated the throne. The Lord of the Vampires looked up as Nyssa entered.

'You wanted to see me?' she asked, as boldly as she was able.

'Yes. Thank you for being so prompt, my dear. Come sit with me.'

Nyssa approached the throne, bobbing a curtsy, and sat primly on the chair nearest to Yarven's. 'Aren't you up rather early, your majesty?'

'I like to see the dawn rise, when I can. It reminds me of immortality. Do you know why stars hurt vampires, little Nyssa?'

Nyssa inwardly bridled at the 'little', but kept her composure. 'No, your majesty.'

'Because when Rassilon slayed the Great Vampire, he banished him to eternal darkness. Rassilon thought of that as being outside of the universe of men, but vampire-kind took him at his word, and that is why we have lived in darkness ever since.'

'Not a very scientific explanation.'

'We are not a very scientific people. At least, we haven't been. However, that is changing. Do you want to be a vampire, Nyssa?'

'No. Not at all. I don't want to hurt anybody.'

Yarven chuckled to himself. 'They all think that until they do. But I wouldn't dream of keeping anybody in this state against their will. Ruath tells me that the technology now exists to reverse your condition, if applied during the next full moon. That is traditionally the time when the process becomes permanent. Before that, killing the vampire that inducted one into the cause, one's progenitor, as it were, cures one. Now, I don't imagine for a minute that you'd harm the baby – '

'No.' Nyssa shook her head firmly.

'So I'm offering you this chance to be free. Would you

like that?'

Nyssa calmed her breathing. The mention of a cure had been more than she could possibly have hoped for. 'Yes. A great deal.'

'Well then, we shall arrange it. You have my word on it.'

Nyssa paused, expecting the vampire lord to offer her some sort of deal, probably involving betraying the Doctor. None was forthcoming. 'Is that . . . it?'

'Yes. I have no desire to rule over unwilling subjects.' He smiled, showing his teeth, and reached across to lay a hand gently on her shoulder. 'You are only a small fish, and I think we shall throw you back. If you can stand living with us until the moon is right, that is. Please understand, I don't want you running off to summon armies of vampire hunters until then. What you do afterwards, of course, is your own concern. Do I have your word on that?'

'Of course!' Nyssa beamed, and took Yarven's hand in her own, kissing the ring in delight. 'Thank you, your highness!'

'Oh, tush. You may leave us now. I think it's getting a bit early for both of us.'

Nyssa jumped up, still smiling, and dashed delightedly out of the room, turning to clasp her hands together and bob appreciatively by the door.

Ruath opened one eye and looked up at Yarven. 'Did you enjoy that?'

'Oh yes,' Yarven chuckled, rubbing the tips of his fingers together. 'I do so adore tormenting the young and innocent.'

Tegan slept late. When she wandered into the console room, the Doctor had just finished sorting things into his cricket bag. 'Good afternoon, Tegan. Now, we just have time for lunch before popping over to see Mr Lang.'

'What are we seeing him for?' Tegan sat listlessly on the wicker chair in a corner of the console room.

'Because he and his group are going to find some of what they call "satanic cultists" tonight. I expect that they're actually vampires, or hypnotized human slaves used to guard them. We may find Nyssa, or some clue to her whereabouts. Besides, without our help, Lang will be in for some nasty surprises.'

'You don't like him, do you?'

'Like? I haven't really thought about it.' The Doctor lifted the bag onto his shoulder, and paused to consider. He took a deep breath, as he often did before venturing an opinion. 'Perhaps he ought to consider the way that organizations like his distract attention from the real problem. Villains don't always have fangs and capes.'

'Doctor . . .' Tegan sighed. 'Do you think we're ever going to find her?'

The Doctor squatted down in front of her and opened his mouth as if to say something. Then he closed it again. 'Yes,' he said finally. 'I don't see why not. Now, chin up.' He bounced to his feet. 'French or Italian?'

'Sorry?'

'Lunch. If we're after garlic, I'm afraid our choices are rather limited.'

Lang pressed the button on his answerphone.

'I live near Alderley Edge. It's a very close-knit community. My uncle and his friends take me out to the Edge every two weeks. And tonight's the night. Please come and get me. You can see them in their robes and things if you want. I'll be at the Edge with them all at nine, and it all goes on until midnight. Please come, I can't take it any more. I'm so frightened. Will I still get into heaven? Please come.'

'She's a very frightened girl, Olivia.' Lang leaned back in his chair, breathing heavily. 'How old do you think she is? Twelve? Thirteen?'

'Bit older.' Lang's P.A. shook her head. 'Sorry sir, but do you think this could be a wind-up? I wouldn't put it past some of the kids around here.'

'No, no.' Lang shook his head. 'To do this once, yes, perhaps. But to keep such a story going, such a series of desperate pleas . . . No. You can hear the despair in her voice. She needs to know that there's light, Olivia. It bothers me that I wasn't here when she called, she obviously couldn't make the set time. Who do we have for tonight, anyway?'

'About thirty of the group. Three minibuses, which New Light are providing. They've got enough drivers.'

'Good.' Lang stood up and flexed his arms behind his back. 'It's good to confront them directly, to see the faces that I so narrowly missed last night. They must feel that Jesus is angry with them.' He gazed at his tired reflection in the panel window of his office. 'But they must also feel his grace and forgiveness.'

The three minibuses, when they arrived, were carrying a flock of stern-faced men, some of them wearing the decorated leather jackets of various radical Christian groups. Tegan and the Doctor had wandered into the reception area at teatime, having spent a long afternoon at a rather high-class Italian restaurant. Lang had shaken their hands warmly and had asked Tegan if she'd like to stay behind with the wives and girlfriends, who were holding a vigil while the men went out on their mission. Tegan had politely declined, saying that she'd feel much safer beside the Doctor. Thankfully she found herself sitting beside the Time Lord in the back seat of one of the vehicles as they made their way in a convoy through the

Manchester night. Lang's bus was ahead, leading the fleet.

'They're going to start singing Cumbaya in a minute,' she whispered.

'I doubt it, Tegan.' The Doctor was peering out into the lights of the city. 'These people are very serious about what they do. They think their way of life's being threatened, and they have a great deal of faith, which makes them rather good opponents for the Undead. Speaking of which . . .' He fished in his cricket bag, and took out a small tin. 'Anybody care for a boiled sweet?' He handed the tin round, and several of the serious young men took one.

'Garlic capsules?'

The Doctor nodded. 'Evening the odds a little.'

'I wouldn't bet on the other side.' Tegan glanced around. 'Looking at this lot, I'm not sure who I'd prefer to meet down a dark alley.'

The journey took over an hour, which the Doctor and Tegan spent playing battleships. The evangelists struck up several rather martial-sounding hymns. At a garage, Lang knocked on the window by the Doctor and raised a proud thumb.

At 8.45, the little fleet pulled into the car-park that served Alderley Edge, a pleasantly arboreal stretch of gravel, the lights of a nearby pub shining through the trees. Only a couple of cars were about. 'Do you think we should ask if they're satanists?' Tegan suggested archly.

The army assembled, the Christians pulling unlikely things like baseball bats and tyre chains from their jackets. Their breath formed clouds in the darkness.

'Gentlemen.' Lang raised his gloved hands for silence. He was dressed in black jacket and jeans. 'Our first priority is to rescue the girl who has been calling for our aid these last few days. I guess she'll come to us. Any other obvious victims, I say we rescue now and face the consequences later. I'll take responsibility for that.' There was general loud agreement. 'After that, those of you with cameras should try and record as much of what occurs here as possible.' He gestured to a couple of the team, who were packing film into their pockets and checking the batteries on flash guns. 'We will pray over the site of whatever practices go on here, and cleanse the place. I don't recommend trying to capture any of the cultists. Remember, the weapons you carry are only to be used in self-defence. Okay, hands.' They all held hands, the Doctor glancing at Tegan warningly. She didn't raise a fuss. 'Lord, keep us safe. Let's win here tonight, and save some souls. Okay? Okay. Let's go.'

As the team marched up the narrow footpath towards the Edge itself, Tegan nudged the Doctor, worried. 'Is this going to be a blood-bath?' she asked.

'I hope not. If I had anything else to go on, Tegan, I would. I'm hoping that at the first sniff of all this mobile and active faith, any real vampires will take off at great speed.'

'Take off? But – '

'Hush.' The Doctor tapped his cricket bag. 'Have faith. Besides, from what Lang says about these telephone calls he's been getting, there may genuinely be an innocent life at risk. And if there are humans serving the Undead, well, we can have a word, can't we?'

Lang fell back, and slapped the Doctor on the shoulder. 'I must say, I admire your bravery, Doctor. This must be the first time you've done anything like this, am I right?'

'You, ah, could say that.'

'And you, Ms Jovanka. You're a thoroughly modern woman. I appreciate that.'

'Thanks.' Tegan glanced skywards, then caught the

Doctor's disapproving glance. 'Have you been on many of these yourself?'

'Yeah. Yes, I have,' Lang sighed. 'You find them out in the woods, doing awful things to children. Things which . . . well, I'm a family man myself, and my daughter's . . . well, she hasn't found Christ, and she's changed her name so people at the gas station don't keep saying . . . but I'd never . . . Hey, sorry.' He clapped his hands together and roused himself. 'I'm babbling. These people still scare me, Doctor. They tip the world upside-down. Sorry if – '

'Not at all.' The Doctor smiled gently. 'I know exactly how you feel.'

The party made their way up through the trees, negotiating the slopes by splitting into groups. The Edge itself was a rather sudden interruption in the flat Cheshire countryside, a wooded and steep-sided escarpment which looked down upon a wonderful view of endless fields. In the cold night, however, it was the rock faces at the base of the ridge that interested Lang's people. Natural basins and overhangs made for ideal camp and bonfire sites. Lovers met here, writers sought inspiration. Various pagan groups found the natural surroundings perfect for their earth-magic ceremonies, and the locals whispered about darker events. Lang's group probably wouldn't have differentiated between the latter two categories.

The Christians came to the top of the Edge in fragmented groups, forming a rough line gazing down at the escarpments below them and the sweep of the frozen landscape beyond. Distant lights shone on the horizon. Silence was dotted with the cry of owls or the love-call of a fox. A low mist wavered above the flatlands.

The Christians grouped together and produced flasks, preparing to wait. The silence of the place hushed them beyond the need for secrecy. The Doctor fumbled with his cricket bag, checking tiny diodes that blinked inside it.

And then there came lights in the valley. Blazing torches, and a low chanting that echoed eerily about the crags of the Edge. A line of hooded men stalked into view, leading a goat by a loop of bailer cord. Behind them, others were carrying a large crate. The line of cultists continued its slow procession.

Lang raised a hand. 'Wait.' His cameramen were already clicking away, relying on the light from the torches rather than risking flashbulbs.

'Doctor,' whispered Tegan. 'That chant of theirs . . .'

'There!' Lang gasped.

At the back of the procession, a teenage girl was being led along, a hood covering her head. The cultists put down the crate and began assembling what it contained.

'Come on. Quietly.' Lang stepped forward and, crouching, led his men down the hillside.

The Doctor put a hand on Tegan's shoulder, staying put. 'What's that you were saying about the chant?'

'I recognize it from somewhere.'

'Where?'

'I don't know. I'll get it in a minute, if they get to the chorus.'

'Tegan, unlike Mr Lang, I don't believe that satanic chants make it into the top forty on a regular basis.'

The cultists had laid out a black cloth on the ground and were ceremonially taking various glittering silver and black implements from the crate. They kept up the chant. The goat had been tied to a post and had started to eat nearby foliage. The girl was turning her head from side to side, as if listening intently for her rescuers.

The Doctor flicked a switch in his bag. 'Well, we may be on a wild-goose chase here, but you never know.'

'Got it!' Tegan snapped her fingers. 'It's from *Evita*. You know, the musical? That's the funeral procession of Eva Peron!'

The Doctor frowned. 'Oh dear. I have a feeling that things may not be quite what they seem.'

Lang's men had gathered in a fern-covered gully at the bottom of the hill. 'Wait until they're prepared,' the American advised. 'We want these photographs to be absolute proof.'

'What's that the bastards are putting together?' Stephen, the leather-jacketed New Light member whispered. His voice was edged with fear.

'I don't know. It could be some sort of . . . magical apparatus?' suggested Lang. 'Whatever. We won't let the girl come to harm. How does everybody feel about the goat?'

There was a general grumble.

'Okay,' Lang nodded. 'We'll act to protect the goat also.'

The Doctor was squinting at the pieces that had been assembled on the cloth. The hooded figures were fixing them together, slotting a long black cylinder onto a silver frame. The cylinder pointed up at the sky, but the cultists were turning a tiny wheel, lowering it to just above ground level.

'Doctor,' whispered Tegan. 'You know, if I didn't know that this was a magical ceremony, I'd say that that thing was a — '

The Doctor sprang to his feet. 'Lang!' he yelled. 'Get away from there! Run!'

Lang looked up, angry at the Doctor's intrusion. 'Go, go!' he shouted, bursting out of cover and sprinting down the hill towards the cultists. The photographers started firing their flashbulbs, turning the action into a strobed sequence of slow-motion flickers.

The evangelists leapt to their feet.

With a crack, something shot out from the cultists' apparatus and hit the ground just downhill from the Christians. Smoke burst from the ground and caught them across their faces as they ran through it, yelling.

'A mortar!' the Doctor whispered. 'They've got a mortar weapon.'

'No shells, though,' Tegan muttered. 'They're just firing smoke.'

'Are they? Stay here.' The Doctor picked up his cricket bag and ran down the hill.

Small explosions were erupting across the hillside as the cultists dropped smoke-bomb after smoke-bomb down the muzzle of their mortar.

Lang, oblivious to the smoke, sprinted across to where the girl was standing. The cultists, he was amazed to see, ignored him, keeping up the barrage of harmless shells. Well, that was fine by him.

He grabbed the hood from the girl's head. 'Madelaine? Is that you?'

Madelaine looked at him sadly. 'Mr Lang,' she said calmly. 'I've been wanting to meet you.'

'Let's get – '

'Away from here? Right.' She put a hand on each side of his waist. 'Hold on to me.'

'If that's what you want.' Lang glanced around him, still amazed at the lack of urgency the cultists were displaying. He couldn't see any of his own men for the smoke. Up on the slopes, the Doctor was shouting something he couldn't hear.

He put an arm around the girl's shoulders, intending to

lead her away. 'This is so bizarre, it's like the Lord himself has intervened.'

'No it isn't.' Madelaine made sure of her grip on him.

They took off straight up. As fast as a firework.

The Doctor gazed up, grimacing at Lang's sudden shout of fear and surprise. He dived a second later to his cricket bag and hit a control.

Down in the valley, awful things were happening.

The Christians, running through the smoke, began to clutch at their throats and mouths. Something was suddenly pulsing through them, a wave of pain and shame.

It was the same for most of them. Mike had fallen to his knees, shivering. He felt distant from the world, an urgent cry changing his body into something that he didn't know at all.

Christ above him on the cross, eyes open.

Mike slammed his fists together, feeling his body being wiped away and replaced by something he didn't understand. It was on the edge of the feelings he associated with speaking in tongues, the slow and torturous buildup that led to a shattering connection with the divine. In those prayer meetings and healing sessions, it had taken hours of prayer and meditation to reach that state, a slow rocking and shaking and repeated intonation. Finally, he'd let the Holy Spirit flood into him, thrown his head back and burst into a babble of outrushing syllables, spending language across his brothers and sisters.

Christ above him on the cross, eyes open.

It was going to happen straight away now. He was going to turn and grab his nearest comrade and push his head into his blood and the two of them would pull in another and another and another until they were one blood and one thing and one grand thrashing mass of life and love and God.

110

Christ above him on the cross, eyes open.

He fastened on the image of his Lord, and felt death or life open behind him. Mike wavered, his body shivering faster and faster. He didn't want to give himself up to this, didn't want to let his flesh go. This was evil, wasn't it? Wasn't it? Wasn't it?

He clenched his teeth and made his choice.

Christ's eyes closed.

Mike's body exploded, the skin bursting to let it out, the flesh expanding into a great flaming ball until all that remained was ashes. Around him, his comrades burst and flared, the valley alight with their ignition.

The hooded men watched as the youngsters burnt. Jeremy Sanders pulled back his cowl. 'What astonishing faith they must have. May their God welcome them.' He turned to the other vampires. 'Leave the mortar and the animal. Bring the shells.'

The Doctor was running down into the valley. 'No!' he was shouting. 'Stop it!'

He stopped. Then clutched his head.

For a moment, the world had swung at a strange angle. Something terrible had happened inside his head, and his time senses had spun like they'd been slapped. The effect was gone as soon as it had come.

He supported himself, hands on knees, panting. Then he made himself stand upright and run again. It was too late. Long before he reached the gathering, the hooded figures had spiralled up into the air, taking a wooden box of ordnance with them. They paused for a moment, gazing down at the flames of faith below them. Then they accelerated off to the horizon.

By the time the Doctor reached the flames, there was only one of the youths left. He was rolling around on the ground, twitching amongst the ashes of his comrades. 'Why couldn't I do it?' he was crying. 'Why did I give

111

up? I wasn't as strong as they were!'

The Doctor helped him up. 'What do you mean?'

The boy stared at him. 'I've been cut off from God,' he said. 'I'm in hell.'

'It's not your fault.'

Tegan had had to drive one of the minibuses, the Doctor being unable to concentrate on the task after all that he'd witnessed. They'd left the boy on his doorstep, Tegan having to physically prevent the Doctor from staying and offering a full explanation. Now they were back at the TARDIS, drinking strong, sweet tea.

'Isn't it?' The Doctor was sitting in the wicker chair in the console room, holding his cup with both hands. 'I could have told them what to expect.'

'They wouldn't have believed you. Besides, you thought that their faith would protect them.'

'It did just the opposite. I'm not sure why, but whatever chemical agent was in those shells made their faith destroy them. Perhaps the garlic played a part as well.'

Tegan took the cup from his hands and put it down on the floor determinedly. 'Well it doesn't matter. We've got Nyssa to save, and there's only a few days left.'

'Yes . . . yes.' The Doctor looked at her and nodded purposefully. 'You're right, Tegan. We can't allow ourselves to wallow.' He stood up. 'You know, sometimes I wonder how I'd get on without you.'

Tegan looked up and grinned. 'Thank you.'

'Probably quite well, all things considered. Now, another cup of tea would be useful.'

Tegan's face fell. 'It's great to feel useful.'

The Doctor had produced a test-tube from the cricket bag. 'This is a rather gory sample I took from the remains of one of Lang's team. I'll conduct an analysis of that later, but first . . .' He hauled out a large device, a parabolic dish connected to an advanced bundle of circuitry. He connected a lead from it to the TARDIS console. 'Vampires produce a unique heat signature, a great concentration of blood, other people's that is, inside a relatively cool body. I set the Heat Source Motion Tracker to plot the course of those leaving Alderley Edge. It should give us some idea of where they've taken not only Lang,' he handed Tegan his empty cup, which she took with a disgruntled grab, 'but also Nyssa.'

Lord Yarven clicked his fingers. 'Silence!' he commanded.

The revellers around the table quietened. In the distance could be heard the chiming of a clock. Yarven pointed to the roof stairwell. With immaculate timing, Jeremy Sanders ran down it, the cowled vampires behind him pulling off their cloaks and swirling them around the room.

'Success!' Sanders cried. 'Everything went according to plan, your majesty!'

'Good! Good! Take the choicest cuts for your team, my most loyal follower! He is on his way, I trust?'

'He is!' Jeremy leapt up to Yarven's side. 'Slowing Madelaine down with his struggles!'

Nyssa looked up from her place beside Jake, suddenly afraid. She'd been sipping from a mug of blood and milk, the blood supplied by Jake himself. Could they be talking about the Doctor?

'Don't worry,' Jake advised, putting a hand on her arm. 'It's not him.'

Yarven stood and indicated several vampires, gesturing for them to follow him. They marched out of the hall with great urgency.

Ruath was standing before a panel of controls, chuckling.

113

Just for a moment there . . . just for a moment, she had had the power of a deity. Those who ruled Gallifrey could have done so much with such abilities. It was only their weakness that held them back. She thought about the reasons behind her mission, of how she felt about Gallifrey now.

The same. When she'd found out the great secret of the Time Lords' future, she'd been reduced to inaction for days, as if a friend had died. As if all her friends had died. But that had become a passionate desire to do something. If only she'd had access to the Time Scoop for a little longer, she might have been able to find out more. The renegades must have discovered the secret in their adventures but none of them, not even Mortimus, had had the courage to try and change it. The Doctor, especially, was wanting in that respect. As always. She tapped a gauge on the newly constructed apparatus before her. The growing sense of achievement made watching all these silly dials worthwhile.

A distant bell rang. Yarven's summons. The plan was progressing. Ruath abandoned her experiments and headed eagerly for the stairwell.

Yarven stalked into a specially prepared room. Overhead was a dome. An attendant vampire pulled a lever and the dome split into quarters, revealing the night sky overhead. The quarters retracted into the roof.

Yarven let out a long cry. The cry was taken up by the handful of the Undead who accompanied him. Distantly, the cry returned on the wind.

'Ah . . .' Yarven breathed. 'The Children of the Night . . . what a wonderful sound that is.'

A speck in the sky resolved itself into Madelaine, carrying a limp figure in her grasp. The Undead lackey pulled another switch and a lid swished open in the floor, revealing a pit beneath.

Madelaine centred herself above the space in the roof of the castle, and let go of Lang. The evangelist fell through the hole and straight down the pit. Ruath ran into the room just in time to watch his descent. She kissed Yarven's cheek happily.

Madelaine fluttered down beside the others and brushed off her skirts. 'He was shouting all the way,' she told them. 'He reeks of garlic, too, which didn't make providing oxygen for him entertaining. Nothing I could have done if he'd wanted to get off.'

'Yes, that's the Doctor's work again,' Ruath nodded. 'That's exactly what I thought he'd do. Was he there tonight?'

'Yeah, I think he was with them.'

'Did he seem to be suffering at all? My experiments have reached a point where he ought to be feeling their effects.'

'I didn't get close enough to notice.' Madelaine pointed to the pit again. 'This one reacted just like you said he would, though. I told him that making himself fall would be suicide, a mortal sin.'

'Good, good.' Yarven patted Madelaine on the shoulder. Ruath closed the dome. From the pit there was rising a palpable ripple of faith, a powerful impulse that was so strong the vampires could almost see it.

They took a step backwards.

'Who are you?' Lang shouted up. He was standing on a pile of mattresses, a circular light source illuminating his predicament. The sides of the pit were supernaturally smooth. The palm of his hand could hardly feel them.

'I am Yarven, lord of all my people,' a dark and cultured voice called. 'This is my castle. I am sorry that the welcome is not all it could be.'

115

'What are you, then?'

'Why, we are vampires, Mr Lang. You know, like in your moving pictures?'

'But vampires don't exist! You can't exist! Madelaine, please! Tell me what's happening!'

'Well, what Yarven says is true,' a familiar female voice nervously intervened. 'I tried to tell you on the way over, but all you could do was shout at me.'

Lang slumped to his knees. 'So it was all a lie? All a set-up?'

There was a pause. 'I wanted to meet you, Victor. I'd still like to talk to you, if that's okay. There'll be time.'

Lang took a deep breath, and made himself answer calmly: 'Of course, Madelaine. You can always talk to me, whatever's happening. But please, will somebody tell me, what do you want with me? Why have you put me down here?'

Yarven squared his chin and walked to the edge of the pit, feeling reality ripple around him at the force of the man's faith. He glanced sternly at Madelaine, and she turned away.

'In answer to your first question, Mr Lang, all will soon be revealed. As to the second, we've put you in a pit because you are, forgive the expression, stuffed with garlic. We're waiting for you to sweat it out. All right?' He gestured to Ruath. 'Cover it up.'

Ruath pulled the switch again and the cover of the pit swished closed, cutting off a pitiful shout from below.

'Now,' Yarven smiled, 'does anybody fancy a spot of dancing?'

Six

As Romana was walking back to her new quarters, she bumped into a fellow Time Lady who was hurrying round a corner.

They exchanged apologies and Romana studied her new acquaintance with interest. She was tall and straight-backed, wearing a neat black trousersuit and a silver belt. Fashions must have changed since Romana was last on Gallifrey. She had sharp inquisitive features, scraped-back hair and she wore a necklace of golden spheres.

'Ruathadvorophrenaltid,' she said formally, adding as one did if one was prepared to be friendly, 'Ruath.'

'Romanadvoratrelundar,' said Romana. 'Romana.'

'I was hurrying to see the Doctor,' said Ruath. 'I heard he'd had an encounter with some vampires, and vampirism is a particular study of mine.'

'I'm afraid you've missed the Doctor,' said Romana. 'But perhaps I can help? I spent quite a lot of time on the vampire planet myself.'

'Oh, really? You know, that would be a help. Could you spare some time to help me complete my research notes?'

'Of course. When would suit you?'

'I'm not busy at the moment.'

Romana smiled. 'Well, let's talk while my memories are still fresh, then. Would you care for a cup of synthetic artificial tea replacement? I'm afraid it's all I've got at the moment.'

Ruath inclined her head. 'That would be very nice.'

'So what's your interest in vampirism?' Romana moved cautiously around the food preparation area in the new quarters she'd been assigned by President Flavia, trying hard not to wince at the colour scheme. She'd have to adjust the contrast knob on the place as soon as she had a moment.

Ruath had seated herself on a plastic lounger and had taken a tiny holo-recorder from her belt pouches. 'I'm writing the definitive history. Everything you ever wanted to know about the species.'

'But were too afraid to ask.' Romana popped her head back into the hospitality area. 'One lump or two?'

'Erm, lump of what?'

'Tea.'

'One, thank you. What is tea, exactly?'

'Human beings drink it. It's a dangerous intoxicant to them, but quite harmless to us Time Ladies.' She popped back, and reappeared with two cups of steaming liquid on a tray.

Ruath took one. 'It's true that I did want to ask you about vampires, but I have to ask . . . you are the Romana that helped battle Agonal in the Tomb of Rassilon, aren't you? The Capitol's full of the gossip.'

'Oh, it was nothing,' Romana grinned. 'The Doctor did most of the work, I just stood back and thought of Rassilon.'

'But how did you get to the Tomb in the first place? Surely there are all those complicated games to get past, if the children's tales are true?'

'There's a very simple way there, actually, straight from the President's Office.'

'Really?' Ruath put down her cup and clicked another control on her belt. When her hand reappeared, it had

118

a staser pistol in it. 'Show me.'

'Oh, not you as well . . .' Romana sipped her tea, frowning at the pistol. 'There's not much villainy left to be done over there, you know. Everybody's had a go.'

'It's not the Tomb I'm interested in,' Ruath told her. 'It's something on the way.'

There was never a Chancellery Guard about when you needed one, thought Romana as Ruath marched her towards the President's Office. Most of them would be out hunting the remnants of the Special Security service. She could jump Ruath, of course, but she wanted to find out what her plans were first. Romana had to admit that it was a clever thing to do, starting a diabolical scheme just as another one finished.

'I take it,' she said, 'that your interest in vampires goes beyond the intellectual? I don't believe I ever actually met a real one on my last visit to the vampire planet, you know.'

'You did,' Ruath told her. 'But you didn't know it. My interest in things Undead does indeed go beyond the purely academic. That's how it began, of course. I was part of a research team studying a number of texts from Rassilon's time. I hadn't a lot else to do, really, considering that I had been left behind.'

'Left behind − ?' Romana interrupted. 'Pardon me. You were explaining your plot.'

'In a certain volume of R. O. O. stories − '

'Do you mean Rassilon, Omega, Other or A. A. Milne?'

'Will you please stop interrupting? I know it's one of the Doctor's old tricks, but − '

'You know the Doctor, then?' Romana felt the staser jab into her back and decided to stop. 'Sorry. I'll be quiet, shall I?'

119

'In a certain volume of those works of legend, there is a marginal illustration of an owl being overcome by a bat. Now, the owl is of course a bird associated with Rassilon, and I needn't explain the significance of the bat. The story itself dealt with Rassilon's battle with the vampires, how he defeated them using his bow-ships, and cast them into eternal darkness. Translating from old Gallifreyan, you can read between the lines, work out certain riddles that older translators have entered in the text. What it all comes down to is that before overthrowing the Great Vampire, Rassilon took something from him. Genetic material. In the most direct way possible, by being bitten by him!'

A Chancellery Guard passed by. Concentrating, Romana just nodded to him. 'But that means – '

'Yes! Lord Rassilon was a vampire towards the end of his life! That's why Time Lords and vampires share ninety-eight per cent of the same genes, why so much regeneration technology is similar to natural vampire traits. Of course, I couldn't keep this discovery to myself.'

'Of course.'

'So I sought out other students of the Undead. Together we found that inside the Capitol, in the ducts and serviceways where none but the workers go, there are vampire shrines even now. Tiny bands of heretics have kept alive the cult of Rassilon the Vampire. It was in their company that I first heard the words Vampire Messiah. Minutes before we met, Romana, I was studying a new discovery I had made in the Panopticon Library, a text that I was quickly translating. Do you know that on board that TARDIS of the Doctor's is the being who will lead the Time Lords back to greatness?'

'If you're talking about Bernice, I don't think she'd be keen on the job.'

'His name is Yarven, he is the Vampire Messiah.'

120

'Yarven? But he was so . . . ineffectual.'

'Mock while you can.'

They'd come to the doorway of the Presidential Office. Two guards stood before it, one of them tall and blond. He grinned at Romana.

'Why, Lady Romana! What can I do for you?'

Romana glanced at the woman behind her, hoping to somehow convey to the guard that she was being intimidated. 'We'd like to see the Lady President, please. If it's not too much trouble.'

'It's a matter of urgency,' added Ruath. 'Connected with the Agonal incident.'

To Romana's annoyance, the guard bowed quickly and opened the door in front of them.

Secretary Pogarel, a lean, precise Gallifreyan bureaucrat, stamped the Presidential Seal on the papers on his desk in front of him and leaned back, satisfied. The vaporization orders for Elar, Morin and Rath. Completed in record time. He'd also prepared a supply of blanks for Zorell's troops as they were caught. Served them right, as well. Pogarel hadn't liked their attitude, swanning into his office at all hours, showing no respect for the intricacies of form and custom. Now that they were being dealt with, everything could get back to normal.

The door opened and Romana walked in. Beside her, once again, was a woman that Pogarel didn't recognize.

'Yes?' he blurted, sitting up in his chair quickly. He calmed himself. Not every companion of this wild adventuress was going to stick a weapon in his ribs. 'How can I, erm, help you?'

'We'd like to see the Lady President, Pogarel!' hissed Romana. It was as if she was trying to tell him something.

'I'm sorry, but even you, Lady Romana, must make

an appointment. President Flavia is very busy at the moment.'

'You misunderstand.' Ruath stepped from behind Romana and pulled Pogarel across his desk by the collar of his robe. She stuck the staser in his ribs. 'Take us to Flavia's office. Now!'

'Oh no . . .' Pogarel sighed, 'not again.'

'What is the meaning of this constant to-ing and fro-ing, Secretary Pogarel?' Flavia rose as Pogarel shuffled through the door, Romana walking beside him. 'Oh, I see you've brought us another visitor, Lady Romana. Tell me, what's so important this time?'

Pogarel glanced at Ruath behind him, and tried to muster his dignity. 'Madame President, may I introduce Lady Ruath. She convinced me that the matter is, once again, of great importance.'

'And did she do this in the usual manner?'

'I'm afraid, Madame, that she did.' Pogarel pointed to the staser stuck in his ribs.

Flavia sighed. 'To admit one psychopathic female to the office of one's President may be regarded as an oversight, Pogarel. To admit two smacks of – '

Ruath snapped the staser up to body height and blasted aside the weapon that Flavia had quietly drawn from her desk. Then she fired again, the silver bolt throwing the Lady President back against the wall. She ran to the door and slammed one of the devices from her belt against the lock. Seconds later, guards began to pound on it.

'Madame President!' Pogarel screamed. 'You've – '

'No I haven't. I used stun setting. Speaking of which.' Another bolt hurled Pogarel across the room. Ruath turned to Romana. 'I only need you now.'

Romana stared at her. 'What sort of diabolical plotter doesn't want to kill the President?'

'One who knows that there are plenty more Presidents where she came from. One who knows the future, perhaps. We'll see. Now show me to the Time Scoop.'

The Inner Council Room was the sort of alcove that the alcove-friendly Gallifreyan architects who built the Capitol adored. It was supposed to be a chamber where the President would gather the High Council to talk on secret matters. It was only used once in a millennium, and generally stood empty. Therefore it had become host to a number of Time Lord heirlooms carrying the tag 'Of Rassilon'. That alone, Romana sometimes suspected, was what kept them from being thrown out for the Shobogans to collect.

Amongst these objects was the Harp of Rassilon: an ancient Gallifreyan harp which stood in front of a painting that depicted a man, probably Rassilon in one of his many guises, playing it. Romana had recently learnt that if you played the notes depicted on the painting, a ballad called 'Rassilon's Lament', a hidden door beneath the picture would slide open. This, she decided, was something that she wasn't going to reveal to Ruath. It was only a matter of time before the Guards burst in and stasered this mad woman. She led her into the Council Room and looked around, trying to locate a delaying tactic. She settled on the portrait.

'Here we are,' she told Ruath. 'This is an ancient painting of Rassilon. If you press his eyes, then a door opens to the Time Scoop. Of course, Flavia knows all about this now. Perhaps she's had it deactivated . . .' She reached up to the portrait.

'I have an ancient relic of my own.' Ruath opened one of her belt pouches and produced a silver ring, which she slipped over her finger. 'This is the sigil ring of the Great Vampire, recognized by the Undead all over the cosmos.

I found it in a book made out of human flesh. It was bound into the spine. And when I say spine, I mean spine.' Ruath walked over to where Romana stood, idly pressing Rassilon's eyes. 'The text of the book said that the ring was made of the command circuitry of Rassilon's lead bow-ship, ripped out of the deck by the Great Vampire himself. It is said that the ring can reactivate any of Rassilon's personal technology. Shall we see if that's true?'

Romana drew herself up to her full height. 'Think about what you're doing. All these things that you've discovered are of great scholarly interest. But vampires aren't the way forward. They're parasites, they reduce civilizations to the level of animals. I've seen that at first hand. Whatever your personal grudges, you can't let evil like that loose again.'

'I can, and I will.' Ruath met her gaze evenly.

'I'll intercede with Flavia on your behalf. It's not too late to turn back.'

Ruath paused, then shook her head. 'It was too late a long time ago.'

'I'm sorry.' Romana lunged for the gun. Ruath caught her under the chin with her fist, and Romana lashed back, her hand smacking across Ruath's cheek. Stung, Ruath fired the staser and sent her flying backwards, collapsing against the painting.

There was the sound of a crash from the President's Office. Ruath held the ring high. 'By Rassilon's command, open the door!'

A tune hummed from the harp at a supernatural speed, and the door beneath the painting swung open, sending Romana's limp form rolling down the steps. Ruath ran after her. 'By Rassilon's command, seal this chamber!' she yelled from the interior.

The door swung closed again just as the guards, led by

Castellan Spandrell, raced into the room.

Spandrell slapped his thigh brutally. 'Drat!' he rumbled. 'If it isn't one thing, it's another!'

Ruath looked around herself in wonder. Things were moving so fast today. It was like she had grabbed the tail of some fast-moving bird, an owl perhaps! She was suddenly a leaf in the wind of destiny, a destiny that had been delayed from so long ago.

Here she stood, in the darkened underground control room that had been host to so many futile grabs for power. They would surely destroy it now. But not just yet. It would take time to activate the giant beam weapons that were housed in the remote Matrix station orbiting the planet. It would take time to evacuate the Capitol. And would a weak leader like Flavia authorize the destruction of so much history? Of course not. She had a free hand.

The great game table stood in the centre of the room, its surface a replica of the Death Zone, the Dark Tower in the centre. 'The winner shall lose, and the loser win,' breathed Ruath. 'I must take care not to win just yet.'

Ruath bent to check Romana's pulses. She was still alive, comatose thanks to the stun setting on the staser. Then she turned her attention to the Time Scoop. The ancient machinery still stood on the other side of the room. As Ruath had counted on, Flavia hadn't numbered destroying it among her priorities. She'd seen the opportunity as soon as she'd run into Romana, and seized it. They'd never have let her into the Temporal Observation Bureau, and then there'd be the matter of escape. This solved both her problems.

She hit a control on the Time Scoop experimentally. Nothing happened. Ruath sighed, raising the ring once more. 'By Rassilon's command, activate!' The machine came alive. She adjusted controls, and a silver-haired old man in severe Edwardian dress appeared. 'You got so old, Theta!' Ruath spat. 'You hung on for so long before betraying me!' She spun a dial and the picture swirled through many times and adventures, the image of the Doctor changing several times. Ruath stared at the final image. 'So that's what you become!' she gasped. 'Well, that's no good to me.' She reversed the dial, and spun back to the Doctor's most youthful-seeming incarnation, the impulsive cricketer. Ruath knew that it was forbidden, and thus generally impossible, for Time Lords to meet each other out of temporal sequence. That was Rassilon's First Law of Time. 'But she who has the . . . oh, what the Omega, the Ring of Rassilon, can do such things. And I certainly wouldn't want to take on the Ka Faraq Gatri . . . Show me the path of the Fifth Doctor's TARDIS.'

The screen lit up with a series of cosmological maps, showing the TARDIS's flight out of the formation of the universe, to a deserted planet, through deep space, Deva Loka, Earth several times, Gallifrey and then Manussa. 'Stop!' Ruath commanded. The TARDIS icon was blinking away on Earth once more. The Doctor was at his most vulnerable there, on his favourite planet, possibly without other foes to get in the way. She had an instinct about this moment in time. And if she had an instinct . . . She made a brief search of events around the time. Yes, there she was, stepping out of a TARDIS! She had to see more, see if she succeeded in her plans –

Romana threw herself across the room and spun the dial. The picture fluttered backwards as the two Time Ladies grappled. 'You shan't do it!' Romana called. 'I won't let you!'

Ruath gave Romana a savage shove across the room and stabbed a control on the Time Scoop. As the elegant

Time Lady struggled to her feet, a shining black obelisk spun into existence and swallowed her. For a moment, she was frozen in the gleaming darkness. Then she and the obelisk spun away. Romana appeared on the screen of the Time Scoop a moment later.

Ruath regained her composure and glared at the image. 'You have interfered enough!' she spat. 'Go and play with . . .' she flicked the dial through random images. 'Oh yes. One of those!' She hit another control, and Romana spun away into the vortex.

From high above the ceiling, an explosion erupted. They were using heavy blasters on the floor of the President's Office. How bold of them. They might soon find a way down. The transmat booth in the corner was whining too, as if its one-way link to the Dark Tower was being forcibly reprogrammed. Spandrell must have taken a team out there by capsule. He was wasted as Castellan. Perhaps she'd persuade the Messiah, Yarven, if he was open to persuasion, to keep him on.

Time to go.

Ruath preset the controls of the Time Scoop and pulled a tiny object from her belt pouch, placing it on the control deck. The obelisk spun down and engulfed her, then spun away again. As the whine from the transmat increased in volume, the Time Scoop controls spun and clicked into place.

As the first of Spandrell's Chancellery Guard burst into the room through the transmat booth, Ruath's bomb went off. The Time Scoop erupted in flame, and the chamber filled with choking smoke. The guard swiftly reset the controls of the booth, throwing a gloved hand up in front of his face as the fire consumed the oxygen in the room. A moment later, he vanished.

The power source of the Time Scoop exploded.

* * *

127

Flavia and Pogarel watched from a nearby tower as the Presidential Office blasted upwards into a ball of flaming debris.

'Oh dear,' the Secretary breathed, his knuckles in his mouth. 'Madame President, please forgive me!'

'Please don't worry, Secretary Pogarel.' Flavia patted him comfortingly on the shoulder. 'I was thinking of having the Presidential Chambers redecorated anyway. All that lead. I'll commission something less martial immediately.'

Pogarel sagged. 'Thank you, Madame!'

'But if another strange woman comes to visit,' Flavia murmured, 'particularly in the company of the Lady Romana – '

'Yes, Madame President?'

'I'm out.'

The black obelisk carrying Ruath spun back into normal space inside the Capitol's TARDIS bay. Nobody was present to see it. The destruction of the Presidential block, on top of the events of the last few days, had caused a Gallifrey-wide panic. Most Time Lords were of the opinion that a full-scale revolution was in progress.

Ruath felt for the key on her belt. Her study group, long ago, had been given access to a Travel Capsule for research purposes. She'd never taken advantage of it until now, but it would be quicker than breaking into one of the capsules. A smile crossed her lips. Nostalgia.

She looked along the line of plain white capsules until she identified the one for which she held the key. She placed it in the lock.

'Stop right there!' The voice was old and gravelled, with a guttural accent.

Ruath turned around. Castellan Spandrell, alone, pointing a staser rifle at her. 'Very good, Castellan.'

'Oh, it was nothing,' Spandrell shrugged, keeping his aim steady. 'As soon as my guards reported from the Tower, I guessed this is where you'd come. You don't want to end up on some alien world without a TARDIS, do you?'

'Indeed not. So, Castellan, we're both holding stasers – '

'Ah, but mine is aimed and ready.'

'True. So one of us is going to fire, and the other is going to die.'

'That, dear lady, is also true.'

'Except, Castellan, that I've seen the future. I know I'm going to go to a place called Earth. I haven't done that yet, so . . .'

'I see. Well, forgive me for trying.' Spandrell fired, flipping the setting to stun as he did so, in case she was telling the truth.

Ruath had already dived aside, snapping a shot as she went. The killing blast caught Spandrell dead centre, and the old lawman fell to the floor, the rifle clattering from his hands.

'I told you,' sighed Ruath, unlocking the TARDIS and going inside. 'You can't avoid the future, old man.' The box faded away, rending time and space.

Spandrell opened his eyes and sat up, pulling the staser-proof vest from his bulky torso. 'True as well,' he sighed. 'But sometimes you can see it coming.'

Romana stared up at the Drashig.

The Drashig stared down at Romana.

It was at times like these that she rather regretted that it was beneath her dignity to emit a really good scream.

Drashigs were huge, snake-like creatures, with a cluster of tiny eyes atop their ridged bodies. Their main feature, however, was a vast number of incredibly sharp teeth.

The thing was, the Drashig kept on staring. It didn't lunge or roar or anything. So Romana didn't do anything either, regarding the situation as a reasonable default. She realized that the Drashig was sniffing the air. If she remembered correctly, the creatures hunted by smell.

She reached into the pocket of the jacket she wore and extracted a tiny scent spray. This would require the sacrifice of a silk handkerchief. She slowly took one from her top pocket, keeping her eyes on the Drashig all the time, and balled it up around the spray, kneading the rubber ball of the spray until the entire contents of the bottle were impregnated into the silk.

The Drashig rolled its head, trying to focus on the molecules of strong scent that were arriving at its many and various nostrils.

Romana replaced the empty scent bottle and took careful aim. 'Go on boy,' she called. 'Fetch!'

She threw the balled handkerchief right past the Drashig's head, and ran.

The monster turned with incredible speed, snapping at the tiny target. It missed, and twisted its whole body round to locate the powerful smell that was so engaging its senses.

Romana was dashing across the soggy ground, heading for the grey slope of a rock-face up ahead. There was a cave at its base, a cave far too small for that monster's snout.

A terrible scream erupted behind her, and a shadow fell over her.

Another one of the monsters had blasted up from the ground. She must have scampered over its tail. Mud splattered around her from the bulk of the thing's body.

The shadow grew, and Romana felt a great gust of fetid breath. The Drashig's repulsive head swayed down towards her. She threw herself to one side, and one of the many rows of teeth snapped closed where her head would have been.

Struggling to her feet, Romana raced for the rock, making herself turn at random intervals. She could feel the weight of the monster behind her, trying to adjust itself to the speed and manoeuvrability of its prey.

The cave mouth was just ahead. She took a chance and sprinted straight for it, diving the last few feet as, screaming, the Drashig's head swept at her for the killing bite.

It butted its head against the cave mouth and Romana dived through, landing in a sprawl against a wet rock.

After a moment to get her breath back, she turned and watched curiously as the giant monster tried to stick its mouth through far too narrow an opening. She smoothed a hair back from her brow and smiled. 'Thanks, Coco.'

It took a while for Romana to realize that there was something strange about the rock she was sitting on. It wasn't hard or stone-like or, well, rocky at all really. It was smooth and warm and made a hollow sound when you hit it.

It was made of some sort of plastic.

Romana got to her feet and followed the cave back into the hillside. She was beginning to have her suspicions about this.

Sabalom Glitz rubbed his hands together joyfully, grinning at his latest prize. The hold of the Nosferatu (technically the Nosferatu 2, but Dibber couldn't get his tongue round the name, resulting in a number of embarrassing communication problems) was a dank and dripping place, but somehow it was right for the object that Glitz was staring at with such delight.

'A Miniscope,' he purred. 'And that old fool thought that the crate just had a load of tinned fruit in it. Grotzi city here we come.' Glitz's head was spinning with the possibilities. Miniscopes were tiny environment-containment devices, miniature zoos that could pull a crowd in any part of the universe you cared to name. The smart thing about them was that no feeding was required. The individual environments were held in chronic hystere-chronic hyst-time loops. So what if the devices were banned under intergalactic law? That was virtually a prerequisite to any of Glitz's fortune-making schemes. He'd been in a bit of a turmoil lately, what with Mel going home. He'd come to rely on her skills in the subtle bank jobs that they'd come to specialize in, but perhaps it was for the best that she'd gone back to Earth. Time for Glitz to get back to good honest dishonesty. In light of that, the Scope was Grotzis from heaven.

He pulled an oily rag from his pocket and gave the console of the device a rub. Here, that was a laugh. He remembered a story Mel had told him about some young Zobzer who'd got his hands on a magic lamp, and instead of pocketing it, he'd –

He found himself jumping backwards, his arms flailing behind him.

The woman had appeared out of nowhere, right in front of him. She ought to be careful, doing that could get you in serious trouble. With catlike grace, he lowered his arms from the killing Venusian Aikido position they'd automatically adopted.

She didn't look like a magical spirit, bit too much mud for that, but you never knew. He raised a finger and remembered the three wishes he'd kept uppermost in mind since he was a child. 'I'd like an everlasting bag of crossbank galactic credits, a Draconian fiefdom and the rights to Mav Hasker's back catalogue. Ta.'

The woman stared at him. 'I'd like a cup of tea with milk and no sugar, a shower and a quiet sit-down. Of our

132

two sets of wishes, I think mine's going to be easier to achieve, don't you?'

By the middle of her third wish, sitting grumpily ignored on a rear seat of the Nosferatu's flight deck, Romana had sorted out what had happened and what she had to do.

Having found that the rock corridor became a metal corridor and then a series of circuit boards, she'd made her way out of the Miniscope, got beyond its containment field and shot up to her full height in front of this ruffian. Luckily he seemed to regard her silence about the existence of the machine as a fair price for her wishes.

She was somewhere in deep space on the other side of the galaxy, with no TARDIS. Meanwhile Ruath had presumably escaped, with every intention of attacking the Doctor in his fifth incarnation. She could not, of course, go to help him, even if she'd wanted to, having met his seventh persona recently. If you started to cross timestreams like that, reality ended up looking like a badly knitted jumper.

There was only one thing for it. She would have to warn him. There was no law against communicating with incarnations out of sequence, at least not that she'd heard of. Besides, rather like physics, Gallifreyan law let you get away with virtually anything if you did it subtly enough. She sometimes thought that the main purpose of the statute book was to prevent embarrassment.

Romana stared deep into the swirling fractal pattern on the surface of her tea and concentrated on the idea of the Doctor's fifth incarnation. Her time brain, under a Time Lady's frontal lobes, reached out across the continuum, searching through the vortex for the spiderweb trails of a particular TARDIS.

She found it surprisingly quickly, used to the Doctor's particular psychic signature. Instinctively she managed to tune into the time location that would matter most, a little while after Ruath's arrival on Earth.

The connection nearly made her drop the teacup. The Doctor's brain at this point was under terrifying temporal strain. It was like trying to shout through a storm. Somehow, time around the Doctor was being ripped apart. It was as if . . . no. Surely not. Not even Ruath would be conceited enough to try that.

Romana shut down some of her less important body functions and threw all her energies into one message. She wasn't sure, but she thought she was getting through. The gap across time had opened for a moment and, she was certain now, a burst of pure thought slipped into the Doctor's tormented mind. But had it made sense to him?

She tried again, focusing all her strength on –

On –

Somebody was shaking her.

'Wake up! Hoi! Wake up!'

The voice made her break the connection and open her eyes.

Glitz was standing in front of her, trying to look concerned. 'You'd stopped breathing,' he told her.

'Try it.' Romana sipped her tea in irritation. 'You might enjoy it.'

'I wouldn't mind, normally,' Glitz whispered, his eyes glittering. 'Only,' he raised his voice again, and threw back a hand, revealing what was behind him, 'some friends of yours are here to see you!'

Lady President Flavia, Castellan Spandrell and a squad of Chancellery Guards stood on the flight deck of the little spaceship, looking around and trying not to laugh. Behind them was a glittering new Type Ninety TARDIS.

Flavia stepped forward and helped Romana to her feet, taking both hands in hers. 'My dear, thank goodness we've found you!'

134

'We managed to recover the destination recording device on the Time Scoop,' Spandrell added. 'Decoding it and following the trail here was a matter of routine.'

'I'm worried about the Doctor,' Romana told them, following Flavia back to the TARDIS. 'I don't know what score Ruath's got to settle with him, but I think he's in terrible danger.'

'Don't worry about the Doctor!' laughed Spandrell. 'Danger is what he knows best!'

'The Doctor?' Glitz's ears pricked up. ' 'Ere, wait a minute . . .' He tried to signal to the Gallifreyans as they trooped back into their capsule. 'He's an old friend of mine. If he's in trouble, perhaps I could help, for a small consideration of course . . .'

'I'm sure the Doctor will be fine,' Flavia was saying. 'Besides, we have done all we can for him. It's in Rassilon's hands. Now, Lady Romana, since you've been through so much in the service of Gallifrey, I was wondering if you'd be interested in a seat on the High Council?'

The doors of the machine closed before Glitz heard the Time Lady's answer. The box faded away.

He raised his hand to ask a question and then lowered it again. 'Story of my life,' he muttered. Then he perked up again. They hadn't, after all, taken the Miniscope. 'Dibber!' he called to the flight deck. 'Take us somewhere where they've never heard of Drashigs!'

Seven

While Tegan slept, the Doctor worked at the console. It took some time to calibrate the readings from his device and feed them into the TARDIS computers. Finally, at around eleven in the morning, he had it. He pressed a button, stepped back and stretched, glancing up at the screen.

Alderley Edge was a cluster of graph lines across the bottom of the screen. First one, then a confused tangle of bright lines sped upwards from it, heading straight up into the sky. Each represented a vampire in flight. The frame scrolled upwards, following the first blip, Lang and his kidnapper.

The line continued straight up and stopped. A moment later, the other lines hit the same height and hung suspended. A message appeared on the screen: *Parameters exceeded. No further information available.*

'Straight up,' the Doctor whispered. 'They went straight up out of range of the detector.' He hit another control and confirmed what he suspected. 'To the edge of the atmosphere. A suborbital hop. They could be anywhere.' He switched off the screen. There wasn't much time left, and he was running out of avenues to explore. For a moment, the Doctor leaned heavily on the console. Then he snapped himself upright. 'Brave heart, as I keep telling Tegan. Still the sample to analyse.'

He was on his way out of the console room when he heard the noise. It started as a tingling in his ear, and for a moment he thought that he was going to fall victim to another spasm of the kind that he'd experienced at Alderley Edge. But this sensation was quite different. There was no pain, for one thing. Last time, he'd reeled, his time senses suddenly askew. This was more in the nature of –

Ah. Communication.

The Doctor put his hands to his brow and closed his eyes, concentrating. What had been a tingling resolved itself into a voice. Unimaginably distant, across space and time, but a voice nonetheless. It was so faint that he couldn't even recognize the person calling him. It must be another Time Lord, of course, or perhaps one of the other High Evolutionaries. The fact that it was so faint indicated that it was being sent across the centuries, perhaps even across his own time track. It might even be one of his other incarnations, calling for help. No, there was something familiar about the voice, certainly, and his previous selves wouldn't feel familiar at all.

He dropped into a sudden cross-legged sitting position and devoted his whole being to hearing the message. He closed his respiratory tract and shut down a number of minor organs, letting his mind drift out onto what humans called the astral plain.

There was the source of the message! She was standing at the edge of the darkness, broadcasting a tight and disciplined beam. In a moment he would be able to identify her, because it was a she. And what was that she was saying? It was something like . . .

Oh no.

'Doctor, wake up!' Tegan was shaking the Doctor's shoulder violently.

The Time Lord opened his eyes and looked into the middle distance ruefully. 'Tegan, have I ever told you

137

about disturbing somebody when they're in the middle of astral communication, hm?' He looked up at her. 'I might have got lost altogether.'

'You'd stopped breathing!'

'I had more important things to think about. Which reminds me – ' He took in a great sucking breath. 'That's better. Now – ' he jumped to his feet, 'since you did interrupt a message which might have been the key to our whole dilemma, I trust you won't mind making the tea this time?'

'Kettle's already boiling. I was on the way to ask you about toast. Who's sending this message?'

'I was about to find out.'

'Could it be one of the vampires?'

'I doubt it, they're very limited telepaths. I think this is one of my own race.'

'The Time Lords? What, are they going to pile in and help us since you knocked off Omega for them?'

'That's not how they work, Tegan. The Capitol hasn't "piled in" to help anybody since . . . well, not for a very long time, anyway. And I did not knock anybody off. Now, you mentioned toast?'

Madelaine sat on the steps of the machine, her head in her hands. The great shining globe above her in the sky hurt with its reflected sunlight, but she was too distracted to care.

Jake rubbed some dust from a plaque. ' "We came in peace for all mankind",' he read. 'Smart. I always wanted to come here. It's nice to have somebody to do things like this with.'

Madelaine stood up and walked down the steps of the lunar module. 'You're just trying to distract me. You always try to distract me.'

'You think about things, let them play on your mind.

138

I'm not like that.'

'No.' Maddy studied the silvery surface of the Sea Of Tranquillity, and watched a low cloud of dust shift slowly along. Even the light steps of the vampires had been enough to disturb the airless lunar dunes. They'd left before sunrise on Earth, speeding west out over the Atlantic before they arched upwards and out of the atmosphere. 'Can you be sure it's safe, though? Where's the sun?'

'Round the back. Old lad I met down on the east coast used to come up here all the time, he'd worked out the times that are okay. Gave me a copy. I found it the other night. Thought you'd like a surprise.'

'It's good here, thanks for bringing me. When I was little I always wanted to go into space. It's just – '

'Just that you're worried about this Lang bloke.'

'Not worried. Interested.'

'Now that worries me, like.'

'Oh, not like that, stupid.' Madelaine gave him a quick hug. 'He's old and American, and he'd want to exorcise me or something. No, I'm interested in what makes him tick. When we flew off, it was as if he half wanted to come along with me. There's something he's more afraid of than he is of us.'

'Has your boss told you what he's going to do with him?'

'My boss? You're the one who wanted us to get involved in the first place. No, Yarven doesn't tell me anything. He only confides in that alien tart. Hey, could we go and meet some aliens?'

'Only if they're hanging about the solar system. Take us months even to get to Pluto, never mind other stars.'

'Well, we could go to Jupiter or something.'

'After this is over we'll go on holiday there. We'd need to take a packed lunch.'

'Lang?'

'Anybody but Lang. Besides, I don't think there'll be much left of him by then, do you?'

'No,' Madelaine sighed, walking carefully along a line of astronaut's footprints. 'No, you're right there.'

Nyssa judged that the moment was right. She carefully pushed back the covers and stood up beside the bed. After seeing Yarven, she'd pretended to go to sleep with the approaching day, but had made a mighty mental effort to stay awake. The windows of the castle had darkened to black and the vampires that shared the room were curled in corners, dead to the world.

She retraced her path down the stairs, avoiding those Undead lying there, who were clutching meat from the previous night's feasting. What was she going to say if she was caught, that she woke and went for a glass of water? Surely even Yarven and his consort would have retired to the master bedroom by now?

Even if Yarven was as good as his word about curing her, and even the faint hope of that had lifted her heart and filled her with bravery, she would still tell the Doctor all she could about the castle. There were two areas she particularly wanted to explore. She took her bearings at the foot of the stairs. When Yarven and his people had raced out of the dining hall to an urgent summons, they had turned right, which meant that whatever was so important must be somewhere in the east wing. She knew so little about Earth architecture. On Traken, a great house like this would have been open and airy, with no mysteries to it.

Nyssa ventured carefully into the eastern reaches of the castle, remembering her path as she went. All about her were sleeping vampires, lying in whatever niche they could find. The castle must already be home to hundreds of them, and more arrived every night.

Three doors were ahead of her. Well, she could only explore so far randomly. Perhaps if she had got so far into Yarven's confidence he would show her whatever had so excited the Undead. She didn't doubt that Madelaine and Jake would have, but they weren't here and, silly as it was, she didn't want to get them into trouble. They had been good to her, in their way.

There came a cry from behind one of the doors. The one to the right. Nyssa tried the handle and found that it opened easily.

The young Trakenite stepped into the domed room. The covered pit immediately caught her attention. From it there came loud speech. It was an incantation of some kind, a prayer. As she moved closer to the metal hatch that covered the pit she started to feel afraid. Now that was strange, this was hardly the most fearful situation she had faced since arriving at the castle. She found that she couldn't take another step. Whatever was in the pit was somehow terrifying. But it sounded just like a man.

'Hello?' she asked nervously.

'Hello! Who's there?' a voice called back eagerly.

'My name is . . . it isn't important. Who are you?'

'Victor Lang. My name is Victor Lang. Are you one of the . . . creatures?'

'No.'

'Then help me! We must get out of here, we must get back to the city and warn them! They only brought me here last night. I don't know what they plan to do to me, but I don't want to be around to find out! The controls for the cover are somewhere on the wall, I distinctly heard a lever being pulled. Hurry!'

His voice sounded so confident, so commanding even when trapped. It was as if the man was the hero of some great story, and knew it. He was . . . terrifying.

Nyssa shook her head, fighting the urge to run from this place. Instead she went to the wall. There was indeed a very obvious set of pit controls, including a large lever of the kind that the castle's electronic systems seemed to favour. She pushed it up to its original position.

The great metal lid swung back from the pit on a hydraulic hinge. Thankfully it made little noise.

'Quickly!' Lang whispered urgently. 'There'll be guards.'

Nyssa couldn't make herself step towards the pit. 'There are no guards,' she said. 'They're vampires, and this is daytime.'

'Vampires? Yeah, I must say I got that impression. Can't get over the fact that they're real. Are you finding a ladder or something?'

Nyssa took a deep breath. 'No. I can't come any closer to you. Can't you get out on your own?'

'No!' Lang called, and Nyssa winced at the frustration in his voice. 'The walls of this thing are perfectly smooth. What do you mean, you can't come any closer?'

'I just can't. Something's stopping me.'

'Well . . . well, what do you think that might be?' Lang had made a great effort to speak reasonably.

'I think it's your . . . faith. When I said that I wasn't one of these creatures . . . well, I suppose I am now. For the moment, at least.' No reply came from the pit. 'Mr Lang? Are you all right?'

'I'm fine. God bless you anyway, and thank you for trying.'

'I'd set you free if I could,' Nyssa called desperately. 'If you could feel less . . . passionate about your beliefs, then – '

'I can't do that,' Lang said quietly. 'Guess you'd better cover me up again.'

Not wanting to say any more, Nyssa swung the lever

again and watched as the pit was closed once more. She felt disgusted with herself. Couldn't she have done anything to help the poor man?

The chanting rose again, and she shivered. There was no use worrying about it. If she wanted to help Lang, she had to take the long-term view. Lang's arrival had obviously been what had excited the vampires so much the previous evening. He must be part of whatever plan Yarven and Ruath were concocting. To find out about that, she needed to find a way down to the cellars.

There was a stairwell leading down near to the control point where she stood. If this was such an important room, then perhaps it had direct access to whatever was down below. She took a few hesitant steps down the circular staircase, and immediately came to a solid-looking metal door. It was locked. Ruath, unlike those who had been vampires for a long time, would still retain the habit of locks and keys.

What a useless trip this had been. 'If only I had the ion bonder,' Nyssa murmured to herself, picturing what one of her everyday laboratory tools would have done to the metal surface. She was about to turn away and head back to bed when a thought struck her. 'If I'm a vampire,' she whispered, 'then why not?'

She concentrated, trying to visualize what she wanted to do, and found that all the reflexes she needed were already there in her head, as easy as holding her breath or closing an eye. Neither of those required verbal thought or visualization, and neither did this.

So Nyssa just did it.

It started at her feet, a slow dissolve of flesh and clothing into mist. The mist rolled up her torso until it claimed her head, and then she was a cloud, feeling just as she'd always felt. Trying to touch the wall, the cloud swirled and separated, and couldn't. Nyssa moved under the door, trying not to think about how she was doing it, and mentally closing her eyes as what she thought of as her head went under. Somewhere inside her, a mental urge to duck had been obeyed, though the mist swept through the thin crack undisturbed by it.

On the other side of the door Nyssa, wondering how she could see, found that after a landing, the stairwell continued. She made herself solid again, thankful that the process was easily reversible, and stepped cautiously downwards.

'So what you're saying is that we still don't know where she is?'

'Tegan, Tegan, Tegan . . .' The Doctor made a pacifying gesture with his open hands. 'Patience.'

'Patience? It's not very long until the full moon, and then that's it, she's part of the fang and cape brigade for good.' Tegan followed the Doctor as he circled the console trying to placate her. It had been a mistake, he thought, to show her the vampire flight-paths.

'I know. But this doesn't help. I still have the samples I took to analyse, and then – '

'What good will that do? Why don't we just go out now it's light, wake up a vampire and make them take us there?'

'It's not as simple as that. We have to – Tegan!'

On her latest circuit of the console, the young Australian had slapped the door release control. She grabbed her coat from the hatstand as she headed for the door. 'Don't mind if I have a go, do you? See you later.'

The Doctor sighed as she departed. Not much could happen to her in daytime, even if she went looking for trouble. He had to concentrate on what was important, the sample. And he had to be ready to receive the mental call if it came again. The best place to do that was in the temporally removed atmosphere of the TARDIS.

He closed the doors again, and rolled up his shirt-sleeves.

Tegan hadn't really intended to go out and find a vampire, and she was sorry for getting worked up at the Doctor. He was doing his best, but her temper . . . Tegan could never bear sitting around waiting for something to happen. Early afternoon in Manchester city centre calmed her, and she was almost reassured by the clatter of people in the autumn cold. There were people selling novelties on street corners, and vans doing burgers. She lost herself in the Arndale Centre for a while, buying toffee and munching it while staring down at the crowds milling on lower levels of the glass and steel complex. One vampire amongst them, and it'd be like a dog in sheep. All the little kids being snatched away, the old people being thrown over. And the adults who'd try to defend them or run away. Helpless.

She left the shopping centre depressed once more, intending to pick up an *Evening News* and see if she could spot anything helpful. She almost walked past the beggar. But what he was putting in his pocket –

He was crouched in the corner of the stairs that led up to the shopping centre, and he had a cardboard sign on his lap that said 'Homeless and Hungry'. Tegan marched up to him and pointed at the anorak he wore.

'What's that you had there?' she demanded.

'What?'

'That bracelet. Where did you get it?'

'I didn't steal it or anything. It's mine.'

Tegan made herself count to ten, aware that she'd rushed in heedlessly again. What would the Doctor do?

Tegan sat down beside the boy and, remembering her training concerning difficult passengers, showed him her widest smile. 'I don't want to take it off you. Look, the truth is, my sister's gone missing – '

'Lots of people going missing these days.'

'Yeah, right. She was wearing something like that, and when I saw it, I thought . . . could I just have a look?'

'I met her. She's okay, you shouldn't worry.' The boy pulled the bracelet from his anorak, and Tegan saw that it was the one Nyssa had taken to wearing, all right.

'Where did you see her?'

'Down near Afflick's Palace. Few days ago. She started asking me all kinds of stuff about missing people. Gave me this.'

Damn. Tegan realized that the boy was talking about the time when Nyssa had lost her in the city centre. 'What did you tell her?'

'Oh, there's loads more since then. And did you hear what happened this morning?' The boy began to reel off a long list of strange happenings, and Tegan listened attentively. Maybe her first impulse hadn't been so wrong after all.

'Interesting!' The Doctor was peering into the eyepiece of a powerful scanning microscope. He adjusted the focus slightly.

The Time Lord had subjected the tissue samples he'd taken from the corpses to a basic biochemical scan and, as he'd suspected, an unknown element was detected. Something had been in the mortar shells which had caused the death of all but one of Lang's group, and had caused the survivor to be deeply disturbed.

The Doctor had separated some of the new substance from the tissue where it had been preserved and placed it in one of the TARDIS's medical pods. This was an upright silver cylinder currently balanced on the end of the bench in the laboratory where the Doctor was

146

working. Its normal use was in case of injury: it could knit together Gallifreyan flesh in minutes. But its current capacity was as a molecular growth machine. Whatever the unusual compound was, it bore all the signs of being organic. The Doctor had made a few adjustments to the pod and left a tiny sample of the bioweapon in it to grow. Hopefully, within the hour a batch big enough to subject to a thorough analysis would have brewed up.

It was at times like this that he missed Nyssa's biochemistry skills. But, as he ruefully thought to himself, that was rather like asking the proverbial horse to help close the gate. He'd prepared slides of tissue affected by the substance and was now examining them, trying to ascertain the cause of death.

The substance was bonded into the tissue at molecular level, that was certain, but as to the nature of those bonds . . . the Doctor squinted at the slide. The chemical lay across the familiar human cell structure like a shadow. He couldn't see any damage. Whatever the stuff was, it was just hanging around the blood vessels, doing nothing. It hadn't even entered the bloodstream. Not the behaviour of a swift-acting toxin.

He raised his head from the microscope and glanced at the pod again.

Churning sounds came from within. 'Still a few minutes,' he muttered. 'Time for another cup, I think.'

Nyssa gazed in awe at the banks of instruments that Ruath had assembled. The technology was beyond her comprehension, she couldn't even begin to guess at the purpose of the device. Whatever it was, it took up most of the cellar. At its centre, in an alcove between the many banks of instruments, was a globe of the Earth. Something about the whole apparatus struck Nyssa as familiar. Then she realized: it had the somewhat gothic look of

Gallifreyan workmanship. Hardly out of place in the circumstances, but unmistakable none the less. She was even familiar with some of the individual components from her recent adventures on the Time Lords' home planet.

Through an arch, another chamber beckoned. Nyssa tiptoed cautiously inside, and found this one to be more familiar. A fully equipped chemical laboratory. A forest of equipment assembled on a series of benches, with formulae scrawled on boards that stretched all round the room. Nyssa started to read them, but swiftly found herself faced with questions. There was chemistry of a kind she knew nothing of here and, she suspected, advanced physics as well. On the far wall, that was surely a wave equation, and what part could wave physics play in chemical science?

Nyssa was startled from her ponderings by a noise from the other room. A chime. She wandered back in and located the source of the noise. On a screen on one of the computer banks, a display had appeared. A clock-face. It indicated a quarter of an hour in shading, and the shaded area was gradually getting smaller.

Nyssa decided that she didn't want to be around when the time was up and whatever was going to happen happened. But surely this was an opportunity too good to miss? A laboratory full of chemicals and equipment. If she could just find a few of the basics . . . Quickly she went back into the laboratory and started to search in the cupboards that ringed the room at head height.

His name was Matthew, and he was very frightened indeed.

He'd told the strange man in the cricket jumper that he was in hell, and that was just how it felt. He'd wandered around his house when he got back, not wanting to wake his parents but not wanting to go to bed either. He'd flicked through the satellite TV channels and seen Roger Moore speaking German, the light from the screen throwing long shadows across the room, because he didn't want to switch the lights on. That would have woken his Mum and Dad up. They were deaf but light did that.

They would have asked him where he'd been, and been sarcastic about Mr Lang. Mike, the leader, had come round to visit them when Matthew had first joined New Light, telling them what the group was all about and inviting them to come to a parents' evening service. But they just made tea and listened and laughed, and said that they were C of E themselves, weddings and funerals. Mum had said to Mike that she believed in some sort of power looking after us, but that she didn't know what it was. When she died, she said, she thought she might go somewhere, but as long as her body fed the trees, that was all right by her. Mike had tried to tell them about salvation, about how without the Lord Jesus Christ there was only death, and Matthew had watched as his Dad grew more and more uncomfortable. After a while, he'd muttered something about 'brainwashing' and wandered off to the toilet.

That seemed like somebody else's life now. Matthew had touched the sofa and the carpet and smelled all the smells he associated with normality and childhood, and felt no sympathy with any of it.

The God he'd found with Mike and the others had gone.

It felt like He'd died, and this was grief.

Matthew remembered the feel of his love, the way that it had filled his head up like a balloon, and made him bounce and laugh with it. Mike and the others who'd died were clustered around Jesus now, accepted into his company. Matthew was in darkness.

He put his hand to the glow of the television screen, and seemed to see light through it. There was a strange taste in his mouth and a tightness in his stomach. He leant his head against the screen and watched pictures made up of three dot clusters: red, green, blue. The remote control in his hand, he hopped channels, faster and faster, panting as something huge thrashed inside him, and then –

He hit the screen and bounced off, his wings sending him fluttering around the room, swerving and shrieking to avoid furniture, a bat or a moth. 'Mother!' screamed the little flying thing. 'Mother!'

It had flapped upstairs.

Now Matthew was really in the darkness. He was full, and it was daytime, so he slept.

Tegan had bought the flowers from a stall in the shopping centre. She had felt almost embarrassed about it, like she wanted to say to the woman 'I'm going to a wedding, honest.'

The boy in the anorak had mentioned something that had happened this morning, at somewhere called Irlams O'The Height in Salford. Tegan managed to get on a bus to Irlam, and spent a confused half-hour there before somebody said, 'Oh, you don't mean Irlam, you mean Irlams O'The Height, lass.' Finally she gave in and took a taxi.

It was still light, thankfully, when she got to where she wanted to go, a quiet-looking street in a housing estate. There was a shock of recognition when the taxi turned the corner. She hadn't paid any attention to the route they'd taken, but if she had then she'd certainly have recognized it. She'd been here last night, dropping off that poor boy. He hadn't told her an address, or she'd have got it immediately. He'd just said 'go right here, and now left here', in that empty voice.

At his gate there was a police van, and in his garden there was a pile of flowers.

Tegan asked the driver to stop at the end of the road, paid him and got out, suddenly unsure of why she'd come here. If what she'd heard was true then she couldn't possibly find out anything. All the details would have been taken down in the early hours of the morning. The police were probably still doing their forensic work and the press would have been long gone.

Presumably they hadn't found the boy yet. Tegan walked up to the gate. It didn't feel right to open it so, after a moment's hesitation, she threw the bunch of flowers onto the pile. There. Almost against her will, she'd become part of a bloody stupid ritual. She should have told the cab to wait. At least this looked like the kind of place where you could get another one.

She started back towards the phone box on the corner, walking over a grating in the pavement. And at that moment she heard a cry, a short, cut-off wail. And it was coming from under the grating.

Tegan looked around. Despite everything she'd been through, she didn't feel able to run back to the police and tell them that she was hearing voices in the sewers. But if it was the kid . . . Look, it was broad daylight. Unless it was a brand new sort of monster that had just happened along, then it wouldn't do any harm just to open the hatch and take a look.

Squatting down, Tegan peered through the bars of the grating. It was certainly big enough to get a child down there. It was too dark to see anything from here, but she thought she could make out some sort of figure. She got her fingers under one bar of the grating and pulled it up, pleased with the ease with which it came away. The curtains would really be twitching now, what with the whole road agitated by the events of the morning.

Tegan leaned forward and looked into the hole.

The Doctor peered into the observation port of the medical pod. He had a gnawing suspicion that he knew what the bubbling green liquid inside the container was. Nyssa would certainly say that he shouldn't leap to conclusions, but if he was right then they had no time for lengthy tests.

There was one way to find out. He turned a valve to drain some of the deadly liquid into another metal container, made sure the lock system was clear of the stuff by activating a vacuum pump, and disconnected the smaller vessel. Thoughtfully he tossed it in his hand, then frowned, aware of what he was toying with. He snapped the observation port on the little cylinder closed and strode out of the laboratory.

Nyssa had gathered all the things she needed. She ran to the door, opened the lock, thankful that it was on a latch system, and stepped outside. She glanced back at the computer clock. Only a minute left. Whatever was going to happen then, she didn't want to know about it. She closed the door behind her and ran up the stairs.

'Hello? You okay down there?' Tegan's voice echoed in the darkness. She could vaguely make out a human shape, huddled in the shadows of the shallow storm drain. It was small enough to be the kid from last night, and it looked like he was wearing the same baseball jacket. 'Remember me? Tegan?' She waited for a moment but no answer came, only a shallow breathing. It sounded like the boy was asleep. 'Now look, I'm not going to come down there with things like they are at the moment. You stay right where you are and I'll go and get some help, okay?'

The child still made no reply, but shifted slightly. He had something in his arms, a cuddly toy or something.

The boy's eyes opened. 'Oh, it's you,' he said.

'Yeah,' Tegan nodded, relieved. 'Everybody's worried about you, you know?'

'Are they?' He still had that terrible empty sound to his voice. 'I'd better come out then. Could you take this, please?'

'Sure.' Tegan reached out for the teddy bear with both hands.

The Doctor looked up at the low sun, shining red above the buildings, and put a hand to his brow to shield his eyes. The silver cylinder was clutched in his hand, and he stood just outside the doors of the TARDIS. No cloud, at least. The sunlight should still be strong enough for his experiment.

He reached down and slid the observation port on the cylinder open.

In the cellar of Castle Yarven, the clock graphic completed its cycle. There was a metallic thud and a low, building hum came from the machinery. In seconds the device had powered up. A shining halo flickered into life around the model globe. A beam flashed from the wall, and the halo glowed blue.

Yarven sat upright in bed, suddenly awake. 'Good evening,' he said to Ruath, who was already on her feet.

'It should be,' she smiled. 'I made it myself.'

The sun slammed down below the horizon.

The Doctor dropped the canister and fell to his knees, clutching his head in agony as his time senses exploded.

Before it hit the ground, the canister burst open. Green

fluid hung in the air for a moment, and then flung itself straight at the nearest living thing: the Doctor.

It slapped itself onto his face, fighting to get into his eyes and nose.

'Catch!' The boy threw something into Tegan's hands. It was round and sticky.

His mother's head.

Tegan screamed and threw it aside, scrabbling out of the hole to find daylight.

But outside it was night.

She turned to run, but something erupted out of the hole and swirled over her head, twisting to land in front of her.

Matthew opened his mouth wide and showed her his fangs.

'Wait!' Tegan yelled. 'Don't you recognize me? I helped you!'

'That,' the boy whispered, 'was before I was damned.'

And he leapt for her throat.

Eight

Yarven and Ruath raced down the stairs, scattering the Undead who had awoken all over the castle.

In ranks they rose and followed their sovereigns, aware that something wonderful was happening. A great tide of vampirekind swept through the structure as more and more of Yarven's followers came to the same conclusion.

They were awake, because it was night. Yet the night had fallen two hours early!

Yarven raised a hand at the door to the cellars, holding his people back as Ruath fumbled hurriedly with keys. 'Wait a while, my loyal subjects. I will tell you what has occurred once we are certain.'

Nyssa stepped forward from the crowd. She had only just had time to shove the spoils of her adventure under the bed before the vampires in her chamber started to wake. 'What's happening, Lord Yarven?'

'The future, my dear,' Yarven smiled, revealing his fangs. 'Quite literally.'

The Doctor stared at Romana, putting a hand gently on both her shoulders. All around them was the characteristic black void of astral communication.

'This,' he told her, 'is not a good time.'

'On the contrary, it's the only time.' Romana brushed a hair back from her brow. 'I've been trying to get through to you for hours. The temporal distance was so great that

155

I nearly gave up but then, suddenly, I found a clear channel.'

'That's because something very disturbing has happened to time. My temporal senses have overloaded and switched themselves off. Also, my physical form is currently in the process of being attacked by some form of aggressive organic plasma so, nice as it is to see you again, I really must − '

'This is important. Listen.'

And she began to tell him her story.

The boy had wrestled Tegan to the ground and was trying to get his teeth close to her neck. Taken off guard as she had been by the fall of night, she hadn't had time to think. When she'd found Matthew, she'd stupidly assumed that he'd been a victim of, or a witness to, the atrocity that the homeless guy had related to her. She'd thought that the vampires had come after him.

Bloody typical Tegan not to consider the idea that he'd ripped up his mum and dad himself. 'The trouble with me is,' she yelled into Matthew's ear, 'I'm too trusting by half.'

The creature that Matthew had become only hissed in reply. Tegan tensed as he slammed her arms flat to the pavement. They were actually quite similar in strength. Maybe it took vampires a while to get strong.

He lunged to bite her neck.

She butted his nose with her forehead. He reared back, screeching, and something caught him across the side of his head.

A spade.

'Get off her, you little bugger!' A rosy-cheeked man in overalls brandished the garden implement before him. Beside him were a group of similarly armed men and a few dangerous-looking women with kitchen equipment.

Matthew clicked his head back into position and stared

at them. He still held Tegan down like a dog with a bird, but he was sizing up the opposition.

'I told you, get off! We've had enough of you!' The man gave a few experimental lunges with his spade. At the end of the street, two uniformed policemen were trotting up.

Matthew shook his head, flustered, and returned to his task. Oblivious to spade impacts on the back of his skull, he seemed intent on suckling Tegan's neck.

His teeth sped forward to their target and Tegan cried out.

The Doctor's body sprawled inert on the pavement, a green mask fitting tightly to every curve of his face.

The plasma was trying to get into his nose and ears, and around his eyeballs, but everywhere it advanced, non-porous barriers had erected themselves. The Time Lord had stopped breathing a long time ago, but the plasma could sense that he was still alive.

It was fighting a vicious battle on a molecular level, sending tiny battering rams against the Doctor's bodily defences. Sooner or later, it knew, something would give. Then it would feast on what was inside.

Ruath ran to the globe, enveloped by the ray, and cried out in laughter: 'I did it!'

Yarven stood beneath a grating in the roof of the cellar and looked up. 'The night,' he breathed. 'The blessed night. At my command. Indeed, my dear, you have done magnificently!'

There came a crackle from the machine. A blue spark leapt across a junction and there was a small explosion.

Yarven leapt back from the grating.

Just in time. The ray vanished from around the globe and late afternoon sunlight blazed through the grating, catching the hem of the vampire lord's cloak. He snatched it away and glared at Ruath.

'Teething troubles,' she told him.

The sun had leapt back up from the horizon.

Matthew had been breathing on the skin of Tegan's throat, stretched as it was by their combined efforts. His head was a mess, probably. He hadn't looked up as he felt the dull impacts of the weapon. And in the last few seconds people had started to pull at his clothes, but he was too hungry for blood to notice.

But when the sun came up, he felt it.

Every hair on his head flared with the pain, like all his human wounds had been bathed in salt water.

The crowd jumped back and he staggered upright, looking around himself and at his skin.

His hand was on fire.

And there was tremendous heat from his back, like he . . . He was on fire all over. Patches of his face started to smoke, and the old sensation . . . pain. Pain was back.

He screamed. He changed.

A fast unshaped creature sped down into the sewer where Tegan had found him. In one liquid movement, he was gone.

The man with the spade helped Tegan to her feet. The policemen were staring at where the apparition had been. 'Arthur,' the man said. 'We're the Neighbourhood Watch.'

'Thanks,' Tegan gasped, rubbing her throat. 'Can anybody tell me . . . what happened just now?'

Arthur shrugged. 'Night fell just like that, then day came back on again.' He turned to an old lady in the crowd and put an arm round her shoulder. 'End of the world, me and Iris think.'

* * *

158

The Doctor sat up and put his hands to his face. They came away covered in ashes. He blinked and rubbed at his skin more fiercely until most of the grey dust had come away.

'Interesting!' he whispered, and glanced up at the low sun. He'd anticipated a fight for his life when returning to consciousness, but whatever had altered time was obviously on the blink. For now anyway.

And the plasma hadn't been able to stand sunlight, which confirmed his theory, at least. Newton would have appreciated the nature of that experiment. But then old Isaac tended to drink whatever mercury compounds he was working with and had gone mad as a hatter as a result.

The Doctor headed back to the TARDIS, carefully gathering ashes in his handkerchief. He hoped that when he found her, Nyssa appreciated these efforts on her behalf.

'So what happened?' Yarven was enjoying a working breakfast, a goblet of blood, as he watched Ruath examining the banks of equipment. Outside the castle, the sun had sunk towards the horizon on its natural course.

'As I suspected, the electronics are faultless, it's the processor that's shorted out.' Ruath opened up a hatch in the front of the machine and revealed a dead sheep, its head shaved and the skull bolted to several electrical terminals. Thin coils of smoke rose from its eyes. 'Couldn't handle the size of the concepts required. Which is surprising, really, because I thought an animal might manage it better than a human. Too tied in to the natural rhythms of the planet, though. Poor little thing.' Ruath glanced up at Yarven, wondering at his lack of concern. Didn't he appreciate what was expected of him? That, like an old human king, his place was as sacrifice to the future? Perhaps he just had tremendous courage.

Yarven was chuckling. 'Give it to Nyssa, she'll eat it.'

'Don't be cruel, my Lord. By the way, did you notice her expression when she crowded with the others at the door?'

'I did. I do believe that we have read the book of that young Trakenite rather well. I will show her the sheep, as a matter of fact, it'll add to her discomfort. How do you think she'll do it?'

'She'll find a way. The people of Traken have a vastly creative scientific class, of which she's a prime example.' Ruath began to disconnect the sheep. 'With her help, he'll soon be here.'

'He will come like – '

'A lamb to the slaughter.'

'Hah!' Yarven threw back the contents of the goblet. 'You took the words right out of my mouth.'

When Tegan ran into the TARDIS, the Doctor was wiping the final traces of ash from his face. The sight of him stopped the rush of information that she was about to unleash. 'What happened to you?'

'A hands-on experiment. Unfortunately, it got its hands on me. Still, I learnt a lot from the experience. And you?'

Tegan threw her coat onto the hatstand and closed the doors. 'The kid who survived Alderley Edge is now a vampire. He thought I looked like supper, or maybe breakfast, because then the lights went out. What the hell is going on, Doctor?'

'Somebody is playing a very dangerous game, altering time. How, I have no idea, as yet. But I think it's obvious why they're doing it.'

'They want it to be night?'

'Exactly, Tegan. They want it to be night all the time.'

* * *

160

Lang had been pacing the pit, praying and considering the Bible. Vampires, if they were real, must be demons. And, dear Lord forgive him, he'd always thought that demons were kind of, well, metaphorical. He'd thought of demons as those things that good men find in bad places. Demons of alcohol or drugs or sexual gratification.

But the good book did not deal in metaphors and, Lang now realized, when Christ had met Satan in the desert, he hadn't met doubt and hunger and thirst. He'd met the guy with the forked tail.

'Easier, isn't it?' The lid had swung back without him even noticing. Obviously he was getting used to captivity. Sitting on the edge of the pit, swinging her legs, was Madelaine.

'I beg your pardon?'

'It's easier when demons are solid. I read your mind. Sometimes that's easy to do. Sorry.'

'That's okay. A man's thoughts ought to be things he doesn't mind the world hearing.'

Madelaine laughed. 'You're really old-fashioned. How are you getting on? Me and Jake just got back from the moon.'

'Really? What was it like?'

'Like it is on telly. Good fun, though. We had a ride in the moon buggy. Terrible gears.'

Lang opened his mouth and then closed it again. 'I don't know what to say to that,' he ventured. 'I'm sorry.'

'Have they been treating you all right?'

'They've given me some food. Roast lamb, I think. It was okay. Madelaine, what are they going to do with me?'

'I don't know. That's up to the King. But, I tell you what, if they were going to eat you, they'd have done it by now. You've been sitting there getting all worried, calming down for a bit and then getting stressed again.

161

You'd taste really crap. And they wouldn't have fed you. If they'd wanted to mature you, they'd just have ripped open your throat and hung you over a bucket.'

'Thank you. That makes me feel better.'

'Good. So, what's your secret, then?'

'My . . . secret? What do you mean?'

'You've got a secret. There's a corner of your mind walled up and hidden away. That's quite odd in such an open person. It reminds me of a girl who used to pick on me at school. Me and Jake found her and dropped her through the roof of a cathedral. She had a lot of secrets, and she couldn't wait to tell me them, while we were holding her there at three thousand feet. But we didn't listen.'

Lang sat down. 'I never know when you're threatening me.'

'I'm not threatening you. Why do you think I'm doing that?'

'Because you're talking so casually about such violent things. You sound like a gangster, talking sweetly to some victim.'

'Yeah, I see what you mean. Like the villain's being really nice to somebody and you know that any minute they're going to kill them? No, it isn't like that at all. I've just spent so much time with our lot, you know, the Undead, that I forget this stuff seems bad to people.'

'Bad? It's evil, wicked, whatever you want to – '

'Oh come on, do you really want the PC lecture? What we do to you is what you do to cows, and all that?'

'But cows are just animals.'

'So are you. We're not. We're not just higher up on the evolutionary scale, we're off it altogether. Sooner or later you're going to die, but we aren't, necessarily. If you were one of us, wouldn't you just take the food and get on with it?'

'If I was one of you I'd kill myself.'

'That's what they all say. Nobody does. Still don't want to tell me your secret, then? What's your personal demon?'

'I don't have any secret to tell.'

'You're lying, but that's okay. I'm not interrogating you or anything. Whoops.' She hopped to her feet and glanced conspiratorially down at Lang. 'Here comes the boss.'

Yarven had stridden in, and glanced suspiciously at Madelaine when he saw that the pit was open. He took a look over the edge. 'Ah, Mr Lang. Glad you're still with us. By the smell of you, you've rid yourself of garlic. You'll be glad to hear that you're going on a journey.'

'Where?'

'Initially,' Yarven produced a tiny capsule, and dropped it into the pit, 'into the arms of Morpheus.'

The capsule broke on impact and a bloom of anaesthetic gas filled the pit. Lang fell onto his side, unconscious.

'Bring him to the operating theatre.' Yarven gestured to Madelaine, and swept from the room.

Maddy floated down into the pit. 'Who died and left you in charge?' she whispered.

Tegan stared down into the microscope. 'What am I supposed to be looking at?' she asked.

'Well, what do you see?' the Doctor replied. He'd bustled Tegan into the laboratory and sat her down in front of the instrument with the air of Louis Pasteur in a dairy.

'Some black things fighting some green things.'

'And are the black things winning?'

'Yeah. Well, they're getting inside the green things. And now – ' Tegan looked up from the microscope. 'The green things turned black.'

'Exactly, Tegan! Do you see?'

'Yeah. Right. Bet on black things, tell any green things you meet to be careful. What was I watching just then?'

The Doctor grabbed a plant pot from a nearby bench, and thumped it down on the lab table, exasperated. In it was a Busy Lizzy. 'You were watching cells from this being taken over by the compound which was released at Alderley Edge. The compound that turned that young boy into a vampire.'

Tegan looked at him in amazement. 'So it has the same effect on plants?'

'On all living cells, Tegan. And no, we don't have to worry about Undead begonias, I've only exposed a tiny sample to the substance. It's a vampire DNA compound, every cell of it a miniature bioplasmic vampire. I was foolish enough to concentrate it, but it's dangerous enough in a gaseous state. It could only infest a Time Lord through prolonged and violent contact, but in the case of a human being, it would diffuse straight through the cell wall. The merest brush with it, a drop landing on the skin, and it's like they've been bitten.'

'My God . . .' Tegan whispered. 'That's what must have happened to Lang's kids. They got it on them, but – '

'They were full of faith and garlic. Instant vampires, or instant death to anybody who's armed themselves against the Undead. Quite a weapon, isn't it? Still, there's one consolation.'

Tegan was amazed. 'What's that?'

'They haven't used it yet.' He held the sample slide up to the laboratory lights. 'I wonder why?'

The setting of the sun in its natural course brought panic to the city, perhaps even more than the two minutes of unnatural darkness had done. Across the northern hemisphere, experts were arguing about what had happened and religious leaders were making declarations. In the southern hemisphere, of course, things were exactly the opposite. Those up early had experienced a false and brief dawn. There, the talk of coming apocalypse wasn't quite so intense.

What the people who lived in the city were wondering, along with where their children were, and who had any authority any more, and if anybody still loved them, was if this night would end. Over the last few weeks, it had felt as if real darkness was encroaching with winter. In the shadows were things that the older folk hadn't expected, that they felt nothing to do with. It was like being in Rome, somebody said, and seeing the barbarians at the gate. It wasn't just that you were going to die, it was that your whole way of life would go with you.

So at the start of that long night, the Arthurs and Irises of Europe, and plenty of them there were still, grouped together and found each other and knocked on doors to meet people they had never enquired of previously. Tea was made, and old wine uncorked, and those of religious inclination actually found a smile to face their God with.

In America, some cities burned and the pendulum swung both ways; those who'd never had anything looking forward to the great scythe of levelling, those who had something taking up guns to protect it, and those who just wanted a television or a toaster going out and taking one.

Nobody had told these people that the world was coming to an end, but then nobody had explained the thing that defied all physics. The day had stopped and started again. That made everything they'd taken for granted into a frightening fiction.

And, oblivious to the news that the sun had stopped in

165

the Old Testament once, the Children of the Night went about the world and *partied*.

Nyssa had put on gloves, mask and apron, and had persuaded Jeremy to let her into the operating theatre.

'If you're thinking about a rescue attempt, old thing . . .'

'Of course not. I want to help.'

'All right. I believe you.' He'd let her pass and smirked after her, as if he had some secret knowledge which was denied her.

Ruath was staring down at Lang's open torso when Nyssa entered, a scalpel poised in her hand. 'I know it looks delicious,' she was saying, 'but I'll be checking your pockets on the way out. Don't even lick your fingers.' Three other vampires were standing by, similarly dressed in surgical gowns, holding various bloodied instruments.

Nyssa swallowed back some bile. She'd watched and assisted in some minor ways in operations on Traken, and she wouldn't normally expect to feel nauseous at such a sight. But it was hard to maintain clinical detachment when you were so hungry. The way Lang's colon was tantalizingly exposed . . . Horrified at herself, she concentrated on the instruments around her.

The vampires had an incredibly advanced surgical area, with many devices she didn't recognize the function of. Beyond Earth technology, once more. But why would the Undead ever require such facilities?

She realized that Ruath had noticed her. 'Why, it's little Nyssa! What are you doing here?'

'I hadn't anything to do, and wondered if I could help. I have some medical training. Has somebody been injured?'

'Not yet. This is Mr Lang under here, enjoying his general anaesthetic. You're welcome to watch, but the

166

procedure's very simple. It won't take a moment.'

Nyssa moved up to the head of the bed and looked down at Lang's face, his mouth moving with random silent syllables. She put her hand on his forehead and gently traced the creases of his brow. 'He looks very peaceful.'

'Does he? Well, he isn't. He's been shouting things out in his sleep.' Ruath quickly slipped something out of a silver pouch and placed it carefully inside the body. She made several connections with a staple gun, and began the lengthy process of tidying and closing the surgical wound.

'What have you done to him?'

'That's a secret, I'm afraid. I'll tell you when you're permanently one of us.'

Nyssa stopped. 'But Yarven said – '

'Yarven says many things,' Ruath muttered, busy stitching. 'I've learnt not to believe all of them.'

'But he's a noble man, he promised!'

'He's noble to members of his own species, my dear. What sort of promises do you make to your dinner, eh?'

Nyssa put her hands on Lang's scalp, as if holding herself upright. She concentrated on her doodlings, shivering slightly. 'I don't believe you.'

'He told you that you could be changed back on the next full moon, but if things go as planned, that may not be for months. And when we get to the point where we let time go forward again, you silly thing, there won't be much point in being human again, because everyone else will be a vampire.'

Nyssa shouted something and ran from the room, throwing her gloves onto the floor.

'Pick those up . . .' Ruath told one of her assistants. 'By Rassilon, it's easy to manipulate these primitives.'

* * *

167

Nyssa ran through the castle, damning her gullibility. Just because everybody with power on her homeworld was honest and generous, she'd seen the shape of that power and assumed the heart to be true as well. Well, she'd seen enough. Her curiosity had been satisfied. If Yarven had broken his word, Nyssa could break hers.

She ran up the spiral staircase of a tower, remembering from her first view of the castle that all such turrets featured large windows. This one was no exception. A stained glass portrait of Yarven, no less, in various shades of scarlet and black.

Nyssa dashed up to the glass and pushed against it. Useless. She needed something to smash the glass with. In the corner there was a trunk, perhaps there was something heavy inside. All she needed was a tiny hole that she could pour her gaseous form out of.

She opened the trunk.

Inside it, the Child smiled up at her. He reached out an arm before she could slam the lid, throwing it back with his supernatural strength. He floated up out of the box, getting between Nyssa and the window.

Ruath appeared in the doorway. She carried a strange-looking gun. 'Shall I leave her to you, Child?'

The baby burbled. Nyssa turned to Ruath accusingly. 'Are you planning to keep me prisoner?'

'Until you are a prisoner of your biology, yes. We've been monitoring you all through the castle. We assume that you've fulfilled your function for us.'

'Which is?'

'To contact the Doctor and tell him of our location. You've certainly had access to all sorts of transmitting equipment in your path through the castle. That's why Yarven promised to free you, my dear. He wanted to delay you until our plans were complete. Now that the party's prepared, I hope that you've invited our guest.'

Nyssa didn't let her expression give away the horror she felt. Well, at least they didn't know how she'd done it. 'What do you want him for? What are you planning?'

Ruath glanced up to the corner of the room, and Nyssa realized that she was performing this scene for an audience. Probably Yarven. 'The Doctor is an ancient enemy of the vampire race. The Books of Prophecy declare that he must be sacrificed over seven days for the rule of the Undead to come to pass. He will regenerate at least once a night and maintain a state of regenerative trauma until he dies, as befits the one who killed the Great Vampire.'

Nyssa shivered. 'You don't really believe in these prophecies, do you?' she asked, looking Ruath in the eye. 'You're just – ' She grabbed the foot of the Child and flung him at her.

Ruath toppled backwards, but the Child swung up and headed straight for Nyssa. She grabbed the chest and hauled it two-handed at the window.

It impacted, smashing the glass open and sending shards flying into the night.

The Child swept through a cloud of gas, looked around in puzzlement, and then faded into gas itself. Two struggling clouds of vapour billowed towards the window.

Ruath had got to her feet again. 'Child!' she shouted. 'Leave her to me!'

Much to Nyssa's relief, the tiny vampire regained his solid form. The two of them had been colliding and wrestling on a molecular level, the Child's form trying to surround and compress Nyssa back into flesh, and what misshapen flesh it would have been. In other circumstances, the young Trakenite might have found the idea of a gaseous combat interesting, but at the moment her only thought was of escape. The cloud that was her swished straight for the gap in the window.

Ruath aimed her pistol and fired. A fanlike beam of golden light caught Nyssa's gaseous form and held it, frozen in the air, for a moment. Then Nyssa found herself being pulled back into the pistol by tiny increments. All her strength, unused as it was to moving gas, couldn't escape the pull of the beam. Finally she gave in and was sucked back into the gun.

The last thing she thought of was the Doctor, and the suffering that she had bequeathed to him. Then she was gone into blackness.

Ruath tapped the pistol with her finger. 'Glad I came up with that,' she smiled.

The Child backed away, raising its hands in sudden fear.

'Don't worry, I'm not going to use it on you. Oh.' The exclamation was caused by a sudden shadow that had swept into the room.

Yarven was standing before her, almost there, his features a charcoal sketch against the shattered scarlet window. 'I did not know of such a weapon,' he whispered.

'I made it while studying vampire lore, my Lord,' Ruath told him nervously.

'There are other such devices?'

'No. Forgive me, I didn't think of this as a secret. I have no secrets from you.'

'Don't you?' Tiny pinprick eyes turned to look at Ruath and, not for the first time, she felt scared by how alien Yarven could be. 'No,' he concluded. 'You are devoted to me. You have not lied about the sacrifice that lies ahead of me, and it must surely have occurred to you to do so.'

'I'm your servant, my Lord.'

'I gave Nyssa my word, you know, Ruath. Once, the word of a nobleman would have meant something one could trust, beyond riddles and mere literal truths.'

'It will again.' Ruath approached the shadow and put her arms around its coldness. 'In the world that we will establish.'

'It will be a world founded on deceit, then. On many deceits.'

'Why then,' Ruath kissed the darkness, 'it will be a world like any other.'

Victor Lang lay unconscious on a bench in the pit room. Yarven indicated him to Jake and Madelaine. 'Take him back, leave him somewhere appropriate. You know the city better than I.' Then he left, sweeping his cape behind him.

'All right.' Jake looked down at the sleeping man. 'Wonder what they did to him?'

'Not our problem.' Madelaine lifted the evangelist into her arms. 'I'll miss our conversations, though. Perhaps I'll go back and visit him.'

'What, before or after our lot rule the world?'

'I'll believe that when I see it. Do you find all that . . . I don't know, frightening?'

'Change always is frightening. We'll get used to it.'

'I suppose so. Okay then, pull the lever.'

Jake did so, and they rose out of the dome as it opened, into a beautifully clear night sky. The moon shone down on the forest, a shade off full.

Lang opened his eyes and looked up at Madelaine. She glanced at him and smiled, giving him a little hug. 'You're going home.'

Their eyes met. And Madelaine knew. 'Oh . . .' she whispered. She stared back into him and hit his brain with a serious thought.

You *will* tell them, you bastard. And then you'll be free.

171

'Problems?' Jake asked, moving up alongside.

'Not mine,' Maddy assured him, looking at Lang sadly. 'Come on, let's finish this.'

The Doctor and Tegan were up early, walking the streets of the city just before dawn in what Tegan took to be a futile search for a slumbering vampire. The Doctor had refused to despair but Tegan could see that he had very few options left. The city centre was going about its business despite itself, comforted by the lightening sky.

'There's going to be another dawn after all,' Tegan opined. She could imagine the vigils that were coming to an end all across the country.

'Yes . . .' The Doctor had his hands deep in his pockets, and was staring ahead, lost in thought. 'Possibly the last one, though. There haven't been any more time experiments, but I can't see why they don't just . . .' His thoughts eluded him again. 'Doughnuts. Must keep the blood sugar up.'

They were walking across the square in front of the Town Hall, and the Doctor had spotted a doughnut trailer, its owner oblivious to the apocalypse, which had opened up to catch the first businessmen.

As they bought coffee and doughnuts, Tegan noticed something happening on the steps of the Town Hall. A small crowd was forming. A lot of homeless people, but quite a few of the early risers of Manchester's working life too. They were clustering around the base of the steps, and on them a figure was standing, proclaiming loudly.

The Doctor nearly spilled his coffee. 'I recognize that voice!' he murmured. 'Come on!'

They raced across the square. Sure enough, on the steps of the Town Hall stood Victor Lang, dishevelled and swaying. He was preaching with all the skills at his

172

command, his powerful voice echoing out across the square.

'I have been lost these last few days, ladies and gentlemen, and you have been lost also, am I right? Lost in the darkness, lost in a night that you thought was never going to stop? Well, I'm here to tell you, I got back, I came back from that pit, and even there, Jesus Christ our Lord did not desert me. He is coming! He is coming. And that is why I am opening the gates of my service, free, to anybody who wishes to attend. We will stand through the next long night together, and together we will see in the dawn!'

The crowd had started to gasp and point. 'A sign!' one of them yelled. 'A sign!' She was gesturing at Lang's forehead.

There, a cluster of red letters and numbers had started to appear.

'What does it mean, Doctor?' Tegan whispered.

The Doctor was grinning broadly. 'I think I know,' he replied. 'But first I have to find an Ordnance Survey map.'

Nine

The Doctor raced around the TARDIS console, tapping in co-ordinates to feed the computer map that was forming on the viewscreen. He squinted at the finished map and then, like a meticulous dinner-party host, reached across and hit a final control. The map flipped on its edge and became a three-dimensional projection of hummocky, wooded countryside.

'Staffordshire, Tegan, the wooded areas surrounding a small town called Leek. They do a rather good oatcake, so the TARDIS tells me. All being well, we'll be able to share one with Nyssa by the end of the day.'

'Did Lang tell you anything useful?' Tegan had moved back out of the crowd earlier as the Doctor had attempted to draw the evangelist aside.

'No, he'd got rather carried away with enthusiasm and wouldn't talk to me for more than a few minutes. He did say, however, that he'd been kept in a pit for most of the time, and knew his captors mainly as a series of voices. He doesn't even know how he got away, which worries me, but still . . . I don't honestly think he could be of much use to us. Except as a message-carrier, that is. Nyssa must have been able to get some sort of heat-activated chemical onto Lang's skin. Similar to invisible ink, I should think.' He looked up at Tegan suddenly. 'So what are you going to do while I pop over and get her?'

Tegan stared at him uncomprehendingly for a moment. 'Oh, now, wait a minute, you can't just go walking in there without me!'

'I'm not going to argue with you. I seem to be like a bad juggler at the moment, trying to keep three things in the air at once.' The Doctor had looked aside, not wanting to meet Tegan's gaze.

'You don't have to worry about me. Listen – ' Tegan grabbed the Doctor's shoulder and gently made him look at her. 'What happened to Adric isn't going to happen again. You can't leave me behind. We're in this together.'

'Are we, hm? Yes, I suppose that perhaps we are. Well, while daylight is with us perhaps we'd better be on our way. I think I can persuade the old girl to get us to the exact place, but I'm going to have to translate the map reference into co-ordinates, and that's going to take a while, so – '

'I know,' sighed Tegan. 'One lump or two?'

Lang pulled the tie smoothly about his neck.

New shirt, new suit. Bathed, shaven, clean. He'd spent three hours ranting from the steps of the Town Hall, and had assembled quite a crowd before the police had asked him to move on.

Ordinarily, it wasn't the sort of publicity he'd have liked, but damn it. *Damn* it. This was what he'd been born for. He'd somehow escaped from that castle, illusory or real as it had been. Maybe the girl Madelaine had got him out, because he remembered her face. He'd been delivered back to humanity to speak to them of the last days of the world.

Olivia knocked on his office door and he opened it, welcoming her in. 'How are you?'

'I'm fine, but what happened to you? There have been so many stories. And, let me say, we've got the world and his uncle on the phone. Is it true you're throwing the doors open tonight?'

175

'It is. And to hell with the Council, pardon my language. I don't think they could stop us now if they wanted to, insurance regulations or whatever.' He stood up and walked to the window. 'This is the big one. Tonight is the last night of man on Earth, Olivia. Do you believe me?'

The young woman sat down. 'Yes, I do. Something odd's happening to the nights, and they had all these scientists on television, but they were all contradicting each other. And everybody knows that there are creatures out there. I don't know what they're supposed to be, but – '

'I was with them. I saw them. And, though I'm sure they don't know it, they're part of the great plan.'

'Which is?'

'The end of the world. The great reckoning. The dead will return and be judged, Olivia. They'll be selected for heaven or cast down to the fire.' Lang spread his arms wide, gazing down at the sunlit city below. 'In that stadium, we'll be getting as many of them through customs as we can.'

Tegan didn't find that making the tea distracted her very much from what was about to happen, but she managed to warm the pot and strain the brew to just the right strength for the Doctor.

When she returned to the console room, carrying the tray, she found him hacking away at the hatstand. Coats and hats had been scattered everywhere as the Doctor used a laser blade to slice up the wooden construction. 'Ah, most welcome.' He finished his task and splintered off a long length of wood. 'I realized that my vampire-repellent kit was missing something.'

'A stake?'

'It's a drastic solution, but at the moment I don't see

176

much of an alternative. There hasn't been a full moon since Nyssa was bitten. That means that if the vampire that did so is destroyed – '

'She's free of it. Make me one.'

The Doctor frowned at her but, having taken a slurp of his tea, resumed his task. A few minutes later he handed Tegan a sharpened stake. 'This is only to be used in the last resort, or when and where I tell you.'

'No worries.' Tegan pricked her finger on the point. 'Hey, that's sharp.'

'That is the general idea.' The Doctor turned back to the console and activated the co-ordinate keypad. 'Now, let's go and see what they've been getting up to, shall we?'

The familiar wheezing, groaning sound vibrated from the console and the central time rotor began its rise and fall.

The TARDIS faded away from the backstreets of Manchester and spun into the vortex.

Nyssa's eyes opened.

She was awake. It didn't feel like night yet, but it was dark. Absolutely black. There was a smell of wet wood all around her.

She tried to move a hand up to her eyes but it encountered something immediately. A surface, right above her. Wood. Nyssa slid her hand up over her body and found that there was a gap of only an inch or so between her and the ceiling.

She tried to turn, and her shoulder hit the ceiling too.

She lashed out with her arms and hit the sides of her prison, left and right, only a few inches away. Behind her head was a board as well. She inched down a bit, and her feet encountered a similar one.

Nyssa was in a box only slightly bigger than she was.

She fought down the urge to panic and start screaming. She placed her palms against the upper surface and pushed, gently at first, then harder.

The wood creaked slightly. She pulled up her knees and tried to exert upward force with them as well, but that didn't help much.

She made a fist and swung it at the ceiling, hitting it with a solid thump.

A tiny dollop of soil fell through a crack onto her face.

At that point Nyssa began to scream.

The woodlands around Leek were basking in an autumn afternoon, rooks clattering back to their nests overhead and the business of nature continuing in the great drifts of leaves that had accumulated in hollows and gulleys.

Nowhere was the forest really deep, surrounded as it was by the green sweep of farmlands, but it was relatively isolated, much of it owned by the National Trust rather than individual landowners. The trees were orange and gold now in the sunlight, and through them distant hills and farmsteads could be spotted.

The TARDIS materialized, sending a great cloud of leaves into a flurry around it. The Doctor thus stepped out into a windfall, shooing them away with his hat. He carried the cricket bag that contained his vampire equipment. Tegan followed, looking around the damply sunlit glades without enthusiasm. 'So,' she muttered, 'where's the coach with the driver who won't take us to Castle Dracula?'

'No coach, Tegan, but I've put us down about a mile or so from Nyssa's map reference, which is – ' he moved his finger slowly from left to right, 'that way. Shall we?' He moved off at a brisk pace.

After a twenty-minute hike Tegan stopped, leaning on a

tree to get her breath back. 'Hey, wait up. We've got a lot of daylight left.'

The Doctor jogged back. 'Not necessarily, if the time experiments are still continuing. Still, I know what to expect now. I should notice some unusual curvature in timespace well before any major changes occur, and I haven't sensed anything yet.'

'Garlic time?'

'No. They might release the gas.'

'Right. Tegan Kiev. Not a pretty thought. Hey, did you get that call you were on about? The telepathy job?'

'Yes. An old friend. She wanted to warn me, but she was under very strict instructions about what she could and couldn't tell me. Gallifreyans looking over her shoulder, I suspect.'

'Anything useful, like who this Yarven bloke really is?'

'Not that, exactly. But a couple of hints that might prove useful.'

'What do you reckon this lot are up to anyway? What do they want?'

'To rule the world, I assume. That's the usual job description. I wonder if any of them ever consider what a tiresome job that would actually turn out to be.' He gave her a reassuring grin and patted her on the shoulder. 'Come on. Can't be far now.'

Grudgingly, Tegan hauled herself up.

Five minutes later the Doctor pulled himself up a bank by grabbing hold of tree branches, and pushed aside the foliage of a bush. He stopped. Tegan clambered up beside him and grasped his coat-tails to steady herself.

'Wow,' she gasped. 'Hey, do you think that could be what we're looking for?'

Castle Yarven basked in the sunlight, its darkened windows sucking in the glare and its long shadow sweeping like a pendulum as the day ticked away across its low valley.

'Come on,' the Doctor murmured grimly and scrambled down the dirt hillside.

Nyssa lay exhausted, panting, her hands covered with lacerations. The fear came and went in waves. How far underground was she? Were they going to leave her here permanently – she suppressed another shout – or just until after the full moon? Wouldn't that be horrifying enough if she couldn't sleep?

Sleep. She wasn't asleep because . . . because she was a long way underground, and a new vampire needed reference to the sun for its sleep cycle? Perhaps. Perhaps this was the vampire version of . . . what had Tegan called it? Jet lag.

If she was underground, where was the air coming from? Nyssa took a few experimental breaths, then realized. No air. She was breathing from habit, not having noticed whether the older vampires had given it up. The creatures were obviously capable of ignoring basic biological needs altogether. If there had been air, there would have been an air vent and she could have flown up it as a mist.

She tried for a moment to diffuse through the roof of the box. The mist rose up to the wooden surface, but the soil was packed tight, full of thousands of tiny passages but none that Nyssa, at least with her clumsy learner's instincts, could navigate her whole gaseous form through.

Still, being in that shape felt more comfortable.

The worst thing was the hunger. It came in waves beside the fear, a red tide. Nyssa felt empty and strained, and terrible carnivorous fantasies kept tugging at her mind. The frustration of it was building in the background all the time.

Surely they must let her out before she started to . . .
would she eat her own flesh? Would that even be
satisfying?

The mist floated in the box, waiting.

The moat was going to prove a problem.

The Doctor and Tegan walked around it once, looking
up at the castle from time to time for any sign of life or
movement. There was none.

'We could strip off and swim for it,' suggested Tegan,
with little enthusiasm.

'I'd prefer not to,' the Doctor replied. 'Not all of this
place's defence systems will be vampiric in nature. I'm
sure quite a few of them will be up and about and waiting
for us.' He picked up a twig and threw it out into the
middle of the water.

After a moment there was a sudden concussion and the
twig vanished, leaving only a ripple on the surface.
'There are few creatures as paranoid as a sleeping vampire, and with good reason. Together with all their other
vulnerabilities, their aversion to daylight is what stopped
them taking over the galaxy centuries ago.'

'Why do they have all these problems, anyway? I
mean, you'd have thought they'd have evolved out of
them or died out?'

'Good point, Tegan. You're starting to think like a
scientist. No, the Undead don't evolve as such. They still
obey the physical laws that were laid down for them in
the first few seconds of the universe. They're the sort of
beast that the Black Guardian delights in, creatures with
random flaws and perfections. Yes, I think it would take
an intelligence like his to put in that bit about the full
moon. However, none of this gets us over this moat.'

'Right. And I can't see anything that would.'

'Patience.' The Doctor squatted down on the leafy soil

and fumbled in his coat pockets. 'I'm starting to have my suspicions about this castle. Tell me, when you were young, did you ever steal a car?'

Tegan frowned and squatted beside him. 'There was an old combie that we liberated once, but that didn't really belong to anybody. They don't look kindly on you having a criminal record when you go into the air travel business.'

'In that case . . .' the Doctor had extracted his spectacles and balanced them on the end of his nose, peering at the TARDIS key, 'you won't identify with what I'm about to do at all.' He took a small needle-like device from his pocket and used it to attach tiny drops of liquid metal to the key. 'There are times,' he murmured, 'when I rather miss the sonic screwdriver. I really must get around to making another one. There!' He looked up. 'This is the key to our problem. Now, what does every key need?'

'A lock.' Tegan stood up and looked around. 'As in canal?'

'As in door. But where?' The Doctor bounced up, dropping his glasses back into his pocket. 'Let's see if we can find it, shall we?'

He jogged off round the moat again. Tegan followed, her breath starting to form faint clouds as the afternoon drew on. Either they were getting somewhere or the Doctor's troubled brain had finally thrown in the towel.

The Doctor slowed for a moment beside a small hillock that looked like it might have been made by moles, and then ran on. He finally stopped at a group of three small trees growing together at the edge of the moat. 'Of course!' he grinned. 'I should have seen it before.' He briefly inspected the tree trunks and shook his head. Then he began to scuff at the spot between the trees with his feet. 'Come on Tegan, help me.'

Tegan joined in. 'What are we doing, Doctor?'

'Looking for a lock. Ah!' He bent suddenly and brushed some final dirt away with his hand. Revealed was a bright new lock, set in metal that seemed to run under the trees. The Doctor fitted his altered key into it. 'Ready? When I say run . . .' He turned the key. 'Run!'

Tegan followed the Doctor, who'd just as swiftly jerked the key out again and ran towards – towards the moat?

Which was flapping up and down like a ribbon.

Tegan stared at the physical impossibility of water, water that she had seen to be deep, rippling up and down, leaving great shadowy gaps between it and the ground like it was a loose groundsheet or something.

The Doctor ran back and grabbed her by the hand. 'Come on!'

Together they sprinted under the moat.

A moment after they'd got to the far bank, it crashed back down again and became a stretch of deep water once more.

Tegan turned to look at it. 'Should I even ask?'

'I'll explain later. We haven't got much time left.'

Tegan rested for a second, leaning her hands on her knees. 'Were you good mates with Moses or something?'

'For a while.' The Doctor looked earnest. 'But he didn't like my corrections to those stone tablets of his.' He grinned, then turned and headed towards the castle.

'You know,' Tegan muttered to herself, 'I never know when he's being serious.'

Lang stood before an empty stadium and took the microphone in his hand. 'Testing, testing. The Lord is my shepherd. I shall not want. One, two, three.'

'And high,' a technician called from backstage.

'La, la, la. Sorry, I can't go that high.'

'That was high enough. And low . . .'

Backstage, Olivia was on a portable phone, staring at a clipboard. 'What do you mean, you thought it wasn't going to happen? You know that Mr Lang goes into retreat a few days before each event. Now, you get your crew down here and we'll say no more about it. All right?' Olivia had had her job made infinitely worse by the town council, who had insisted that no more announcements concerning free entry and the gates being open be made. The police, it was said, were going to be denying entry to those without a ticket. Olivia was aware, however, that the word had got onto the streets, mainly thanks to New Light. At some point in the evening, she'd have a word with the officer in charge and point out that letting them in was less of a hazard to public safety than keeping them away. The police were already busy with rioting on some of the estates, they wouldn't want to risk a major incident that they could avoid.

Stewards from the New Light group were already going about their business, being briefed in groups by their leaders. Prayer sheets were being distributed in the seating, which had taken up most of the football ground, and technicians were wandering the stage, checking the sound balance of every microphone. Behind Lang, a huge white cross was being erected by carpenters, and lighting crew members were running a wash of white light across it.

Lang turned back and looked at the cross, a mixture of apprehension and awe on his face. 'Not long now,' he said, and his voice echoed across the stadium.

The Doctor had pushed at a side door, found it unlocked and gone inside. A moment later he came out again. 'Come on through,' he told Tegan. 'But hold on to my hand and keep your eyes closed.'

Tegan took his hand. 'What's in there?' she asked.

'The kitchen.'

'Oh.' She closed her eyes. As she was led through the dark, she whispered, 'Where did this castle come from, anyway? Something like this would be on all the tourist routes, wouldn't it?'

'Indeed. I don't think it's been here very long.' Tegan heard a door closing. 'You can open your eyes now.'

They were in a dark hallway. Tegan let go of the Doctor's hand and put her hands on her hips. 'So what was so terrible that I couldn't see it?'

'The Undead's idea of *haute cuisine*. Not very pleasant. Now, I think we've got about three hours until the sun sets. This is when vampires are in their deepest sleep.'

'Good news.'

'So we'll split up.'

'Bad news.'

'Tegan, we need to cover an entire gothic castle in under three hours, and then get back to the TARDIS safely. We don't have time to stay together. Here.' He handed her a pen-sized object. 'That's a directional transducer. If you find Nyssa, or anyone who looks like they might be in charge, press the button and I'll follow your signal. We'll meet back here in two and a half hours.'

Tegan took the transducer. 'Wait a minute. If I'm going to wander about a vampire-infested castle on my own, I want some protection. Give me a stake and a hammer.'

'Tegan, you are not to go staking vampires without – '

'Just to make me feel better, huh?'

'All right. But try not to wake anything up.' The Doctor reached into his cricket bag and produced the relevant objects.

'As if,' Tegan grinned.

* * *

185

They set off in opposite directions, Tegan tiptoeing apprehensively along the hallways, the Doctor setting off upstairs.

Tegan met her first vampires where the hall intersected with another. They were lying along the wall under a line of portraits, a gang of straggly teenagers, their clothes caked in old blood. They looked dead, no movement disturbing their sleep, but Tegan knew better than to check.

She inched past, stepping carefully over the outstretched hand of one of the boys. As her shadow passed over it, the limb twitched upwards, narrowly missing her ankle with its reflexive movement. Tegan contained a squeak of fear and stepped swiftly along to the end of the hallway.

A vast banqueting hall lay before her, with rugs stretched across a marble floor. On the chairs, tables, and floor itself lay what must have been over a hundred of the Undead. A great stain of blood began on the table and spread in thin lines across the room. In the blood were remains.

Tegan did her best to ignore the feast. At the end of the table a great throne stood, ornately carved and inlaid with gold. Now that would be where the boss sat. Pity he wasn't still in it.

Something crunched under Tegan's heel. She looked down, hardly daring to wonder what she might have stood on. Soil, a thin trail of it. It had dribbled out of the hand of one of the young creatures that lined the hall. He had a fistful of it. Clutching it like a security blanket.

Well, that bit in the movies must be true. Vampires did like their home soil. And where do you find soil?

Tegan turned around and looked for a stairwell that headed downwards.

* * *

The Doctor, meanwhile, was picking his way through the bedrooms, more than a hundred of them. He knew enough about gothic architecture to put him on course for the most important suites, but the contents of the rooms fascinated him.

Undead in numbers. That in itself was a frightening thought. In the normal way of things, these creatures had skulked around the margins of civilization, one or two in every fifth star system. Now they were as prolific as a viral plague, and just as lethal.

He came to the bedroom that contained Jake and Madelaine and stood at the end of their bed, looking down at the couple curled round each other. There was a space between them, an enforced depression that suggested a missing person. The Doctor reached forward and plucked a brown hair from the pillow. He rubbed it between his fingers and sniffed it.

Nyssa's hair. So this was the home she'd found. But where was she now? He almost felt like waking the vampires and asking.

The Doctor carefully examined the sleeping Undead that littered the room, and even glanced under the bed. Where on Earth could she be?

Angry at such a near miss, he finally moved on, carefully replacing the hair on the pillow.

He wondered, as he did so, whether the two vampires missed her presence as much as he did.

Tegan had found her way to the pit room, and peered down the pit as she walked past. Obviously some place that they kept prisoners, but it was empty right now. She found the downwards stairway and opened the door. Unlocked. Far too many unlocked doors in this place. Still, if they didn't expect anybody who couldn't fly to get in . . .

She stepped down into the laboratory. This was getting more like an old horror movie every minute. Where was the monster and the electrodes? She glanced at the globe of the world. Something important was going on here. If only the Doctor was about, he might be able to work out what.

There was nobody down here, though. Certainly no Nyssa. Tegan slumped against the wall.

And fell straight through it.

The Doctor had come to a locked room. Now, amongst a people with such slight regard for privacy, that was a very rare thing indeed.

He worked at the lock with a small metal implement for a few seconds, and it clicked open. Cautiously, he entered.

The master bedroom. At least, it had been. There was no bed in the opulent room, but up against one wall stood two tall silver cabinets. The modern version of coffins.

The Doctor crept across to them. Left or right? He fumbled for a coin, flipped it, and slapped it on to the back of his hand. Left it was.

Carefully, he put his fingers to the edge of the door of the left-hand cabinet, these things not being designed with handles, and levered it open.

Inside was a tall, slim, elegant man with a neatly trimmed beard. He lay against red velvet, fully dressed, his hands folded across the black silk of his shirt.

This, presumably, was the vampire called Yarven. Not that the Doctor recognized him in the slightest. He was probably personally responsible for the existence of a great many of the vampires in the castle.

The Doctor wondered if the thought crossed his mind out of anger, but then he put such doubts aside. This was no time for moral scruples.

He went to his bag and found his stake and hammer.

One stroke, a moment of decision, and these creatures would be a leaderless rabble; many of them, those Yarven had bitten within the last month, waking to find themselves human again. That number might include Nyssa.

He poised the point of the stake over Yarven's heart.

Tegan tumbled down a short flight of stairs into a scene that she found quite familiar.

It was the console room of a TARDIS.

Different in some respects, certainly. The panelling was of oak and leather, and the console itself looked rather more advanced than the battered old version that the Doctor kept on about reconditioning.

But this meant that the whole castle . . . Tegan slapped her forehead. That was what the Doctor had meant about stealing cars. He'd realized that the castle was a TARDIS and had sprung the lock somehow. The moat must have been part of the whole . . . whatever. Tegan had seen enough mind-boggling changes in TARDIS structure to know that virtually anything was possible.

Various items of equipment stood in the corners of the console room, including what looked like an electric chair. Well, Tegan wasn't going to take a rest in that. The illusory wall had put her on her guard.

One of the TARDIS's internal doors stood open.

Tegan took a deep breath and walked further into the craft. If Nyssa, or indeed the boss, were going to be anywhere, this was as good a place as any.

After a short stretch of corridor, she came to another open door. A blank room. For a moment, Tegan thought that it might be a Zero Room, but the chamber had none of that place's calming effects.

Then she looked up.

The roof was made of soil. At intervals across this tiny

189

inverted field, little gold chains hung down, with handles on the end. One of the handles had a tag attached, like you might use to mark a seedling in a more ordinary garden.

'All right, I'll buy it.' Tegan reached up and grabbed the tagged handle, standing well back. The thought struck her that this might be the vampiric idea of a nice soft bed, so she took the hammer in her free hand and shoved the stake under her arm.

She read the tag. *Subject One.* Very helpful.

'Here goes nothing,' muttered Tegan. She pulled the chain.

A torrent of earth spilled down from the roof, in a limited area. Obviously it was held up by some sort of forcefield. The rain of soil continued for some time. Then there was a clatter as a trapdoor swung open.

To Tegan's delight, Nyssa fell out of the ceiling and landed in a heap on the floor.

'Nyssa! Thank God!' Tegan ran to the dazed girl and started to brush the soil off her dress. 'Come on, we're getting out of here.'

Nyssa stared up at Tegan, blinking the earth and light out of her eyes. They were full of red, full as her stomach was empty.

She had been left hungry for so long.

And now here was meat showing its fat neck to her.

Nyssa closed her eyes and mouth, screwing everything up against the rage and lust that were erupting inside her. But her mouth burst open in a scream across her fangs.

Tegan staggered backwards and found her gaze locked by Nyssa's. Her eyes were blank red, and they pinned her to the wall.

Nyssa swept forward and slapped Tegan sharply across the face, one nail drawing a splash of blood from her cheek.

190

Tegan couldn't even react to the blow. She stood in the middle of a movement, her muscles screaming with adrenalin, but unable to do anything to get away.

Nyssa knew it. She watched as the cut on Tegan's face swelled with new blood.

Then she stepped forward to lap at it.

The Doctor raised his hammer and placed the stake gently on the centre of Yarven's chest.

In doing so, the very end of the wooden spear broke an infra-red beam.

The message flashed through the castle at the speed of light.

Inside a box in the cellar laboratory, Jeremy Sanders jerked awake, his brain afire.

He knew that this would come, but had hoped that it wouldn't awaken him. Concepts and patterns slammed into his brain, faster than he could see or hear, taking over all his senses until the world became a blur of roaring colour.

Jeremy focused, and dedicated his life to the cause.

Ruath had explained it to him that day, had asked him if he wanted to do this, without pressure or evasion. Her honesty had touched him and he had agreed. All his Undead life he had hoped for the Vampire Messiah, and the great change that he would bring. He had hoped for a real civilization for his people.

It was an honour to give all he had for that.

Time halted, clenched for a moment in the centre of Jeremy's mind. Then he spun it forward, calculating things that he couldn't hope to understand in the parts of his unconscious that had been used for dreaming and smelling and remembering faces. His brain bubbled under the strain and a vision spun by, clouding his eyes for a moment.

191

Mother and Father, smiling proudly at him in their polished pre-war kitchen. They finally thought he'd done well. Then, just as quickly, the smell, touch and sight of the vision were boiled away, as the senses themselves were quickly after.

Outside the castle, it was suddenly night.

Victor Lang spun, his arms held wide, as the sun flared like a comet down over the horizon.

'Open the gates!' he bellowed. 'Let them come as they will! Let them all come into His grace!'

He gazed up at the giant white cross that shone like a beacon in the stadium. Already, from the streets outside, he could hear the panicked crying of car horns and factory hooters.

He hugged the cross to his body, filled with a steely determination. 'The night of revelations is at hand!'

The Doctor swung back his hammer, and winced as time haemorrhaged around him. With a yell, he flung his arm forward, hammer connecting to the butt of the stake.

Nothing happened. He opened his eyes, staring against the pain.

Yarven was holding the shaft of the stake, smiling horribly at him.

'Doctor,' the vampire Lord purred. 'We meet at last.'

He threw aside the stake and grabbed the Doctor by the throat.

Ten

Yarven drove the Doctor back against the wall and held him there by his throat. 'At last!' he cried. 'That I, Yarven of the House of Yar, should hold the life of the great scourge of my people in my hands!'

The Doctor choked on a reply. The vampire's grip on his throat was tightening.

'My Lord, no!' The door of the other cabinet had swung open. Out stepped a woman that the Doctor recognized, in the uncanny way that Time Lords had of ignoring the various bodies that each of them might wear.

'Ruath!' he gasped, as Yarven let go. 'What are you doing here?' He sounded groggy, his senses still reeling with temporal confusion.

'You may very well ask,' Ruath smiled, turning to her consort. 'Yarven, my love, restrain yourself. You know what fate is in store for the Doctor. Don't ruin it, not when we're so close.'

'You are right.' Yarven visibly controlled himself. 'I will enjoy his suffering at a distance. It will make the pleasure of it even more . . . extreme.' He grabbed the Doctor once more, and hoisted him over his shoulder like a sack of potatoes.

The two vampires walked downstairs to the pit room, and Yarven unceremoniously threw the Doctor into the pit. He landed awkwardly on the padding, and stared up at them. 'Ruath . . .' he whispered, then collapsed, unconscious.

* * *

Nyssa had been licking Tegan's blood from her wound for a few minutes, toying with her prey. The kill would come in a few moments, when the wave of appetite washed over her again.

Ruath entered the room and laughed, putting her hands on her hips. 'Well done, Nyssa! I see you've become one of us already. It normally takes a few days underground to persuade doubters of their true nature. No more escapes now, eh? No, you've been reduced to a bundle of instincts, and you'll stay like that until the full moon. But leave her alone now, we need her alive. I'll find you something else. Come on.' She gently interceded between Nyssa and her food, smiling at the girl's little growl. 'Oh, aren't you fierce?'

She attached a pair of tiny pods to Tegan's belt and clicked a control pad. Tegan, still paralysed, hovered out of the door. Ruath wandered after her, beckoning for Nyssa to follow.

The Doctor woke to find Tegan lying beside him, rubbing her wrists and ankles. She was white, either from fear or lack of blood.

'Tegan . . .' he croaked, 'have you been – ?'

'No. Just this. Nyssa did it.' She indicated the cut on her face, healing under the effects of Nyssa's saliva. 'Damn it, she's way too far gone now, Doctor.' She was shivering, trying to slap some life back into her cramped muscles. She was also very scared, but that wasn't something that Tegan was fond of showing.

The Doctor thought for a moment, pulled out his handkerchief and dabbed at the cut. 'I managed to erect some mental barriers while I was unconscious,' he murmured, 'so I shouldn't be quite so affected by the temporal concussion. Still, this hasn't gone very well so far, has it?'

'Did you find the guy in charge?' Tegan blinked back her tears.

'Yes . . . and I've never met him before. He, however, regards me as an enemy of his people. He does have an associate that I have encountered before, however. This is her TARDIS.'

'I'm glad you remember me, Doctor.' The languid voice drifted down into the pit. Ruath lay on the rim, pouring blood into a goblet from a decanter.

'I do.' The Doctor got to his feet and frowned up at Ruath. 'But the Ruath I remember was sincere and compassionate.'

'I was in the class of '92, at the Prydonian Academy. The year above you.'

'We used to break into capsules together. Which is how you knew I'd get into this castle of yours. You know, I do believe that you were the first to lead me astray.'

'Oh yeah?' Tegan glanced up at the beautiful vampire.

'That was when I was young and wild, Doctor. My contemporaries and I grew up to take our responsibilities seriously.'

'Ah . . .' The Doctor nodded. 'Unlike my year. I begin to see.'

'Yes.' Ruath warmed to her subject, sipping from the goblet. Her eyes never left the Doctor's. 'Mortimus, the Rani, that idiot Magnus. And you, Doctor. All graduates of Borusa's Academy for scoundrels.'

'I am not a scoundrel!' The Doctor sounded genuinely aggrieved. 'It was a very difficult decision for me to leave Gallifrey.'

'Difficult?' Ruath nearly spat out a mouthful of liquid. 'How much more difficult do you think it was to stay? I made the decision to live out the troubles and contribute to our society.'

195

'Of course . . . and giving an army of Undead parasites access to Gallifreyan technology is the height of civic responsibility, hm?'

'You know nothing!' Ruath leapt into the pit and confronted the Doctor face to face. 'Do you know what percentage of genes Time Lords share with vampires?'

'No, I can't say – '

'Ninety-eight per cent! Haven't you ever considered how similar the two species are? Both maintain regenerative information in a bioplasmic field around their bodies, both can recycle the entropic process to prolong their lifespan. How do you think that all this happened?'

'Parallel evolution?' The Doctor and Ruath were inches apart now.

Tegan wasn't sure that she liked the way that they were concentrating on each other so much. She suddenly felt very human and very ignored. So, being Tegan, she tried to butt in. 'You mean that Time Lords and vampires evolved from the same creature?'

Ruath didn't look at her, continuing to stare into the Doctor's eyes. 'I can put a name to him. Rassilon. In the dark times, he became an initiate of the Great Vampire, itself merely a mutation of a natural creature. He took on the blood of that bat-like being, and became the first humanoid vampire. And do you know why he did it?'

'I can't possibly imagine.' The Doctor seemed to be considering Ruath's thesis very seriously.

'Because of what you renegades choose to ignore. You know that, relatively speaking, the civilization of Gallifrey is far in the past of this time continuum. You know that TARDISes are prevented from entering what the Minyans call the Constellation Of Kasterborous after a certain date. At the point where we stand, there is no sign of there being an active Gallifreyan civilization. Apart from you renegades, running about the cosmos playing

196

out your adolescent conflicts, where have all the Time Lords gone now?'

'You're asking about the future of Gallifrey. I always think it's best not to know one's own future. It gives you a certain sense of mortality.'

'You fool!' Ruath grabbed his lapel, crushing the celery. 'I'm talking about the mortality of our whole race! The destiny of the Time Lords!'

'Assuming that they have one. Presumably you intend to impose one of your own?'

'The one that Rassilon foresaw and prepared for. The one that he created Agonal to set in motion, the one that he lies in his Tomb, Undead, waiting for! The one that I have worked centuries for!'

'You've just finished three sentences with a preposition,' the Doctor murmured. 'I do hope that it's in a good cause.'

Ruath ignored him. 'Rassilon knew that the Time Lords had retreated down an evolutionary blind alley. He knew that the Undead would come to be the dominant life form in the universe. Together, the two species will unite and form an empire that will return Gallifrey to her old glory!'

'I see. And how do you intend to achieve this?'

Ruath lowered her voice to an insane whisper. 'By raising a planetary army of vampires on Earth and using them to take the Capitol.'

'Of course.' The Doctor smiled. 'You know, this all makes a good deal of sense.'

Despite herself, Tegan had the awful feeling that he might mean it.

Victor Lang stood in front of a backstage monitor, watching the faithful trooping into Old Trafford. Well, more than just the faithful. The great mass of the C of E also, those who hadn't thought of God beyond christenings,

197

weddings and funerals, but didn't feel themselves to be hypocrites in the slightest.

And he'd got them, thanks to signs and portents. God's design in His mercy, to bring the uncertain to the gates of Heaven. He only had to shepherd them in and, in the morning, for a kind of morning would come, they would all sit warmed by the light of the Lord.

Olivia took his arm, gently. 'They're being let in. The policemen at the doors have given up arguing. We're going to be sued by the council, though.'

Lang laughed, a full, healthy roar. 'Oh, let them sue me in the Hereafter. I'm sure the public defender there's a good man!'

Olivia smiled too. 'I haven't seen you so happy in ages, sir.'

'It's good to get it over,' Lang patted her shoulder. A strange frown shadowed his features for a moment. 'It's good to get it out.'

Nyssa had been promised food by Ruath, but she'd just led her to the kitchens and pointed to the various joints of meat that lay around.

Nyssa wanted real food. Fresh blood.

She loped along the hallways, shrugging past the Undead who were assembling in the Great Hall. There was word of an announcement from Lord Yarven shortly. Nyssa was deaf to it all.

Some instinct drove her forward, in the last fevered trance of her transformation. Many of the younger vampires recognized her condition, and gave her wry smiles or a pat on the shoulder as she passed.

She stumbled down the stairs towards the laboratory, breezing into a vapour to slip under the door. Not a thought in her head, she materialized again and found herself staring at Yarven.

He had opened a panel in the wall and was looking at the body of Jeremy Sanders, the devoted vampire's skull shaven and dotted with surgical connections. The burnt cross on it stood out like a brand.

The expression on Sanders' face was one of intense concentration, his teeth resolutely grinding against each other.

Yarven turned and smiled at Nyssa. 'This is what my Queen would have for me, Nyssa. Ugly, isn't it?'

Nyssa raised a hand in a vague gesture. She remembered that she had some reason to hate this man, but couldn't recall it.

Yarven walked over to her and ruffled her hair. 'Come with me, little creature. While I'm making my speech, there's something I'd like you to do.'

Yarven entered onto the balcony above the great hall, and gazed proudly down at the mass of vampires gathered below him.

'My friends, my loyal subjects, we are ready at last.' He stepped off the balcony and floated smoothly down to stand on the end of the great banqueting table. He kicked aside a limb and snapped his fingers. 'Stephen, the screen!' At the other end of the hall, a young vampire pulled a lever and a giant screen unfolded behind Yarven. It showed the planet Earth hanging in space, one side in darkness, the other in daylight. 'Imagine,' Yarven whispered, 'an eternal night. One half of this globe without recourse to sunshine. Would that not be a place of glorious feeding?'

There was a roar of agreement from the vampire horde. At the back, Jake and Madelaine gave a noncommittal cheer. They'd made a quick search for Nyssa in the last few minutes after waking, and were still scanning the crowd for her.

'That night is nearly upon us.' Yarven nodded to the

assembly. 'Thanks to Ruath's time technology, we have plunged this planet into what she calls – '

'A Time Freeze!' Ruath told the Doctor triumphantly. 'A miniature Time Loop, if you like, holding the Earth's rotation, its local time in terms of the solar system, on a second-long repetitive cycle – '

'But not affecting time for the inhabitants! Interesting!' The Doctor stared into Ruath's eyes, his glance flicking to the silver ring on her finger every now and then. 'Tell me more.'

'The night side of Earth will be the new kingdom of vampirekind!' Yarven bellowed. 'The day side will become dry and cracked, its ecology and civilization destroyed! When, and only when, we have converted or eaten every human being on the night side . . .'

There was a roar of approval.

'We shall allow the world half a day's rotation, and fly with the night, falling on the other hemisphere as one, gigantic horde. But, my people, our mission shall not be accomplished by force alone . . .'

'We will release the vampire genetic material into the air in aerosol form, into the stratospheric currents over Europe. It will spread round the globe, converting or destroying on contact. The process of conversion will take mere weeks.' Ruath was trembling now, the words spilling obsessively from her lips.

'Ruath,' the Doctor put a hand on each of her arms, 'this is wonderful, you've achieved so much. But what's my part in this?'

'Ah.' Ruath reached up and stroked his cheek. 'That depends on who you ask.'

* * *

'The Time Lord known as the Doctor will give his blood, over the course of a week-long torment, over the course of his remaining eight incarnations. He will give his blood so that as many of you as possible will have the blood of the Time Lords in your veins.'

The picture behind Yarven changed. Another world hung in space, a world of huge cities and vast deserts. 'That will prepare you for the rigours of time travel, for our assault into the universe at large. Together, the Undead will conquer Gallifrey, and then be free to feed over all space and all time!'

The crowd burst into frantic cheering. 'Well,' Jake whispered to Madelaine, 'that's us booked up for the next few weeks.'

'Yarven has my symbiotic nuclei in his blood,' Ruath explained. 'He will take over from the fanatic Sanders, become the biological component of my Time Baffles – '

'And extend the long night infinitely!' The Doctor grinned. 'Yes, it would take somebody with the blood of a Time Lord to do that. The brain of any other life form, even a vampire, would burn out after a few days. But that still doesn't explain why you set a trap for me.'

'Doctor, I have high hopes for you. Since Yarven will not be joining us for the assault on Gallifrey, I thought that perhaps you might stand beside me, as my new consort.'

'You've got to be joking!' Tegan exploded. 'Why would he want to join your lot?'

'Tegan, Tegan, Tegan . . .' The Doctor raised a hand. 'Don't be so hasty. Ruath's made a good strategic choice. I am, after all, Lord President of Gallifrey, at least in theory. As we've recently seen, my Presidential access codes are still valid. And there would always be at least a few Prydonians willing to follow a President of their own

College, even if he had fangs and sinister intentions.'

'Why, Doctor, I had hardly dared hope that you would be so sympathetic.' Ruath spun, and pointed a long-nailed finger at Tegan. 'Will you become one of the Undead, Theta? Will you share this human's blood with me?'

'Doctor . . .' Tegan muttered, uncertainly.

She was horrified to see the Doctor produce his coin, and spin it in the air. He slapped it onto the back of his hand. 'Heads I will . . .'

Lang, his arms wrapped around him, watched on the backstage monitor as his audience started to file into the stadium. The darkness was illuminated only by the light of the screen.

They were running in, some of them, looking around at the walls of the stadium as if they were a guarantee of safety.

Maybe so. Maybe this strange choice of place was going to be the last fort against the dark. There was surely something reassuring about the great football lighting gantries that shone across the ground.

He winced as he felt a slight pain in his stomach. That old ulcer again. Couldn't let it get the better of him now. Tomorrow he'd be in an ideal body, with all his friends and relatives together in the sight of God. His daughter would be reconciled with him.

Maybe. He didn't want to think of that, though it forced itself to the front of his brain more and more.

He was going to go out there and minister to this crowd.

He was going to lead them to redemption.

And he would get there himself. Of course he would.

'Heads!' The Doctor looked at Tegan apologetically. 'I'm terribly sorry, Tegan, but she's right, you know. I've always wondered what was going to become of the Time Lords, and Ruath offers an elegant solution.'

Tegan backed away. 'You can't . . . not after all this!'

'The trouble is,' the Doctor continued, 'you've always thought of me as a human being. Even fooled yourself into thinking that there could be some sort of friendship between us. In reality, I've always seen you more as . . . what's a good analogy? A pet. Like an affectionate dog or a cat. They can be relaxing to have around, but when the time comes for them to be put down, well, only a child would make a fuss about it.'

Ruath laughed as Tegan looked between them. 'Yes, my dear. Gallifreyan loyalties run deep. Now Doctor, do you want to, or shall I?'

The Doctor waved a hand. 'By all means.'

Ruath grabbed Tegan by the hair and exposed her neck, bending to bite it.

Tegan screamed and reached behind her.

Using all her strength, she used both hands to smash the woman aside, and ran at her with the stake she'd slipped down the back of her jeans.

Ruath smacked the wooden spar aside and halted Tegan with a look.

Tegan watched the Doctor's face as Ruath approached. She didn't think that she would feel the teeth entering her throat. A great despair had welled up inside her, and her heart felt like stone. If the Doctor was going to go over to the side of the vampires, then what was her life worth? His expression as Ruath bore down on her was distant and empty, focused on the vampire. Then he seemed to make a serious decision.

'Ruath,' he called, just as the Time Lady was about to make the first incision. 'I've made up my mind. Forget the human. I'll show you my loyalty to your cause in the most direct way possible. Take me now.'

Ruath spun from Tegan, her eyes full of excitement. She advanced on the Doctor. 'Bare your neck,' she said. 'And be my next consort.'

The Doctor undid a button on his cricket shirt. 'Do be careful,' he advised. 'I have enough trouble washing the collars as it is.'

Yarven's audience had climbed the stairs of the castle with him, up to the roof of one of the turrets. Stacked there were a large number of black canisters, each about the size of a fire-extinguisher, fitted with a screw-top aerosol release nozzle.

Yarven pointed to the canisters. 'The fruits of Lady Ruath's research, my people. Take them now, up into every level of the atmosphere, and release the genetic material inside. Do not worry about the sun, Sanders has a few hours before the end of his glorious sacrifice, and long before that . . .' he paused, glancing at some of the faces in the crowd, 'I shall have made sure the day will not come again. Now, go!'

The vampires flew to the cylinders, grabbing them and spiralling up into the sky, hundreds of them rising like a flock of bats against the near-full moon.

Yarven watched, delighted, as they went. He was aware of a weight on his hand, and looked down to see a death's-head moth sitting there.

It flew up and blossomed into the humanoid form of Nyssa. She panted, her eyes glowing with the blood madness.

'Be still a moment, and then tell me what you have seen and heard,' Yarven advised her. 'Then I shall give you the blood you desire.'

Ruath raised her head. Her fangs were covered with gore.

204

Tegan stared. The Doctor had stood gamely through the whole experience as if he'd been waiting at a bus stop. Now, he glanced down.

'Finished? Oh good.' He pulled out a handkerchief and dabbed at the twin wounds in his neck. 'I can't say that was a pleasant experience, but it was certainly an interesting one.'

Ruath laughed and licked her lips. 'I always wondered what Time Lord plasma would taste like. Yours is delicious.'

'I got the impression that you didn't like the vintage. What with my compatriots and I going out to see the universe and all that. But if I remember correctly, you were considering coming along as well.'

Ruath turned aside. 'I don't want to talk about that. Not now, when everything's so close to being perfect.'

'My dear, what are you doing down there?' Yarven was standing on the edge of the pit, smiling warmly.

'I was . . . debating our plans with the Doctor.' Ruath waved a hand airily while the Doctor turned aside to hide his wounds. 'He can't bring himself to agree. Look what his ape tried to do to me!' She playfully tossed the broken stake up into Yarven's hand.

Tegan had come round from her paralysis. She looked carefully between Ruath and Yarven. 'Hey,' she muttered, 'what's going on here?'

'These evil beings are toying with us, Tegan.' The Doctor tried to take her aside, but she shrugged his hand from her shoulder.

'What, you mean you don't want me getting in the way of your sweet little deal with Vampirella here? I'm not going to just shut up and letglummff – '

The Doctor had plucked the mashed-up celery from his lapel and pushed it into her mouth.

Luckily Yarven didn't seem to have noticed. He was

helping Ruath from the pit. 'The children have started to seed the wind,' he told her. 'Soon, my love, we shall have all we ever wanted.'

'Indeed we shall, my Lord,' Ruath grinned.

'Seed the wind?' The Doctor frowned at Yarven as if Ruath hadn't explained anything to him. 'What are you up to?'

'Scattering genetic material, Doctor. Vampire DNA. One drop of it on human skin, and within minutes that individual will be a fully developed vampire. We're being rather efficient too, now I think about it, releasing it on the night before the full moon. Once our community is fully established and there are more vampires than humans, I shall allow the cycle to progress by one day, and seal all our new conversions in their fate.'

'My dear . . .' Ruath put a hand to his breast sadly.

'Ah yes, I was forgetting. By then I shall be insensible, and after our plans for Earth are complete, I will give my life that the Undead may prosper. Such a pity that I shall never see them rule the stars.'

'This genetic material,' the Doctor asked casually, 'has she taken it from you yourself?'

'Why yes,' Yarven replied proudly. 'This generation of the Undead shall literally be my children. A thought to take to my grave. Now, we must see how the seeding is progressing. When I return, Doctor, prepare yourself to suffer torment beyond endurance. Until then . . .' He let the sentence trail off as he marched Ruath to the door.

'Until then,' the Doctor murmured grimly.

Tegan spat out a lump of mashed celery. 'What the hell are you up to?' she demanded.

'Just taking advantage of circumstances, Tegan. Ruath's totally insane, of course, but from our previous association, I thought she might still retain some fondness for me.'

Tegan raised an eyebrow. 'So you're not going over to their side?'

The Doctor sighed. 'Tegan, do try to keep up. What's better, do you think, being Ruath's consort or being tortured over a period of days?'

'Give me your coin and I'll tell you. What did you two get up to back on Gallifrey, anyway?'

'Oh, we introduced cats into the Gallifreyan eco-system, altered the local gravity in the Panopticon so that a graduation ceremony took place in mid-air . . .' A nostalgic grin spread across the Doctor's face. 'Do you know, once we even electrified Borusa's perigosto stick.'

'Charming. So she stayed behind and you went away?'

'Yes, and I think that's what's been irritating her all these centuries. She's been brooding on it so long that I actually think she believed my rather sudden conversion. I suspect that I fulfilled her dearest wish.'

'Certainly had me fooled. How did you fake the bit with the neck, anyway?'

'Fake?' The Doctor dabbed at his wounds once more. 'Tegan, I hate to tell you this, but if we don't get this sorted out soon, you may have to start locking your door at night. I wonder what it's like, being a vampire?'

Madelaine and Jake had flown higher than their comrades, up over the countryside until all the cloud was below them and the Earth's atmosphere was a curve shining with moonlight.

They looked at the cylinders each one carried. 'How do you operate these things, then?' Jake asked.

'You just unscrew the top and pull off the toggle,' Madelaine murmured absently. 'I hope they're ozone-friendly.'

'Not going to be important, is it, when the world's all vampires?'

'No. You're right. It's not.'

Jake stopped his fumblings with the tap on his cylinder. 'Do you want to do this?'

'I don't know. Just because this lot are vampires . . . I haven't liked every vampire I've met, have you?'

'Not most of them, really, no. I just thought that it was all right that somebody was on our side for once. I'm sorry.'

'I did my share, Jake. All that stuff with Lang.'

'So what do you want to do? It won't make any difference, two cylinders, will it?'

'No,' Madelaine sighed. 'No, I suppose it won't.'

Yarven and Ruath had gone to check on the state of the temporal baffles in the laboratory, heading down into the depths by a circuitous route through the cellars. It might have crossed Yarven's mind that Ruath wasn't just enjoying walking with him, but was actively trying to waste time.

Then again, it might not.

'Poor Jeremy . . .' Ruath sighed at the laboratory door, fumbling with her keys. 'He cannot have long left now.'

'Indeed.' Yarven opened the door and ushered her inside. 'Let us see how he's managing. I wouldn't want to miss my great destiny.'

Before he followed her, he reached into his waistcoat pocket and removed a little moth on the end of his finger. He blew at it and it flew off. 'Go,' Yarven whispered. 'Do as I bid you.'

He turned back to the laboratory and followed his consort, rubbing his hands together in gentle anticipation.

The Doctor turned to Tegan. 'Well, rather remiss of them to put two of us in here together, don't you think?'

'Why?'

'Because at least one of us has shoulders, Tegan. I suppose I could dissolve into a mist, but I'm not sure how long it takes for a novice vampire to learn to do that sort of thing. Up you get.' He bent and allowed Tegan to clamber onto his back. 'Ready now? Hup!' He stood upright, and Tegan leapt over the edge of the pit.

'There's nobody about!' she whispered. 'Grab my hand and I'll – '

Nyssa appeared behind her and felled her with one blow.

The Doctor stared up at the creature his companion had become, a look of horror washing over his face. 'Nyssa . . . I'm so sorry.'

Without a word in reply, the young woman snarled and leapt into the pit. She reached for the Doctor with both hands.

The vampire genetic material poured into the night sky, spilling into the winds like fine rain. The older vampires, masters of the stratospheric currents, advised the younger ones on how to disperse it.

The deadly liquid would be spread randomly across Britain within the hour. Within what had been days it would work its way across Europe and eventually into the daytime of Asia. There, it would cause the initial panic that would serve as a prelude to the greater horrors the night would bring.

And there would be more. Flasks for the Americas and Africa, scatterings across the globe until everybody knew what this life of darkness and doubt was like.

Until everybody was a vampire.

Yarven stared sadly at the blistering forehead of Jeremy Sanders.

'He was a good servant. He deserves more than this.'

'He was a willing sacrifice. When I explained the principles to him, he leapt at the chance to prepare the way for you.' Ruath straightened up from the sensors she'd been checking. 'Complete cerebral decay will happen at some point within the next three hours. The chance gets greater every moment.'

'And when that happens?'

'It's day again. To keep the device powered up indefinitely, we need somebody who can instinctively calibrate temporal conditions, somebody with symbiotic nuclei in their bloodstream.'

'Somebody such as myself.'

'Indeed. That is why I gave you my blood, my Lord.'

'Just so.' Yarven turned to the window and stared into the night sky. 'Have I ever told you, my dear, about my second encounter with the spirit called Agonal?'

'Second?' Ruath stopped, suddenly fearful. 'But you said – '

'That I only met him once? Well, a King must have secrets, even from his most . . . trusted confidantes.'

Ruath took a deep breath. 'Indeed, my Lord.'

'I was stumbling away from my encounter with that idiot Tarak, making my way out of the forest with an arrow in my chest. I was thinking only of escape, of that reflex of ours that calls us to our native earth in times of peril. When I got back to the inn, the man in black, the one who had shown me the shed where Ivo kept his tools and told me to use them on Veran . . . he was waiting for me. He told me that he was called Agonal, and that he was my real father.'

'What!' Ruath exclaimed. 'But Agonal was merely a disembodied energy matrix, a spirit, he – '

'He had come to my mother as a shower of rain,' Yarven explained impatiently. 'I knew that my parentage and my great destiny would be revealed to me eventually.

210

All my life I had anticipated that. Agonal showed me where to hide and explained my coming to Earth. Agonal told me all that I needed to know.'

'But I came to do that, I am the messenger of – '

'He said that I would rule all vampirekind, forever. That I and I alone would be their King.'

'Well, that's true, in a sense. As Vampire Messiah you'll rule in proxy, while doing your people a great service . . .' Ruath smiled and moved casually across the room.

'Agonal said nothing of that.' Yarven didn't turn from the window, his voice remaining level. 'But he did say that my Queen would betray me. And you've just done that, haven't you?'

Ruath froze, her hand on a wall panel. 'What do you mean?'

'Your conversation was reported to me.' Yarven spun, bellowing, 'The Time Lords would use the Undead as breeding stock, would they? A noble of the House of Yar isn't good enough to rule Gallifrey, is he?!'

'My Lord, no, you've got it all – ' Ruath snatched the gun she'd used on Nyssa from the wall and fired it at him.

But Yarven wasn't there.

A great shadow swept over Ruath and she froze, looking up into the Lord of the Vampires' piercing eyes and shivering like a rabbit. 'Silence,' he whispered.

The doors burst open, and in rushed the masses of the Undead, Nyssa amongst them. They carried the Doctor before them.

Yarven turned from the paralysed form of his consort, and bared his fangs at the Time Lord. 'Doctor . . . I gather you were expecting a wedding. I fear you have been misled. You see, I have come to a very obvious conclusion. If a vampire with symbiotic nuclei can hold the night forever, then surely a Time Lord can do that

211

just as well? While you're having your brain burnt out over the centuries, I can get on with my destiny. The conquest of Earth, Gallifrey, and then all time and space.'

There came a cry from inside Ruath's machines. Sanders was in the last throes of his agony. Yarven pointed to the Doctor. 'Give him to the machine.'

Eleven

The spotlight picked out Victor Lang as he walked onto the stage.

The crowd roared and applauded, but he waved the applause aside.

'My friends . . . I know you're frightened. We're all frightened. But I'm here to tell you, after night there is dawn. And after such a night as this there will be *such* a dawn. The dawning of God's city on Earth, when all evil will be swept away. It's true, it's simply true, I'm here to tell you that it's true.' The applause washed over his words. He could feel their need as he extended his arms, an embrace to them all.

But as he made the gesture, he felt something give inside him again. It didn't matter. It didn't matter if he was dying. He had this job to do. 'I have a daughter,' he began, and he found himself thinking of Madelaine's eyes and of the way she'd looked inside him. 'And she's far from here. She's far from me in spirit, as well as in the flesh. I want us all now to think of those who aren't here. Ask for their protection. Ask for them to be shown the way of the Lord, while there's still time.

'You see, she berates and threatens me, calls me up and threatens to tell the papers about us, about our love, and yes sir, I would call it love – '

He stopped, realizing what he'd just said.

The audience's love had snapped off like a light. And the stadium was dark. He could hear whispers and

213

scattered shouts and a scared, embarrassed silence.

They were going to crucify him, he thought giddily.

The air was thick and full, really full of something.

And then something split inside his stomach lining. And he started to laugh. 'What unites us all?' He guffawed, picking out individual faces as the spotlights remorselessly swept the audience. He coughed and tried to stop giggling. 'What unites us all? Let me tell you, ladies and gentlemen, let me tell you the only thing that any of us in the glare of the last crummy years of the twentieth crummy century have in common.'

He grabbed the microphone stand in front of him and found a sharp edge on it. 'This is it, folks, this is all that we've got in common! Saints and sinners like we all are! Just the blood!'

He made a slicing motion, and felt a huge surge of relief as the liquid spouted from his forearm. He watched it go, and thought of his daughter's voice.

The crowd was shouting, a noise of terror and wanting.

Lang felt their fear and their pleasure, and the last traces of secrecy died inside him. With a roar of laughter, he hit the control in his hand that ordered the cameras to zoom in.

He opened his mouth, and showed his fangs to the audience.

They cried and wept and shouted. They loved him for it.

Lang dived forward, scattered screaming altar boys from an on-stage table, and seized the cups that were ready for communion. 'Come and get it!' he bellowed, filling them with the glorious warm liquid. 'Drink of the blood of common ugly humanity, eat of its flesh! So I'm not perfect, so neither are you! What a revelation that is, huh?'

214

The crowd screamed and swayed, and Lang in his ecstasy couldn't be sure if they wanted to hurt him or cheer him on. A number of them were climbing up onto the stage.

The spotlights swung up into the night sky and locked on something.

A tiny shape was floating down into the heaving auditorium.

A naked baby, spinning and laughing as it flew towards the stage.

The audience were fighting now, and mounting each other, and yelling in tongues. It was the air, Lang realized somewhere deep inside, the air was changing them. Like whatever they'd put into his stomach had changed him.

The baby, illuminated like a star, floated into the circle of the stage. It reached for the cup and drank a long, hungry draught of Lang's steaming blood.

The lights of the stadium flickered upwards, and the audience gasped.

Standing around the walls of the stadium was a circle of shadowed figures. Evenly spaced, they stood there grandly, waiting.

'They've come for us!' Lang laughed. 'Our children have come for us, our children, to take us away!' He grabbed the baby by the hand, and allowed himself to be hoisted up into the air, kicking his heels. 'They don't care if we're monsters. Look into your hearts, good people.' Lang laughed in delight as the Child swung him around the stadium, gazing down into the great, mauling, blood-letting, copulating mass below him. 'Look into your hearts and see!

We are the monsters!'

The Doctor frowned as Yarven connected the terminals to either side of his head. 'Are you sure you know how

215

to work the controls?' he asked.

'Oh, I think so . . .' Yarven glanced at the frozen and sweating figure of Ruath. 'I've secretly been learning the basics of Ruath's technology. I can't pretend to understand how it works, of course, but I think I know which buttons I have to push.'

'Do you really think I'll co-operate with this?'

'There's no need for you to co-operate. The machine simply uses your time-sensitive brain as a power source. You will be able neither to help nor hinder the process. But I gather it will be painful.'

'You'll never get away with this, you know.' The Doctor addressed his words to the assembled audience of vampires. He had been imprisoned in a similar box to the one that Sanders still sat in. Nyssa was standing in that mass of the Undead, close to Yarven, and the Doctor thought that it was obvious who Yarven intended to be his new consort. 'What makes you think that the Earth will just give in? They'll fight you on every street corner.'

'Oh really, Doctor, you are a romantic. We live on every street corner. We're staging what might be called a show of strength in the city near here at the moment. And it's a show that should rather shake the faith of the population. We placed a slow-release package of my DNA in Victor Lang's stomach. As we speak, he should be experiencing the delights of vampirism in front of an audience of thousands, a good proportion of whom, thanks to my airborne seed, will be transforming themselves. From what you know of humans, Doctor, do you honestly think that, within a few hours, there will be any form of human civilization remaining?'

The Doctor lowered his head. 'No.'

Two of Yarven's lieutenants dragged in a recovered Tegan. She gasped when she saw the Doctor's predicament. 'My God, Doctor, what are they doing to you?'

'Ah, Tegan. Glad you could make it.' His gaze fixed on Yarven and his voice became harder. 'I hope that she's going to remain unharmed.'

'You may hope. Personally, I was thinking of having both Miss Jovanka and my dear Ruath made into soup.'

There came a cry from the other box. Yarven looked up sharply. 'No more delays, Doctor.' He checked the linkages to the Time Lord's temples, making sure that the Doctor was connected to the circuitry of the laboratory. Then he grabbed the lever that would transfer the power demand from Sanders to the Doctor. 'Any last words?'

'Yes,' the Doctor shouted. 'By Rassilon's command . . . dematerialize!'

The ring on Ruath's paralysed finger glowed silver.

Lang had returned to the stage and was fighting off a great horde of people who had scrambled up to drink from his cup. 'There's enough for all!' he was calling. 'Sinners, sinners, let my blood wash your guilt away!'

Amongst a squalid knot of writhing vampires, a pool of blood forming around his feet, stood a boy who was staring at the stage. His head was a wrecked mass of blood and hair. His face was terribly scarred, and there were callouses on his hands. The marks of sunlight.

Matthew was looking at the giant cross as Lang danced around it. He'd come up out of the sewers when the night had fallen, and had made his way with so many of his new brothers to the stadium.

Watching Lang, Matthew made a decision.

He started to walk towards the stage, jumping over the bodies and the corpses and the transforming Undead. There were quite a few semi-digested piles of ashes too, where the passionately faithful had taken on the vampire DNA and set themselves ablaze.

Matthew's walk became a determined run.

217

'Say it loud!' called Lang. 'We're guilty, and we're proud!' He had leaned back against the cross, its shining white silhouetting him. There was no faith in it now to hurt him. The baby had perched on his shoulder, blood dripping from its mouth, as more and more of the ordinary folk of Lang's congregation leapt up to drink from his cup.

Matthew was nearly at the stage when it happened.

The sun appeared back in the sky.

Two o'clock in the afternoon it had been.

Two o'clock it was again.

There was a moment of silence. Then the fire began.

Russet light sparkled off Piccadilly station, ran in a great amber river down Oxford Road, made the crescent estates of Moss Side into tangles of lengthening shadows. A wave of it swept across the stadium and the greater city outside it, and the country and continent outside that. The Undead who had come to treat the world as their place to walk free caught fire and exploded.

In the stadium, bodies thrashed to and fro with the flames. A mass of decaying biology smashed against itself and flared again, a spiral of ashes winding into the bright sky.

Around the walls of the amphitheatre, the watching vampires flared like candles, burning where they stood or falling into bundles of cinders off the walls.

The Child stared, its face suddenly red with sunburn. It took a deep breath, its first in decades. Then it exploded in a ball of flame.

Lang looked around in terror, wondering if Christ had come to chastise him. Looking at the devastation before him, he felt something else give inside him.

Burning tears started to trickle down his cheeks.

'My Lord. My girl,' he whispered. 'I'm so sorry.'

Matthew was on fire as he sprinted up onto the stage.

He grabbed the microphone stand from Lang, and spun to face him.

The evangelist looked him in the eye. 'Well then?'

Matthew ran at him. The microphone stand pierced Lang's chest, sped through his heart and embedded itself into the shining cross behind him.

Matthew's momentum couldn't be abated. He careered into Lang's arms, a disintegrating bundle of ashes.

Lang held onto him, comforted by the strength of the cross behind him as his flesh began to blaze into clouds of dark and sickly smoke. To his comfort, he suddenly realized that the wood at his back was burning him too. 'He forgives you,' he told the evaporating boy. 'He forgives us both. Despite everything.'

The blaze grew higher and higher, engulfing the two of them until they were only shadows inside it. And then they were ashes, and the ashes blew away on the rising breeze.

The cross stood surrounded by debris, a microphone stand piercing its heart. The cloud of heat rising from the stadium condensed the moisture from all the blood and vapour in the air.

It began to rain.

From backstage stepped Olivia, untouched. She stared at the empty stadium, its seats full of the scattered remains of humanity. She stared at the cross, electrical cables shorting out all around its charred frame.

She stared until she was soaking wet.

And then she went back in to get an umbrella.

Castle Yarven had dematerialized, taking its Time Freeze with it.

The feudally designed TARDIS whizzed through the vortex, the moat spinning around it.

Inside, the Doctor leapt out of his seat, ripping the

219

connections from his head. The vampires around him were staggering, disorientated by their sudden plunge into the timeless netherworld of the vortex.

'Doctor, how did you – ?' Tegan gasped as the Doctor grabbed her hand.

'You can't confine a vampire, Tegan! My hands were just a mist for a moment there.'

Yarven recovered first, and grabbed the Doctor by the shoulder. 'What have you done?' he bellowed.

'The right thing!' the Doctor replied, his voice just a little too high to carry conviction. But his fist did. It caught the vampire Lord across the chin, sending him staggering backwards. The Doctor wrenched Nyssa from his grasp. 'Come on Nyssa, people to see, places to go!'

The three of them raced up the stairs from the laboratory, the Doctor slamming the door behind them and locking it.

'After them, you fools!' bellowed Yarven, stumbling to his feet. 'After them!'

The Doctor and his companions jogged through the pit room, passing as they did so a bundle of staggering vampires.

'They won't be disorientated for long, but the journey's a short one!' the Doctor gasped.

'You mean you know where we're going?' Tegan asked.

'I'll explain later. At the moment, we need a turret, some way to get out!'

'I know of one,' Nyssa spoke up. The other two stared at her. She was back to her normal self, full of dignity and poise.

'Nyssa!' Tegan exclaimed. 'You're – '

'Human again,' Nyssa smiled. 'Yes.'

'The vampire who bit her must have been destroyed,'

the Doctor grinned. There came a crash from the laboratory. He grabbed his companions by their shoulders again. 'Come on!'

The stained glass window in the turret that Nyssa had found before had been repaired by Ruath. A quick adjustment to her chameleon circuit was all that had been necessary. Now it was shining with psychedelic colours, the glass prisming the butterfly blues of the vortex outside.

'I managed to send the navigation circuits the co-ordinates for a destination and the chameleon circuits the idea for a new shape.' The Doctor shrugged off his coat and rolled it around his arms, silencing Tegan's questions with a stern gesture. 'It shouldn't be long now.'

'But Doctor,' cried Nyssa, 'this tower is very high. How are we – ?'

'Hush, Nyssa, we have to time this just right.'

The blues and purples of the vortex faded from the window. Tegan and Nyssa waited for the familiar clunk of landing, but before it happened, the Doctor shouted, 'Ready? *Now!*'

He ran at the glass and jumped through it, his arms before him protected by the coat.

'Geronimo!' Tegan grabbed Nyssa's hand and jumped after him.

The three adventurers leapt out onto a strange landscape. A distant sun was sinking fast, its violet light diffused through the gaps between the mountain tops, and reflected off the slopes of snow and ice. A cluster of grey trees stood in the middle of the snowy plain.

Tegan shouted, expecting a long fall.

But they hit the snow after a moment. They'd jumped only a few feet.

She looked over her shoulder at the castle.

But it wasn't a castle any more, it was a flat, open disc of metal, with a TARDIS console standing in the centre of it.

And on that disc stood hundreds of disconcerted vampires. They hissed and held their hands up to shield themselves from the sun, but swiftly realized that it was setting. Within seconds, the planet's surface was dark. The sun had set. The vampires straightened up and rumbled with anger.

The Doctor turned to face them. 'We jumped in that second when a TARDIS is deciding on its new shape,' he whispered to Tegan. 'Stay where you are, by the way. There's nowhere to run.'

Yarven stepped forward, pointing a finger at the Doctor. 'You did this!' he shouted. 'How?'

'Rassilon was rather a control fanatic, I'm afraid,' the Doctor called. 'Circuits for his personal operation have always been fitted into TARDISes and, like a lot of Gallifreyan tradition, there seems to be a method to its madness. A friend of mine told me about that ring that Ruath wears, how it's a key to Rassilon's devices. Odd that it should become an item of reverence for the Undead, hm?'

'For all your Gallifreyan conceit, Time Lord, you still seem to have miscalculated!' Yarven snarled. 'Did you not mean for us to land here in the daylight?'

'I wanted to make you an offer. I gather that my companion Nyssa went some way towards developing an artificial blood substitute, at least, if the traces she left in the TARDIS labs were anything to go by. The two of us, perhaps with Ruath's help, could work to devise a mass-production process. You could have a permanent and harmless food source, and we could find you an uninhabited planet to make your own. This one, if you like it.'

He looked at the splendid night sky that had spread above them in the darkness. 'You have the chance, Yarven, to really make a difference for your people. To turn them into a true culture, rather than a race of parasites that preys on others. What do you say?'

Yarven drew in a great breath. 'I say . . . *die*!' He launched himself forward, his cape billowing into great wings as he leapt the hundred yards or so between him and the Doctor.

He caught the Time Lord by the throat, and the two of them struggled. Behind them, the vampires rushed forward. Nyssa and Tegan could only stare at the Doctor in terror.

'You haven't much time left, Yarven!' the Doctor shouted. 'Consider my offer, while you still have a chance!'

'To live on one world, supping swill and settling things with endless debate and argument?' Yarven matched his strength against the Doctor's, trying to reach his throat. 'That is not the way of a noble race. Haven't you read Ruath's books? We are destined to – '

A certain heat touched the back of his neck, and Yarven stopped. He released the Doctor and turned to see the terrible reality. A few feet from Nyssa and Tegan, the vampire army had seen it too. Across the crags, a new light was shining.

'No!' Yarven bellowed. 'It cannot end like this! It cannot!'

A second sun broke from beneath the horizon, its giant body shimmering through all the hues of the spectrum.

The vampires cried out in fear. Some dashed straight up and flew, attempting to outrun the dawn, but the speed of the planet's revolution was clearly faster than Earth's. They shot up like fireworks, to explode in flames high in the atmosphere. Those on the ground became a sea of crumbling fire, the ice surface reflecting the sun into every crevice where they might have hidden, boiling them away into a blaze of screaming bodies.

Yarven began to crumble, his skin giving way and fluttering off into ashes. He did not cry out. He straightened up and looked at the rising star calmly. 'So, Doctor. Destiny is not all it is reputed to be.'

'It never is. I'm sorry.'

'Are you really?' Yarven raised an eyebrow as his flesh caught fire. He looked down at the scar on his chest, the wound he'd taken so long ago. It had been erased as his flesh fell away. He opened his arms to embrace the rising star. 'I am not. It was a glorious design. It should have succeeded. The Children of the Night will have their moment still, Doctor. When they do, you will not be able to contain them. You were a worthy adversary. Until we meet in the next life, I bid you farewell!'

The Lord of the Vampires exploded.

His flesh billowed into a ball of flame. It flared bright blue for a moment, and then collapsed back to a withered skeleton. The skeleton fell around its axis and withered into a pile of bones on the icy ground. And then the bones were only dust, and the dust fluttered away on the wind.

The Doctor lowered his head.

A horrible thought had struck Tegan. 'Doctor, get under cover!'

'What?' The Doctor raised a hand and winced. It was red with sunburn. 'Of course, I hadn't thought of that. But that means . . .'

'Shut up and get out of it!' Tegan pulled the Doctor's coat from his shoulders and threw it over his head, adding her own pullover to it a moment later. She grabbed the resultant bundle and fell to the ground with it, smothering the Doctor.

'Tegan,' Nyssa murmured, 'I think that from my own experiences I can safely say that exposure to sunlight doesn't destroy somebody who's been a vampire for only a few hours.'

'Doesn't it?' Tegan looked at the bundle in her arms. She sat up and pulled the pullover from the Doctor's face. 'Why didn't you tell me?'

'You didn't give me a chance,' the Doctor sighed, 'but thank you for your concern.'

It took a few minutes to locate all the dazed and shaken people in the mass of organic debris. Jeremy Sanders lay against the console, his body a crumbling husk. Those who had been novice vampires, like the Doctor, were suffering from nothing more than sunburn and had returned to their human state. The process of being bitten wasn't as ruthless that way as ingestion of the genetic material would be. There were over a dozen of them, and they initially reacted to the Doctor and his party with fear.

'It's all right,' the Doctor told them, his hat carefully placed on his head and his hands stuffed in his pockets. 'All we want to do is get you home. If that's where you want to go.'

There was general agreement. 'We didn't want to be vampires,' one of the young boys ventured. He was brushing the ashes off his jacket. 'We never bit people or nothing. We got carried along with it all.'

The Doctor looked at his shoes. 'There's no need to explain.'

'We were just – '

'I said – ' The Doctor's voice had risen in tone for a second. He calmed it again and grinned. 'There's really no need. Let's get you home.'

* * *

225

They stood around the console of Ruath's TARDIS, and the Doctor tapped out some instructions on the chameleon circuit controls. The walls folded upwards to form a neat white cabinet, and the ex-Undead crowded around the console, until they realized that the space inside was just as great as it had been previously. The Doctor set to work on the co-ordinate controls. With a screech of technology, the box faded away.

The big sun set, less than an hour after it had risen. By now the ashes had scattered far across the planet, and there was nothing to be seen of the army that had once threatened the cosmos.

There was only peaceful and starlit night.

The Doctor left the children in the centre of Manchester, in daytime, and watched as they staggered off into the streets, leaning on each other for support.

He sniffed the air. It was going to be a fresh and rainy day, a cold wind coming down from the north. The city was recovering, the forces of business and family forcing people back into the regular patterns of their life. There was something muted about the place, perhaps. It wasn't going to enjoy its first natural night. But at least there would be a dawn to follow it.

'Doctor,' asked Nyssa, 'are there any vampires left here?'

'Oh yes, I dare say a few got away.' The Doctor closed the doors of Ruath's TARDIS and selected a new destination, setting the capsule in flight once more. 'But their numbers have been cut back to below what they were when this all started. They've resumed their place in the natural way of things. Any that have been created since then, remember, will have been freed.'

'And now that Yarven's dead, those infested with his genetic material won't turn into vampires?'

226

'Indeed not. If they were sheltered from the sun, they'll be fine.'

Nyssa hugged him. 'Thank you,' she whispered and began to cry, the tears that she'd held back for so long finally fighting their way to the surface. 'The things I saw, the things I did . . .'

Tegan hugged her too. 'Hey, we all do stuff we regret. Usually when somebody else is in charge.' She smiled up at the Doctor.

But he was deep in thought.

Ruath's TARDIS landed in the forest, a few yards from the familiar police box shape of the Doctor's own vehicle. For a few seconds, it stood there, then a bizarre change in shape occurred. A thin liquid arm sped out from it, and contacted the door of the police box. Just as quickly as it had protruded, it snapped back.

The Doctor ushered his companions outside and ran after them a moment later, slamming the door of the white capsule behind him. 'Three . . . two . . . one!' he counted, and the box faded away. 'Sent it back to Gallifrey,' he explained. 'They can always do with an extra TARDIS or two, and I dare say that Ruath stole it in the first place.' He fished in his pockets and pulled out the TARDIS key to open the door of the police box.

'What a terrible thing to do,' Nyssa opined.

The Doctor gave her a severe frown as he let the two young women enter the box before him. Then he followed them and closed the door.

The TARDIS faded away.

The Doctor was glad that both of his friends were too exhausted to question his condition. They'd headed for their rooms as soon as the TARDIS had entered the vortex. And he didn't blame them. Sometimes their emotional and physical strength astonished him.

He tapped out a sequence of random co-ordinates, his mind elsewhere. If he was still a vampire, then –

Ruath was standing behind him.

She walked out of his peripheral vision, over to the other side of the console. 'Then I'm still alive. I can read you like a book, Theta.'

The Doctor closed his mouth, covering the fangs that had grown there. 'I knew you'd come.'

'As soon as Yarven was distracted enough to relax his mental paralysis, I slipped down through the cracks. A little bolt-hole I'd prepared inside my console. Nice and dark.'

'Why are you still a vampire?' The Doctor frowned.

'Because I haven't stepped outside the null-time field of a TARDIS. I used one of our old chameleon circuit tricks to transfer between vehicles. I think you taught me that one, actually.'

The Doctor ignored her friendly tone. 'Well, since your plans have hit a snag, perhaps you'd do me the service of stepping outside at our next destination. You might be fond of this condition, but I can't say it suits me, I'm afraid.'

Ruath shook her head. 'I wish I could leave all this behind, but it's too late. I have to fulfil the destiny set in motion by Agonal, Yarven and the Great Vampire.'

'How? What strategy can you possibly have left?'

'If you want to be free of this curse, Theta, you're going to take this TARDIS of yours back to the Dark Time.'

The Doctor shook his head sadly. 'You know that's – '

'We're going to find Rassilon, to see what really happened, to bring the Great Vampire into Gallifrey's time zone.'

He stared at her. 'You know, I knew you were

dedicated when I saw you, that last time at the Panopticon Library. I knew that in your hearts you didn't want to leave.'

'Don't try to distract me.'

'That's why I decided not to meet you at the appointed rendezvous. I left you a message.'

Ruath was blinking, her mouth open. 'You . . . you *decided* to leave me behind? I found no message, I – '

The Doctor pressed home his advantage, circling the console, his eyes never leaving Ruath's. 'I didn't think you were up to making all the choices that the life of a renegade demands. I thought that you'd do better for our people as a political rebel, as a voice on the inside.' He stopped in front of her, his face inches from hers. 'And until very recently, I thought I'd made the right decision.'

'So . . . you're saying you should have taken me with you?' Ruath broke into a vast smile.

'Yes,' the Doctor whispered. 'Because then perhaps you wouldn't have let your dedication twist into insanity.'

Ruath roared and slapped at him, but the Doctor caught the blow before it struck him. 'What about the books?' she shouted. 'What about this ring?'

'You always did set too much store by history. Exactly the opposite point of view to my class. Those books might have been lies, written by Rassilon's enemies. Or they might have been half-truths or muddled legends. I don't know what's happened to Gallifrey, if anything has, but I do know that civilizations have natural lives and deaths, and that no amount of empire building or dictatorship can change that. We all make our own destiny. If you're looking for truth, Ruath, don't look at history. History is a lie.'

'You said that you'd take me away! You said you'd save me!'

'And in the Library you said that it was the duty of

229

every loyal Gallifreyan to stay. Typical vampire logic. The rules only apply to other people.'

'I'll kill you! I'll kill you!'

'Listen! We're going to land somewhere in a few minutes. Step outside with me, just step outside. We'll both be free. Please don't − '

Whatever the Doctor was going to say was lost to history, because destiny intervened.

Tegan stepped through the doorway of the console room in her pyjamas. 'Doctor,' she began. 'I just figured it out. Oh.'

Ruath froze the Doctor with a glance and swept at her like a hurricane. Tegan reacted a split second too late, turning to run just as Ruath's blow threw her across the room. The vampire spun and flew at her again, spitting blood.

Tegan staggered up, and found herself leaning against the remains of the hatstand. As Ruath rushed forward, she grabbed one of the remaining spars and swung it up.

It pierced Ruath straight through her left heart. She bellowed and tore the stake out of her chest. 'Two hearts, ape! You need to stake both to kill me! Go on, try! Cut my head off, scald me with holy water, I'll only regenerate!'

Tegan screamed as Ruath launched herself at her.

With an effort of will, the Doctor tore himself out of his paralysis and dived across the console room. He wasn't going to get there in time.

'Ruath.' A quiet voice stopped the vampire in her tracks.

Nyssa was standing by the console. The door activation lever was in her hand. 'Forgive me.'

She pulled the lever.

The doors of the TARDIS opened into the vortex.

The air blasted out.

Nyssa grabbed the console, Tegan grabbed the Doctor and held onto the long spine of the hatstand, which had wedged between the console and the door.

But Ruath had nothing to hold onto.

She roared, and fixed her feet to the floor, an expression of intense concentration on her face. 'I will . . . not . . . give up. I . . . will . . .'

The Doctor let go of Tegan's hand and launched himself at the console. He managed to grab a handhold and reached out for Ruath's hand.

'Take my hand!' he shouted. 'Don't try to – '

A gleam blazed into Ruath's eyes. 'Doctor. Theta. I'll take you with me!'

She jumped for the Doctor's throat.

And shot back out of the doors.

She spiralled away into the butterfly corridor of the vortex, screaming: 'The winner shall lose and the loser – '

And she vanished into the distance.

'Nyssa, close the doors!' The Doctor reached out and forced Nyssa's white-knuckled hand upwards, pulling the lever with it.

Slowly the doors swung closed. The rush of air abated. A red light on the console blinked on and off, showing that emergency oxygen supplies were being pumped into the TARDIS, now that the threat was over.

The Doctor gently led Nyssa away from the console.

'I couldn't let her do it,' she said. 'I had to stop her.'

'Yes . . .' The Doctor sadly put a hand on her shoulder. 'Yes, I think that perhaps you did.'

Epilogue

' "It was all a trick!" bellowed the Great Vampire, as he fell out of space and time. He was very angry with Rassilon, because he thought that they had become friends. But Rassilon had fooled him, because the Great Vampire was very self-important, and it is not hard to fool those who are self-important.

'Omega and The Other both laughed to see the expression on the Great Vampire's face as he fell. They knew that Gallifrey would live in sunlight forever. So Omega made a new sun, which he put in a system that already had one. The planets of that system would now only ever have very short nights, and no vampire could ever live there for long.

'The Minyans and the other peoples of the universe thanked Rassilon and his friends for freeing them from the vampires with their great Bow-ships. They had no need to ever fear the fall of night again.

'And that is the story of how Rassilon slayed the Great Vampire, and let us all sleep safely in our beds at night.' Romana closed the book with the Great Seal of Rassilon on the cover and smiled at the children that were sitting around her chair in a rapt circle. 'Which is what all of you Time Toddlers should be doing now.'

Nurses led the little Gallifreyans away, oblivious to their protests. Some of them stopped to thank Romana or ask questions about Rassilon, and she replied to them all.

As the last one vanished out of the door of her apartments, a familiar head poked around it. 'You might be tired after all that,' gruffed Castellan Spandrell, 'but I think there's something you ought to see.'

They walked through the corridors of the Capitol, Spandrell refusing to discuss the matter any further. In the days since her communication with the Doctor, Romana had immersed herself in study and recreation, delaying even Flavia's persistent enquiries about joining the High Council. It didn't take Spandrell's detective instincts to tell that she was worried about the Doctor.

He led her to a port in the Travel Capsule Holding Area. In it stood Ruath's TARDIS, a plain white capsule, except for one thing. On its door were embossed the words:

All well. Superb as always.

Spandrell fished in the pocket of his robes. 'We found this inside also.' He handed Romana a cricket ball.

She grabbed it with a girlish little smile. 'I'll treasure it!'

'So, now that your mind has been put at rest, have you considered the Lady President's offer?' They began to stroll back towards the new Presidential Suite.

'I'm not certain. You know, last time I obeyed a Presidential Directive, I found myself in serious trouble.'

Spandrell shrugged. 'It's the way things get done here. Thank Rassilon.'

As they walked through the corridors of the residential block, the two Time Lords passed a pair of old men who were sat at a table, apparently considering some serious problem.

One was bearded, and his hand rested on a walking stick, its head in the shape of an owl. He was smiling.

The other was scowling, his hand to his chin. He was staring at the black shape of a wooden raven on the table before him.

233

Romana and Spandrell hardly spared them a glance as they walked by, deep in conversation.

'Yarven . . .' The scowling man looked up hopefully, as if making a move in some game.

'Agonal,' the bearded man smiled back.

'A message!' The man in black slapped a cylinder of parchment down onto the table.

'A ring!' the bearded man chuckled, slipping a silver band onto his finger.

The dark figure thumped the table. 'Hmmph! I shall have to try something else!'

A moment later, Secretary Pogarel, on some urgent errand or other, rushed down the corridor, and he idly glanced at the alcove where the table was. But if there had ever been two figures sitting there, they were long gone now. Pogarel shivered, as one might at some passing breeze. Then he shook his head and moved on.

'You know, Merv,' the Doctor grinned, shielding his eyes from the Tasmanian sunshine, 'I'm surprised that the tournament's overrun so much.'

Merv twitched his moustache. 'Bad light.' He got up from his seat and wandered back inside the pavilion to get another tinny.

Tegan and Nyssa strode up to the Doctor and threw themselves into deck-chairs on either side of him. 'How are you?' asked Tegan.

'Absolutely relaxed.' The Doctor pulled the brim of his hat over his eyes and opened his mouth in a yawn.

Nyssa jumped forward and peered into the chasm.

The Doctor pulled his hat up a notch and opened one eye. 'They're quite the right length, I assure you. I don't think I'd be lying here with my sleeves rolled up if they weren't.'

'So your girlfriend's dead?' Tegan asked.

234

'Probably. The vortex is quite hostile. But to free me of the curse, all she had to do was land in a time after the destruction of Yarven. And she is not my girlfriend.'

'How bad do you think the damage was . . . in Britain and all that?'

'Not as bad as it could have been. Besides, perhaps the crisis will have had positive effects. People are always drawn together by adversity.'

'I have a feeling that we're not going to find out how you knew about that ring that Ruath was wearing,' Nyssa opined.

'And you'd be absolutely right, Nyssa. It's not a good idea to boast about bending the laws of time. Things tend to fall on one's head.'

'Things like apples,' Tegan smiled.

'I beg your parglomp – ' His companion had slipped a Granny Smith into his mouth. He took hold of it and took a bite, unperturbed.

'While you're like that, I might ask how come it took you so long to figure out whether you were going to let me get bitten or not?' Tegan continued, fanning herself with Nyssa's volume of Primo Levi. In the last few days she'd finished reading it, and now she was thinking about starting a Jackie Collins or something. Something meaningless and fun.

The Doctor munched thoughtfully for a while. 'I was considering the chances of Ruath being destroyed or returning to her natural condition,' he finally replied. 'And it seemed to me that there wasn't much chance of that happening, so – '

'So you took the risk instead of Tegan!' Nyssa smiled, looking between her two friends.

'Yeah,' Tegan muttered, looking aside. 'I'm grateful.'

'Well, actually,' the Doctor began, 'my decision was based on who would make the better vampire. If one of

235

us was going to be fluttering about and floating under doors . . .'

'Oh, thanks. I'd have been really bad at it, would I?'

'I did have visions of you still trying to do your make-up in a mirror, yes.'

Tegan flopped back into her deck-chair, losing all posture. 'How are your side doing in this stupid game, anyway?' she asked, gazing out at the white-garbed figures on the cricket pitch.

'Oh, we were knocked out yesterday.' The Doctor finished his apple.

'So we've got no reason to stay?' Nyssa piped up.

'No reason? There's still the interest of the game, not to mention a small wager I have with Merv concerning – '

There came a grand shout from the pitch. The spectators rose in applause.

The Doctor's face fell. 'No. No reason at all.' He counted out a small pile of coins onto his deck-chair. 'I wonder if he'll appreciate Rutan Populas?'

Tegan found herself disarmed by him yet again. 'Of course he will,' she said. 'Do the Rutans drink Fosters?'

They wandered back to the TARDIS as the light started to fade. The grass was looking a little bleached, compared to Tasmania's usual verdant green, but it would recover in time.

Nyssa turned to look back at the setting sun. 'Out of all of the vampires,' she said, 'there were two who looked after me. I think they meant it when they said they wouldn't let anybody hurt me.'

'Well, if you didn't see them under the twin suns, they might have got away.' The Doctor laid a hand on her shoulder. 'There's always good in everybody you know, if you only know where to look.'

236

'Here endeth the first lesson,' muttered Tegan. She let go of the Doctor's arm and dropped his hat back onto his head. 'Ah well, it was good to see Aussie again. Where are we going next?'

'A destination,' the Doctor frowned, 'picked quite at random.' He brightened again. 'But I think I'll narrow it down to somewhere sunny.'

He led his companions into the TARDIS and closed the door. A moment later there came a grinding of machinery, and the light on top of the police box began to flash. With a strange wheezing, groaning sound, the TARDIS faded away from the cricket fields.

The Doctor and his friends were on their way to another adventure.

Somewhere in the outer solar system, a tiny craft flashed through space.

It was a probe called Voyager Two, sent spinning off from Earth to take photographs of other planets. Once it left the sun's family of worlds, it would head off into space, encountering other star systems, perhaps, in the centuries to follow.

It was not meant to carry a crew. But it did.

They'd just managed to catch up with it, at a speed they could never sustain. Jake had grabbed a solar panel and pulled Madelaine on board.

They secured the flasks of vampire DNA to the main body of the craft. Then they found a flat surface and coated it with a thin layer of soil from Earth.

Jake pushed indentations into the soft metal of the probe with his fingers and fastened the grapples into the holes. The two vampires bound themselves securely to the craft and tested their anchors in every direction. They had a long voyage ahead of them.

Jake kissed Madelaine's eyelids as she settled down to

sleep. 'When we wake up, love,' he whispered, 'we'll be somewhere different.'

'A place of our own.'

'A place for us. Are you frightened?'

'No. I'm with you, aren't I?'

Jake smiled. They wrapped their hands together and fell into peaceful sleep.

The probe sped on out of the solar system.

Into the future.

The next Missing Adventure, to be published in September 1994, is *Evolution* by John Peel, which will feature the fourth Doctor and Sarah Jane Smith.